SCORCHED EARTH

by Lisa von Biela

Kevin Oakley leapt to his feet and gave his chair a vicious kick. It smashed into the wall and tipped over. He hated his job with every fiber of his being. Every single day he wished he could walk away from it knowing someone else would take over and do it better. He knew full well he just doomed half of Nebraska—and probably more—by denying Governor Percy the water he needed to fight the fire. But he was responsible for the nation's water reserves. He had no choice but to protect what was left.

The drought had been so severe, and so longstanding, that every source of water had been gravely depleted to levels never before seen. Aquifers that had survived previous droughts stood no chance against this one. Lakes, rivers, and streams. All but the very largest were dry as a bone now.

Most of the potable water now came from desalinization plants on the coasts. Some still came from the Great Lakes, and some from the once-mighty Columbia River in the Pacific Northwest. And that water had to be trucked cross-country for distribution in special tanker trucks driven by pairs of armed guards.

All very expensive. Made even more so by the fuel needed to operate the tanker trucks, vehicles that were far too heavy and too old to convert to modern electric power technology. The drought killed the fracking industry several years back, making the country completely dependent on foreign oil, at whatever price those nations wanted to charge. And they knew a seller's market when they saw it.

Kevin righted his chair and dropped down into it. In some ways, his job was simple. Just say no. With domestic water reserves as low as they were and no foreign countries willing or able to sell their water at any price, no was always the right answer. At least until the drought broke, whenever the hell that might be.

DEDICATION

For David, with love.

SUMMER 2032

CHAPTER 1

Sweat streamed down his face, down his entire body. His clothes lay plastered against his skin like someone had hit him with the business end of a firehose. Nothing new about that. Just another night working the kitchen at Jerry's Steakhouse. No amount of air conditioning ever managed to overcome the sweltering heat that built up in there.

But Jake Morgan didn't care. Not tonight, anyway.

He broke into a wide, giddy smile as he scrubbed down the grill just so. What a night! Adam ran a two-for-one special, and it seemed like damned near everybody in town came by. The place hadn't been that busy on a weeknight in years. Hell, hardly anyone showed up at all these days, even on Saturday nights. But tonight, the orders came in so fast, he had to hustle over the scorching-hot grill like a madman just to keep up.

And everyone wanted the sirloin steak. Rare, well-done, and everything in between. Blew right through their inventory. He tossed the scraper aside, grabbed a pad, and started his list for tomorrow's order: *eight-ounce sirloins, potatoes, butter substitute, medium shrimp, assorted vegetable mix.* Too bad they couldn't get some nice vine-ripened tomatoes—the kind that smelled like summer, the way it used to be. They'd go great with the steaks. But those days had been over for quite a while now.

Jake set down his pencil and shook his head, that brief rush of optimism suddenly as distant as those tomatoes and everything they represented. He could wish and imagine all he wanted, but there would be no fresh tomatoes like that again. Not in the foreseeable future, anyway.

Customers nowadays had to settle for those utilitarian

veggies the BigAg companies invented. Veggies that thrived on untreated sea water. Ugly, pale, malformed-looking things, even if they were supposed to be ultra-nutritious. Took an awful lot of skill and effort to make them look even halfway attractive on a dinner plate. At least they could still get real steaks—though the price was through the roof and getting higher by the day. Adam may have brought in a good crowd tonight, but charging two-for-one prices for those sirloin dinners must have cost him dearly.

Jake shrugged and got back to work. Daydreaming about the good old days wasn't going to help him wrap up for the night and get home to Lexi and Ava. He gave the corners of the grill one last scrape, then stood back and scrutinized his work. Nice and clean, ready for tomorrow night.

To save water, he'd taken to cranking the grill up to the max, turning any residue to a crisp char that came right off when it cooled. Department of Health would never have let him get away with his little trick back before all the trouble started, but it actually worked pretty damned well. Maybe even better than cleaning the old-fashioned way.

But it heated up the kitchen like Hades itself. Big downside, there. Unnecessary sweating was never a good idea with water at such a premium.

"Jake, can you come out to the dining room?" Adam stood in the kitchen doorway, his face pallid and emotionless.

"Sure. I'll be all wrapped up in a couple minutes."

"Now. Please." Adam turned and walked away.

Jake dropped his scraper in the sink and dried his hands on a towel. Something was wrong, terribly wrong. Adam never took a tone like that. If anything, he bent over backwards to keep everybody's morale up, no matter what. Jerry's had been in his family for generations, and he'd cared for it like his own child since he took it over from his parents nearly twenty years ago. Nurturing his staff, keeping standards high—or as high as possible under the circumstances, anyway. Most of the staff had worked there for years, loving the place nearly as much as Adam did.

Frowning, Jake tossed the towel onto the counter and went into the dining room. The rest of the staff stood scattered amongst the empty tables, arms crossed, faces apprehensive. Adam turned and motioned for him to join them. Then he thrust his hands into his pockets and stood silent for several minutes, visibly fighting to keep his composure.

Head bowed, shoulders slumped, he opened his mouth, then closed it. He cleared his throat and tried again.

"I never dreamed I'd have to say what I'm about to say. I've tried everything possible to avoid it." Adam cleared his throat again, raised his head. His eyes glittered with unshed tears. "I ran the special tonight to give our customers—and everyone here—a night to remember. A night like it used to be." He choked and stared down at the floor for several moments before he could continue.

"Because this is our last night."

Everyone let out a gasp. No one said a word. Jake felt like all the air had gone out of the room, as if he couldn't take a breath.

Adam sniffed, looked away, and struggled to get his words out. "I can't make it work anymore. I've tried…and tried. With rationing, I can never get enough water—even if I could afford it. And supplies. I've been losing money with every steak dinner. Every single one." He rubbed his hands over his face. "How can I run a steakhouse when beef's nearly impossible to get? I can't price the dinners so people can afford them." He shook his head. "Can't do it."

Tara, an older woman who'd worked at the steakhouse all her adult life, ran toward the bathroom, sobbing. Crying herself, Jeannie, her best friend, caught up with her, cradled her in her arms and tried to comfort her. Everyone else stood rooted in place, eyes wide, stunned into silence.

Adam reached inside his sport coat and pulled out a stack of envelopes, rubber-banded together. He held the stack in both hands, staring down at it for a moment before speaking once more, his voice breaking this time.

"These're your final paychecks. They cover your hours up through tonight and include a month of severance. I wish I could do more, but it's all I have left." He set the stack down on the table next to him. "I am so sorry." Shoulders trembling, he turned away, strode quickly back to his office, and slammed the door shut.

Jake flinched. The slam of the door jolted him like a physical blow. He glanced around the room at the shocked faces surrounding him. He hadn't worked there as long as many of the others—only eight years—but it still felt like home to him, like he belonged there. Jerry's was a fixture in town, the kind of place people went to for special dinners and celebrations. He loved being a part of that, making sure each meal they served was something to remember. A hollow feeling stole into his gut as the loss began to sink in.

And Lexi had only just returned to work! Her maternity leave had decimated their savings, and they'd counted on getting their finances on track once they were back to two incomes. Fat chance of that now. Jobs in their little town were few and far between, and there was no telling when he'd find something again. They'd have to budget like never before to make that month's severance last.

Sobs and murmurs replaced the silence as, one by one, his coworkers hesitantly approached the table to pick up their paychecks. Most took their envelope and left quietly. Some stood in small clusters around the room, shaking their heads and talking softly like mourners at a wake. Jake wondered what would become of them all, how many would have to leave town to find work. Sighing, he trudged over, took his check, and stuffed it into his pocket without opening the envelope. Might as well go on home and tell Lexi. Delaying the news wouldn't make it any easier to take.

He slipped out of the dining room alone, then paused at Adam's closed office door on his way to the rear exit. Maybe he should say something to him, but he couldn't think of anything the least bit useful. Besides, Adam probably wanted his privacy right now. *He* would, if he were in Adam's position. The pain on his coworkers' faces was unbearable for him to see—and it had to be a thousand times worse for Adam, watching the death of his beloved steakhouse.

Jake opened the back door and stepped outside. It took all his energy to push through the thick wall of hot, humid air to get to his car. The night seemed alive and malignant, like it wanted to trap him in its dark, oppressive hell.

CHAPTER 2

Lexi Morgan indulged in an epic, from-the-core-of-her-being yawn, then bent over to tuck Ava in for the night. And hoped (a girl can hope, can't she?) she would be an exceptionally good baby tonight and sleep straight through for once. She planted a soft kiss on Ava's cheek, then straightened up and eased the kinks from her lower back.

Exhaustion held her firm in its filthy clutches these days, and she wondered when she'd see the end of it. That last trimester had been hell, with the baby squashing all her internal organs—lungs in particular. Pretty hard to sleep when you can barely breathe. Then came the long, difficult birth, and a single full night of delicious, uninterrupted sleep seemed about as elusive as a unicorn sporting a diamond tiara.

Damned vicious cycle, it was. Kept her too tired to get back into her exercise routine, so she hadn't yet dumped the baby fat and regained her usual stamina. She shrugged. No point beating herself up over it. This would pass. Eventually. At some point, Ava *would* start sleeping through and she could get back to her pre-pregnancy body and energy level. Then everything would be easier.

It's not like she didn't know having a baby would be a challenge on all sorts of levels. But knowing it and experiencing it were two very different things. Still, she didn't regret it. Not for a minute. She smiled as she gazed at her perfect, sweet baby girl, already asleep in her little yellow jammies. A tiny, living treasure. And the only baby she would ever have.

Lexi absently rubbed her stomach where the laparoscopic surgery left behind three tiny incisions. Razor-thin, each a deep, fresh, angry red. Reminders of her enforced sterility. Mandatory scars. One baby per woman. No exceptions, no matter what. And good luck to women who had trouble conceiving on their own. To protect the dwindling water supply, the government outlawed fertility treatments of any and all kinds several years ago. Population growth—no matter how small—was no longer an option. Hell, she heard they'd even started rationing certain life-extending treatments.

The constant barrage of doomsday news about the seemingly endless drought had made it all the harder to convince Jake they should have even the one baby. It had been an uphill battle all the way, spurring argument after argument over the past few years. Things got so bad she'd sometimes thought about leaving him, finding someone who really wanted a kid, and starting over before her biological clock ticked off into oblivion.

Kids never interested Jake that much in the first place—and he was such a worrier on top of that. Could they afford the additional water they'd need for a family of three? Could they handle the responsibility? One worry, one objection after another. But at last he gave in and fell completely in love with Ava at first sight.

Exhaustion notwithstanding, it was all good now. She and Jake were closer than ever, both totally devoted to Ava, and they were settling into a normal new-parent routine now that she was back to work. Of course she'd rather stay home with Ava, but with her out of the house on weekdays, their water bill had dropped back to a more manageable level. And they'd soon be caught up on all the bills that had stacked up during her maternity leave. Lexi smiled and tucked a corner of Ava's blanket beneath her little pink cheek. Yep, it was all good.

She turned out the light and padded into the living room to read while she waited for Jake to get home from the restaurant. She wished they could have dinner together as a family more often, but his working the dinner shift had its advantages. He saved them a ton of money on child care by staying home with Ava during the day. And while he was out working, she and Ava had their special time together before Ava's bedtime, then she got some quiet time to herself. Not a bad arrangement, all in all. Her friends with young children led much more harried lives, trying to juggle everything with both parents working during the day.

Lexi curled up on the couch, picked up her e-reader, and let out a long, relaxed breath as she settled in. She missed actual books, the feel and smell of them. The physicality of turning the pages. Another casualty of the drought. Paper had become way too expensive to use for mere novels. She turned on the reader and skipped back a page to remind herself where she'd left off. Then she sunk back into the story, mesmerized by the endless twists and turns of a killer plot.

The sound of the front door closing startled her back into reality sooner than she expected. Frowning, she set aside her reader and glanced up. Eyes downcast, Jake leaned against the wall beside the door and rubbed his hands over his face.

"Jeez, Jake. What's the matter—tough night?"

His body sagged as he let out a long sigh and spoke without making eye contact. "Worse than that. Way worse. Adam's closing the steakhouse. He let us all go tonight."

"What—" Lexi's throat felt tight, like she could barely push out the word.

Jake shuffled over and sank down onto the couch next to her. He shook his head and stared at the floor, elbows on knees, then muttered in a low rush, almost as if he were talking to himself.

"Should have seen it coming, but I didn't *want* to see the signs right in front of my eyes. Fewer and fewer people had been coming in. The place was like a graveyard most nights. I know Adam wanted—*needed*—to raise his prices to cover costs, but he knew he'd lose what little business he had left. I did the ordering. I saw the invoices. Costs kept rising—a lot. For everything, but especially the beef. He had to've been running in the red for a while, and finally had to stop the bleeding."

"He's shutting the place down? For good? After all the years it's been in his family?"

"'Fraid so. I don't see it coming back. I know it killed him to have to do it." He covered his eyes, rubbed them. "I'll never forget the look on his face when he told us. Shattered."

"Well, what now?"

Jake let out a bitter chuckle. "I don't know. Still trying to wrap my mind around it. I doubt I'll find anything similar, though. Hardly any restaurants left open in town and now all of us he let go'll be competing for what few jobs there might be—if there are any at all. I'll start looking tomorrow, see what's out there."

"When's he closing it?"

"Tonight was it. He ran a special, got a great crowd in. Just like the old days. Sort of a last hurrah for the place." He reached into his shirt pocket, took out an envelope and tossed it onto the coffee table. "He paid us up through tonight, plus a month's severance. Took the last of his cash to do it, I'm sure."

Lexi put her hand on her chest, felt her heart pounding like it wanted to smother her. They couldn't weather another income drop right now. They hadn't yet caught up on the bills that had accumulated during her leave.

"I can't believe it. I mean, I know I shouldn't really be surprised. A lot of restaurants—all kinds of businesses—have gone under because of the damned drought. But I never thought Adam...I guess I've been too preoccupied to think about it, with Ava and all." She smiled. "Well, if worse comes to worst, I'm sure my family would be happy to help out."

Jake's face darkened. "No. This is *my* family. *I'm* responsible. I'll find something, no matter what." He clenched his jaw. "I will not take charity. Not from your family. Not from anyone."

"It's not charity. It's what family does. Just because your—"

Jake glared at her. "Don't go there, Lexi. Just don't. We'll get through this, and we'll do it without taking handouts." He pointed at the envelope. "Got a month's pay sitting there. I'll figure something out. I promise you."

Chewing her lip, Lexi stared at the envelope. She didn't doubt for a minute Jake would do everything in his power to get back to work. But he couldn't do the impossible. The job market being what it was, a month was a mighty slim buffer.

About as slim as that envelope.

CHAPTER 3

Teeth clenched, Jake fidgeted beneath the covers. Might as well give up trying to sleep. Pointless to lie in bed staring into the darkness hour after hour. He'd tried it all. Counting backward, yogic relaxation tricks. Nothing was working. Too much to think about. How long would his severance have to last? And where the hell *was* he going to find a job in their dinky one-horse town?

After delivering the bad news, he'd put on a relentlessly confident front the rest of the evening. No sense rattling Lexi any more than he already had. Better to keep his worries to himself. And there was plenty to worry about. The way things were, it could be a long, long time before he found any kind of work at all. What's more, he couldn't get the faces of Adam and all his coworkers out of his mind. They were all in a world of shit.

Lexi lay by his side, breathing softly, finally asleep after Ava's last feeding. He glanced at the digital clock on his nightstand. Four in the morning. As good a time as any to get started.

He slipped out from beneath the covers, careful not to wake Lexi, then tiptoed toward the hallway. He gave her one last look before quietly shutting the bedroom door behind him. No matter what it took, he could not—*would* not—let her and Ava down. He'd find a way to get them all through this.

Jake went into the study, switched on the desk lamp, and plopped down in his chair. Anxious to get started, he opened his laptop and rubbed his hands together. At this ungodly hour of the night, silence surrounded him, and it was still full-on dark outside. Good time to be up and about in the relative cool, now that the hideously hot days of summer were upon them.

He logged in, found a job search site, and typed in the broadest criteria he could think of. Better cast as wide a net as possible.

He glanced at the results and muttered a curse. This was going to be every bit as hard as he thought—maybe even worse. Nothing local came up. Not a single listing. Everything was a couple-hour drive or more away. A commute that long would be a deal breaker in every way. His hybrid wouldn't go that far without backup gas—insanely expensive now that the drought made fracking impossible. And it would make for way too long a day. He had to be able to mesh his schedule with Lexi's, or child care costs would take a huge bite out of his paycheck. The net result wouldn't be worth the effort.

Frowning, he stared out the window into the darkness. If only he hadn't given in to Lexi's constant harping about having a baby. Then they wouldn't have all the extra expense and responsibility, and he'd have far more flexibility in hunting for a new job. Ava was a cute kid—and he loved her—but if he had it to do over again, he wouldn't. He shook his head. Never did understand why Lexi felt so...incomplete...without a baby. Their pre-Ava life had been just fine. Aside from the drought, anyway.

He turned back to his laptop and tried another job site. Same damned thing. Not a good start. Not a good start at all. He'd have to think of some clever strategy, though what that might be, he had no idea yet. To make matters worse, he'd be competing against his former workmates—good people, every single one of them—for whatever jobs there might be. This damned Podunk town. Times like this, he wished he'd never left Omaha. At least in a bigger city, there'd be more jobs to pick from. Not like out here in Smalltown, Nebraska.

That was another thing he regretted letting Lexi talk him into. She just *had* to live near her family. Her big, dysfunctional, annoying family. Every time there was a gathering, he had to grit his teeth and reach for a drink to get through it. They say when you marry someone, you marry their family, too. Spot on, though he wished it weren't. Lexi's father, in particular, never missed a chance to take a dig at him, like he wasn't good enough for her. Like he was incapable of managing his own household.

His family was microscopic by comparison, and that suited him just fine. Nothing warm and fuzzy about them, but they'd taken the job of raising him seriously. Whatever else he thought of his parents, they made sure he understood what it meant to be responsible, and that he had the skills to be self-sufficient. It was a point of pride for him, which made Lexi's father's constant insinuations all the more insufferable.

The study door opened, and Lexi shuffled in, rubbing her eyes.

"What—" She yawned with her entire being. "Are you doing up at this hour?"

"I didn't wake you, did I?"

"No, no. I thought I heard Ava starting up, but she settled back down without me. And now I'm awake." She plunked down in a chair and sighed. "So, what're *you* doing up?"

He gestured toward the laptop. "Figured I'd get started looking for a job."

"Find anything interesting?"

"No, not yet. I'll keep looking."

Her eyebrows rose. "Nothing at all?"

"Nothing local. Closest thing was clear on the other side of the next county. Too long a drive to coordinate our schedules for Ava. And the gas I'd need for a drive like that would eat into whatever I brought home."

Lexi slumped in her chair and yawned again. "Don't worry about Ava. Mom would be happy to sit her if we needed her to."

"No, Lexi. Once in a while is one thing. But I don't want to depend on your family for day-to-day needs like that."

Lexi sat up, scowling. "Why do you have to be like that? They're happy to help."

"Let's not argue about this again. You *know* how I feel about dumping my responsibilities on others."

"It's not dumping! It's their grandkid, for God's sake. They love her, and they *want* to help."

"Like I said, once in a while is one thing. Relying on them all the time to take care of *our* kid is another."

"You can be so fucking stubborn about things."

"And *you* don't seem to understand how important this is to me. Our family is my responsibility, and I'll figure something out. We'll be fine. Trust me, okay?"

Lexi raised her hands, palms out. "*Whatever.* Guess I'm not getting back to sleep now. Might as well feed Ava and go in to work, rack up a little overtime pay." She stomped out of the room and down the hall.

Jake started to say something, then stopped. Lexi's family was the one topic that could escalate into a full-on argument in the blink of an eye. No point in feeding the fire. Especially when he had more urgent matters to attend to. He turned to his laptop to try another job site.

There had to be something out there. He just had to find it and make it work. And soon.

CHAPTER 4

Lexi groaned as her car detected the blockage up ahead and braked. The light at the intersection was as green as it could be. No reason for traffic to come to an abrupt halt. So much for getting into the office early and picking up a little overtime. What else could possibly go wrong?

Blasting the radio usually helped clear her mind. She cranked up the volume and tried to let the music distract her, but this morning, it only stoked her irritation. She turned it off with an angry flick of her wrist, then shifted in her seat and waited some more. Nothing was moving, not even an inch. Lexi drummed her fingers on the steering wheel, feeling trapped and powerless. And not just because of the traffic jam.

Last night was a disaster, all the way through. Hard to imagine it going worse, really. Jake kicked it off with a bang by announcing he'd lost his job. Then somehow, despite that lovely bit of news, she later managed to fall into a deep, restful, dream-state sleep for the first time in forever. It was as delicious as it was short-lived, because, right on cue, Ava started fussing and woke her. For nothing, as it turned out. If it weren't for that, she could have slept another hour or two before she really had to be up instead of getting into another fight with Jake over her family.

She tensed her jaw. When would he get over that independent streak and accept a little help without kicking and fighting about it? Though most of the time, it *was* nice being with someone who took responsibility seriously. Someone she could depend on to take care of what needed taking care of. Not like that wishy-washy lout she used to date before she met Jake. Still.

Sometimes he took it a little too far.

At last, traffic started to inch ahead. Just in time for another red light. Lexi slammed her fist on the wheel and glared at the signal, willing it to turn green. How the hell could traffic get this screwed up? Sure, it was the main drag through town, but for God's sake, it wasn't that big of a town. That's one of the things she liked about it. Rarely any congestion and everything was nearby. Her job, her parents, all her friends. Errands took almost no time at all. A great little town to live in, with none of those big-city problems.

Green. Finally. And the jam appeared to be clearing at last. Lexi blew out a long breath as the car started picking up speed. A couple of blocks ahead, emergency lights awaited. Red, blue and yellow. Traffic was still moving slowly enough for her to get a good look at what was going on.

Three black-and-whites, their lightbars flashing, were parked in front of a run-down house on her right. One of the cars blocked the driveway, and a Water and Power truck was parked behind it, yellow emergency lights blinking. A uniformed Water and Power man stood in the front yard, talking to one of the cops. As Lexi passed by, she saw two other cops hauling a man out of the house in cuffs. And none too gently. The man appeared to be screaming and pleading, without apparent success.

Shivering, she looked away. She was so sick of the goddamned drought. Sick of constantly hearing about it, and sick of living with it and all the damage it had done, all the changes it had brought. And she wasn't the only one. Everyone was getting desperate now, tired of all the water usage restrictions that had been in effect for so long. At first, the powers that be tried to control consumption with aggressive fines. But that wasn't enough. People treated the fines as part of their water bill and soon became more and more bold about their usage. She could hardly blame them.

Now, a nationwide crackdown with some real teeth was in effect. Arrests for water crimes were becoming commonplace. Last year, counties all across the country—hers included—criminalized violations. And harshly. Something that used to get you a twenty-dollar fine became a misdemeanor with up to a year in the local jail. Anything that used to involve a fine of fifty bucks or more became a felony. A year in prison minimum, and it went up from there, depending on the egregiousness of the violation. Water and Power had taken to wireless water meter monitoring to make sure violators were caught and prosecuted promptly.

Lexi shook her head. Crazy, just crazy. Used to be, having a toilet that ran or leaked a little just meant a higher water bill. Now it meant jail time—prison if it wasn't fixed after the first warning. Watering a lawn? You might as well plan on a good long time in prison for that one. She barely remembered how it used to be, back when she was a kid and it was still legal to play in the sprinklers on a hot day. How much worse could it get before it got better?

Would it ever get better?

"We've got you down for ten-thirty next Wednesday for your annual eye exam, with Dr. Reynolds. Remember to bring your insurance card. See you then."

Lexi hung up the phone and stared down at her keyboard. Good thing she could touch-type, because the letters all looked mighty blurry today. If only she'd gotten those last couple hours of sleep last night. She stifled a yawn. Soon. Soon she would start getting more sleep and feeling more normal. This was all part of having a four-month-old baby at home—and a newly unemployed husband. Just hang on, everything would work out. It always did. She rubbed her eyes and tried to focus.

"Lexi? You okay?" Dr. Reynolds stood by her desk, a concerned look on his kind, grandfatherly face.

She waved her hand. "Just a little tired is all. I'll be all right."

"Lexi, if you need a little more leave, we can work something out. I can get a temp for a few weeks, give you a little more time to rest and recover."

"Oh, I'll be fine, thanks." She chuckled. "I'm almost getting used to being awake half the night. I'm even starting to like the night better than the day. So much cooler. And nice to look at something outside other than the sun beating down."

Dr. Reynolds smiled. "Well, if you're sure. But seriously, don't hesitate to ask if you need a little more time. You need to stay healthy for that little girl of yours."

"I know. I'll let you know. Thanks for offering." She glanced out at the waiting room. "Are you ready for your two o'clock?"

"Yes, send her in."

"Alicia, you can go in now."

Lexi took her mug into the break room and poured herself another cup of coffee. She took a sip and closed her eyes, imagining the dark liquid flowing through her veins, washing away the grogginess with its caffeine payload. Awfully nice of Dr. Reynolds to make that offer. If Jake hadn't just lost his job, she'd have taken him up on it in a heartbeat. Some days, the exhaustion felt just like a dark curtain coming down on her.

Nope, she couldn't afford to miss a single day—not even a single hour—of work. Not right now. Until Jake found something new, they'd better watch every single dime.

She topped her mug and clutched it like a lifeline. At least she got free coffee at the office. Nice and strong. And all she could drink.

CHAPTER 5

Jake rubbed his eyes. They felt dry, hot like they were on fire. Like they might crumble into dust if he rubbed them too hard. Aside from breaks to deal with Ava's needs, he'd spent the entire day scowling at his laptop's screen, searching for a job. Or at least a lead on one. An idea. Anything. But all he had to show for his efforts were a serious case of eyestrain and the warning throbs of a headache in the making. Maybe he should just skip dinner and go right to bed.

"Aren't you hungry?" Lexi raised an eyebrow, reached across the table, and poked the edge of his plate with her finger.

Jake glanced at his untouched dinner, tried to muster some enthusiasm. And utterly failed. Lexi's cooking wasn't to blame. No, it was the food itself. Hard to get excited about those limp, flavorless GMO veggies, and ocean cod that was harvested and frozen in mass quantities, so it could be shipped all over the country like car parts. No flavor to be had. And the fish had freezer burn. The culinary skills needed to transform this food into something appetizing simply didn't exist.

"Sorry, I'm just not terribly hungry tonight." Jake picked up his fork, speared a piece of the cod, and made an attempt to choke it down to show Lexi her cooking wasn't to blame.

"It's kinda nice to be able to have dinner together anyway, don't you think?" Lexi half-smiled.

"Wish it were under better circumstances." Jake set down his fork and spit a hardened bit of the cod into his napkin as politely as he could.

Lexi frowned and stared down into her lap. "Sorry. Just trying to make the best of the situation."

Jake reached out and took her hand. "I know you are. I didn't mean that the way it sounded. Of course I enjoy having dinner with you. I'm just…well, I'll feel better when I have something new lined up, is all."

"No luck yet?"

"No, not yet. I worked on it in between taking care of Ava today. Nothing turned up." He forced a smile, hoped it looked good enough to pass for the real thing. "But it's only been one day. I'll get back on it tomorrow. So, how'd your day go?"

Lexi rolled her eyes. "Got stuck in a terrible traffic jam on my way in this morning. Cops, Water and Power. They were just dragging some guy out of his house as I passed by. Looked like they meant business. Must have been a pretty serious violation." She shook her head. "Wouldn't want to be that guy."

"Jeez. I'm all for conserving water, but the cops act like they're paid on commission these days, they're so hell-bent to enforce those water laws. If this damned drought ever ends, what do you bet those laws stay on the books as a nice little revenue-generator?"

"I bet you're right. The cops, the prisons, lawyers, and everyone down the line…they're all making money off those laws, and the legislature won't dare take it away." She shrugged. "But no one's predicting the drought will end anytime soon, so it's probably a moot point."

"Feels like the drought will *never* end." Jake sighed and pushed away his plate. "I'm sorry, I just can't finish this."

Lexi stood and picked up their plates. "I'm not that hungry, either. I'll just put some plastic wrap over these and stick 'em in the fridge. Fewer dishes to wash tonight. That much less water to use. Hooray for us. Master water conservers, we are."

Jake touched her arm as she passed by. "Hey, I'm really sorry about this morning. I know it's hard for you, going back to work with Ava still not sleeping through the night. I didn't mean to make it harder."

"Well, you can make it easier on me—on both of us."

"Lexi, don't press too hard, okay? At least give me a chance to handle our own affairs without taking charity."

She pulled away from him and headed for the kitchen.

"Then don't apologize if you don't mean it."

Jake put his head in his hands and growled, "It's only been one day, Lexi. Give me a goddamned break."

He picked up his glass, swallowed the last of his water, precious and rationed, then slammed it down on the table. Wiping beads of sweat from his hairline, he stormed back into the study without another word.

Jake dropped down into his chair and yanked open his laptop. Better get busy finding a job like his life depended on it. Because it very well might. The longer it took, the more likely Lexi's parents would start sticking their noses into his business, and then he'd have to deal with that on top of everything else. Intolerable.

The only worse scenario he could imagine was running out of his month's severance with no job on the horizon.

He could *not* let that happen.

But it very well might.

He gritted his teeth and tried to push that thought away before it could take root.

Too late.

CHAPTER 6

The daisy-shaped night light cast a soft, warm glow through the nursery. Soothing, peaceful light. Lexi smiled as she gently lowered Ava into her crib. Fed, content, and asleep—for now. Over on the nightstand, the clock's bright green numerals announced it was shortly after two in the morning. Lexi chuckled softly. Back in college, two in the morning was nothing. She'd been a raging night owl, studying until all hours, sleeping until the last possible minute the next day, then rushing off to class.

Those were the days. Back when her schedule was her own, and before the drought catapulted the entire country into a seemingly endless state of emergency. Back in the drought's early stages, when no one yet realized it had come to stay, and all it meant was a few more summer wildfires for the firefighters—not a whole new way of life for everyone on so many levels. She tried not to think about it very often, because she knew all the wishing in the world wouldn't bring back those days.

Now she was a creature of the night once more, but not because of her own youthful energy. And not because she had the freedom to live that way. Ava's needs dictated her rhythms, and there was no sleeping in until a conveniently scheduled afternoon class. Graduating into the working world closed off that option years ago.

Lexi made sure Ava was asleep, then headed for the study. She knew better than to go back to bed right away. By the time she nodded off, Ava'd be hungry again. No point in teasing herself with snippets of sleep. Might as well get something done while she waited for the next feeding.

She switched on the desk lamp and settled in, then opened the laptop and logged on to the bank's billpay site. She winced at the sight of their anemic account balance. Jake had only been out of work for a couple of weeks, and they'd kept a tight lid on their spending. Even so, his month's severance was dwindling faster than they'd hoped.

Lexi frowned as she scrolled through the list of pending bills. The water bill was noticeably higher than last month's. Of course it was. It only made sense their total usage would rise some, with Jake home all day and night now. He was careful about his use and they were still within their allotment—barely—but the per-unit charge kept rising, partly to cover costs and partly to further incent people to trim their usage.

And that allotment was serious business. If they blew through it, they'd be hit with a stiff penalty they likely couldn't even afford right now. And that was for a first offense. If they blew it a second time, they'd be subjected to a mandatory, intrusive water audit—on their dime—to find out why they'd overshot their allotment. If there was a leak, they'd have a very short time to fix it and be rechecked.

And if the excess usage *wasn't* due to a leak or some obvious mechanical problem, the law assumed it to be deliberate waste—a water crime—and imposed harsh penalties. She shivered as she pictured that guy she saw being arrested, dragged out of his house. They'd just have to find some way to economize even more on their usage. She didn't like dancing that close to the edge of their allotment. Way too risky.

Lexi selected the next few bills that were coming due and clicked to pay them. Didn't leave much of a balance. Good thing she got paid next week. They'd likely make it through another cycle without an overdraft. At least she hoped so. Jake had been trying like hell to get a job, but not even a bite yet. His luck better turn around soon, or they'd need to hit her parents up for some cash to tide them over. And of course, that would piss Jake off to no end. Best if it didn't come down to that.

She leaned back in the chair, flexed the tension from her shoulders, and closed her eyes. They felt gritty and raw, like she'd been walking for miles through a hot, dusty desert wind.

Maybe she should have listened to Jake. Before they had Ava, he'd worried about whether they could afford a baby, whether they could stay within their water allotment if they had a child in the house. Maybe he'd been right. They'd have been much better positioned to weather his layoff if it was still just the two of them.

Lexi's eyes snapped open. How could she even *think* something like that? Ava was precious beyond measure. Irreplaceable. Worth whatever sacrifice they had to make for her. She put her face in her hands. She must be way overtired for that sort of thing to even enter her mind.

We'll get through this. No matter what it takes, we will get through it. All of us. Together.

CHAPTER 7

Just for the hell of it, Jake typed *Omaha* into the search box and clicked the icon. Sure enough, the pickings weren't nearly so slim over there, in a *real* city. A couple of screenfuls, in fact. Not like the gaping void he faced when he searched within a decent driving distance. So it wasn't like there were no jobs to be had anywhere. Just none where he needed them.

He closed the laptop, pushed it aside, and gnawed his knuckle. Weeks. Three weeks had gone by, with nothing to show for it but an insidious, escalating tension between him and Lexi. And less and less money. Lexi didn't bring it up, probably didn't want to put more pressure on him than he already felt. But he knew how low their bank account had dipped. That month's severance was nearly gone already, and they didn't have the reserves to hold out much longer before they'd have to pick and choose which bills to pay. Then the late fees and interest would chew up their budget all the faster.

It was just like being trapped in one of those rooms you see in some old movies. The cold stone walls start sliding in, closer and closer, shrinking the room around you until there's nothing left. No matter how hard you fight, no matter how hard you push against those walls, they just keep coming and coming, tighter and tighter, until they crush the life right out of you. Everything was closing in on him, and he felt powerless to stop it.

He shook off the mental image. Can't think like that, can't even let the *idea* of defeat get hold and drag him down. He'd find something, somehow. And damned soon, because he knew what would come next if he didn't. Lexi's parents would get involved, offer to help—undoubtedly with a little behind-the-scenes nudge from Lexi. And that's the last thing he wanted. To be beholden to them. To prove her dad right, that he wasn't capable of providing for his own family. He crumpled up a piece of note paper and hurled it across the room.

Jake went to the window and peered out. A nice enough morning, sunny and bright. Maybe some fresh air and a change of pace would lift his mood, reinvigorate him. Maybe even help him come up with some new ideas to try. He glanced at his watch. If he was going to get outside, better to get out now. Before everything started baking under the merciless mid-day sun.

"Going to the park, Sweetie. What do you think of that?"

Jake pulled to a stop at the red light, then glanced over at Ava, snugly secured in her car seat. She waved tiny fists at him, a trail of drool running down her chin. She looked happy to be alive. Best he could tell, anyway. He still felt like anything but an expert in knowing what went through a baby's mind. But she had no cause to worry and fret. Must be nice being a baby. No cares. No responsibilities.

The light turned green and Jake took one extra beat to look both ways before allowing the autodrive to reengage and propel them into the intersection. He was anything but a reckless driver by nature, but he'd become even more cautious now that they had Ava. Even though she was a few months old now, he still felt a little uneasy with her. Every time he picked her up, he held her like the most fragile piece of rare china. She was such a tiny thing, he was afraid of doing anything that might hurt her.

Jake turned onto the road that led into the municipal park, about the only redeeming feature this one-horse town had to offer. Ten acres, smack in the center of things. Extensive picnic grounds, a baseball diamond, bike trails, a leash-free dog park, and even a stage where they held concerts on summer nights. The fishing pond and the swimming pool had long since gone bone-dry, though. Casualties of the drought. But the rest of the park was still worth a visit when the sun wasn't directly overhead.

He frowned as the car braked to a stop. Black-and-yellow striped wooden roadblocks stood in a line, closing off the park entrance. A sign hung from one of them: PARK CLOSED FOR THE SUMMER. EXTREME FIRE HAZARD! A cop car was parked by the side of the road to emphasize the message.

No point in getting into a chin-wag with a cop about it. No one ever came out ahead—except the cop. Jake sighed, cranked the steering wheel, and three-point-turned his way out of there. Ava smeared the passenger window with her slimy little fist and got that I'm-about-to-cry look on her face.

"Don't cry, Ava. Sorry, nothing we can do."

Ava puckered her mouth, then her whole face reddened and caved in on itself as she let out an ear-splitting wail.

"I'll get you a bottle when we get home. Won't be long," he shouted over her.

Jake clenched his jaw as Ava wound up her cries to a skull-shattering crescendo. He wanted desperately to clap his hands over his ears, to be out of the car, away from her shrill shrieking. Away from everything. But there was no escape until he could get her home and give her a bottle. She'd settle down and sleep for a while after a good feeding in familiar surroundings.

Should have just stayed home. Everywhere he turned, nothing but dead ends of one kind or another. Can't even take a break and get out of the house for a little while.

Goddamned drought. It was stealing their lives, piece by piece.

CHAPTER 8

"I am *so* freakin' tired. We had a patient show up first thing this morning without an appointment. Possible detached retina. Turned out she's okay, but it threw the entire rest of the day off schedule." Lexi trudged over to the couch, flopped down onto her back, and put her feet in Jake's lap. "I'll deal with the dishes later."

"Don't worry about it. I'll take care of them." Jake started rubbing her right foot, digging into all the nasty tight spots, just the way she liked it.

"Mmmm…thanks. Don't know how my feet get so tight. I sit all day at work."

"And tight they are." He switched to her left foot. "Um, Lexi, I've been thinking."

She propped herself up on her elbows. "Sounds serious. What about?"

"Might be a good idea to move."

"Move? Why? I like this house."

"Not houses. I mean relocate. To another city entirely."

Lexi yanked her feet away and sat up. "*What?*"

Jake stared down at his hands and took a deep breath. "I don't think we can go much longer without two incomes." He glanced up at her, anger and frustration plain on his face. "I've looked and looked. Every damned day. There's nothing here in town. What few jobs I've seen would involve a horribly long commute, too long to work our schedules around Ava." He shook his head.

"I can ask for some overtime, just to help bridge the gap for a little while. 'Til you find something."

"No. You work hard enough as it is. No way. Besides, the job's only part of the problem."

"What do you mean?"

"The water supply."

"Oh, come on. Water's a problem everywhere."

"Yeah, but we're in about the worst place possible, outside of flat-out desert. Nebraska's depended on the Ogallala Aquifer forever. But the Ogallala is dried up, dead, gone."

"The drought'll break sometime, and it'll come back."

"Not in our lifetime, I'll bet. Maybe never. So, we're smack in the middle of the country, completely dependent on water being trucked in from other places. It's some of the most expensive water there is, because it has to come from so far."

"So, what's your point? Everyone has to get water from somewhere. It's not like we can't get it at all. *That* would be a problem."

"Lexi, here's the thing. If we moved to a decent-sized city somewhere else, we'd pay less for water—probably a lot less—and I could finally get a job."

"Whoa, whoa. Wait a minute. You cannot be serious." Lexi raised her hands, palms out. "This is the only place I've ever lived. I can't even *imagine* living anywhere else. Come on, the drought has to end sometime, and then everything will be okay again. Besides, my whole family is here, all my friends. My job. I can't just move to some strange place just like that." She snapped her fingers.

Jake took her hands in his, an earnest look on his face. "Lexi, think about it. The drought's been going on for years now. Years! Look at how we live. Afraid to use a drop more water than our allotment. Barely making ends meet." He sighed. "And just today, I tried to take Ava to the park. It's closed! Too dry. Can't even visit the damned park anymore. This isn't living. It's slowly being strangled by the drought."

"But the whole country's in a drought, not just us. Hell, a good chunk of the planet, for that matter. Why uproot ourselves just to have the same problems—and maybe some new ones—somewhere else? It's not worth it." Lexi snatched her hands away and folded her arms across her chest.

"Yes, but at least other parts of the country have better access to what water *is* available. The Great Lakes, for instance. The coasts, with their desalinization plants. Their water's expensive, but not nearly as bad as ours. And not only are we far from those sources, we're in a place that gets hotter than hell in the summer—and humid, too. So, on top of everything else, we're paying through the nose for the electricity to keep the AC running day and night."

"You've been thinking about this for a while, haven't you?"

He tilted his head. "Off and on. More so, now that the steakhouse closed."

"And what would *I* do if we just took off like that? If we leave, then we're *both* out of jobs, taking a chance on some place where we don't know anyone. No. It's crazy to leave a bird in the hand." She crossed her legs and jiggled her foot, hesitated before continuing. "Besides, I know what this is really about. You're afraid we'll have to take money from my parents. You'll do anything to avoid that, won't you?"

Jake's jaw muscles flexed. "Let's not go there now. No, that is not why I came up with this. We really are in just about the worst place possible to ride out the drought and everything it's brought with it. And if we could set ourselves up in a better place, more than likely we wouldn't have to ask them for money. Bonus in my book."

Lexi stood, shaking with anger. "No. The answer is no. I don't want to move to some new place we don't know, where things might be as bad or worse, or bad in a different way. We know what we have here."

Jake glared at her from the couch. "You've never lived anywhere else. Of course you don't know what's out there. I do. And I'm telling you, we could do a whole lot better than this. We could even come out of the drought—whenever that happens—in a really good position. No chance of that here. We're barely scraping by, and you know it. We have to do something."

"Enough! I don't want to discuss it anymore. I'm going to bed to try to get some sleep before Ava needs her feeding." She turned to go. "*If* I can get to sleep after hearing this. Fucking crazy talk."

Lexi stormed down the hallway, her stomach knotting at the very thought of moving anywhere.

No way. No way in hell is he going to talk me into leaving. She brushed her fingers along the wall as she made her way toward the bedroom. *This is my home, our home. We stay, no matter what.*

CHAPTER 9

It was like trying to hold onto a feral cat, all arms and legs and motion, but thankfully no claws. Jake struggled to secure Ava against his shoulder, then gently patted her back until she let out a delicate little burp and settled down. He wiped the drool from her lips with the tiny pink towel Lexi'd bought and put her down for her afternoon nap. She wriggled into a fetal position, planted a tiny fist next to her mouth and yawned. Her eyelids fought a brave battle to stay open—and lost that battle within just a few moments. Just like that.

He stood beside her crib for a while, watching her breathe, watching her face twitch as she dreamed about whatever babies dreamed about. Lucky, she was. Not a care in the world. No clue about anything beyond the here and now. The pleasures of food and dry diapers were probably all that registered in a brain so young. If only life were really that simple.

He'd give anything to not have to worry about everything that might or might not happen, to not have to plan for the future in a world he could not control. And to not have to fight Lexi every step of the way—or deal with having her parents breathing down his neck, questioning his every move.

If it were just him, or even just him and Lexi, it would be one thing. But now they had Ava. On more levels than he ever imagined, having a baby depending on them made it a lot harder to take risks. Even good ones. But if ever there was a time they needed to make a leap, it was now.

They had to start over in a place where water was closer at hand, but he just couldn't seem to get that through to Lexi. If she had her way, she'd live and die in this damned town, never experience anything else, no matter the cost. She'd always been that way, dependent on being physically near her family, like some kind of security blanket. Probably couldn't stand on her own two feet if her life depended on it. And she apparently didn't trust him to take reasonable risks to make their lives better. Hell, she didn't trust him to take *any* risks.

Even when they took a vacation, she never wanted to stray very far from her geographic anchor. And since Ava, she'd gotten even worse.

Jake closed the nursery door, wandered into the living room, and gazed out the bay window. Not a bad neighborhood, really. Looked kind of ramshackle now, with all the grass and other vegetation long dead—a fire hazard lying in wait. Their house was nice enough, comfortable for a modest starter. But they'd probably lose a chunk of change if they tried to sell it. Who in their right mind would want to buy out here now?

The mail truck ambled down the street, reminding him of a big mechanical bee, stopping here and there to visit a waiting mailbox. He wondered when mail delivery would disappear altogether in favor of everything finally going electronic. Bees had certainly disappeared, along with the flowers they used to pollinate.

Jake listened closely for any sound from Ava's room. Nothing. Good time to sneak out and get the mail. Shielding his eyes from the blazing afternoon sun, he stepped outside into humidity so oppressive it made it hard to breathe, then slogged the few yards down the concrete walkway to their mailbox.

He tentatively poked at the metal mailbox with one finger. Searing hot. Covering his fingers with the hem of his shirt, he opened the box, grabbed the few items inside, and slapped it shut. He hurried back inside to the comforting chill of the air conditioner before taking the time to even glance at the mail.

Humid Midwest summers had never been high on his list of favorite things, but they were a million times worse since the drought. Nothing but parched vegetation and dead, leafless trees everywhere. No shade, no protection. And turning on the lawn sprinklers to cool things down would be nothing short of heresy in this day and age. He chuckled. Heresy, hell. Turning on the sprinklers was a flagrant water crime, punishable by way too much time behind bars.

He wiped beads of sweat from his hairline, then flipped through the day's mail. A couple of flyers for local businesses. He shook his head. Stupid waste of marketing dollars, with paper being so expensive these days. Who reads these things, anyway? Then he stopped. A letter from Water and Power. Wasn't the bill. They got those electronically. Couldn't be good. They wouldn't waste paper on something trivial.

Jake ripped open the envelope and pulled out the single sheet of paper. It announced—in accusatory, large-font, bold letters— that they had used twenty gallons more than their allotment in the new billing month. Because it was their first time exceeding their allotment, and because they did so by a relatively small amount, they were only being fined $500. *Only $500!*

Twenty gallons. What was that, a few extra toilet flushes? They already installed super-high-efficiency toilets, and only flushed when they had to. They'd been running close to their limit before he lost his job. Being home instead of at work for however many hours a week had to be the difference. Great double whammy. More water, less money. And now a fine they couldn't afford.

Jake threw the paper down on the kitchen table and paced. What the hell could they cut to get their usage back down? And where were they going to get an extra $500 to pay that fine by the due date?

A wail from the nursery broke the silence. Jake stopped pacing and clapped his hands to his head. Not the goddamned baby again! Not now! Everything was closing in, falling down around him. And nothing he did—or tried to do—made a fucking bit of difference.

They had to get out of here, try someplace else. He couldn't live in this town anymore, imprisoned without any real chance of getting their lives back on track.

But how the hell was he going to convince Lexi?

He clenched his fists and stood in the middle of the kitchen, shifting from foot to foot, as Ava's screeching stabbed at his ears. He wanted to scream, to run from the house and never come back.

But he was boxed in, every way he turned.

CHAPTER 10

Lexi started her car, cranked up the air conditioning, and leaned close to the vent to enjoy the deliciously cool blast of air on her neck. A little taste of heaven compared with what it was like outside. Just the short walk out to her car in that muck, and she felt bathed in sweat. She couldn't imagine ever getting used to the downright vicious heat and humidity the drought had brought.

Murderous weather aside, she couldn't wait to get home and put all thoughts of work behind her for the evening. Today felt like nothing less than a long-distance sprint. Dr. Reynolds had a personal emergency that took him out of the office part of the morning, so she'd had to do some mighty fancy dancing to get everyone rescheduled with the minimum possible disruption. She'd been running nonstop all day long, so busy she had to wolf down her sandwich with one hand while she worked through lunch.

She switched on the news station and started for home. At least she had a super-short commute before she could kick back. So much more pleasant than living in a big city. Or at least than what she imagined big-city life to be like.

Temperatures throughout Western Nebraska are predicted to rise significantly by this time next week—likely to record levels—and public safety officials are warning this heat wave is expected to turn deadly. Water and Power tells us the power grid is already struggling to keep up with demand from heavy reliance on air conditioners. They anticipate system overloads and widespread power outages.

Without air conditioning—and with stringent water rationing in effect—the very young, the very old, and those with pre-existing health conditions are expected to fall victim to heat stroke and heat exhaustion at an unprecedented rate. Smaller towns lack sufficient ambulance and hospital-bed capacity to handle the anticipated demand. Widespread deaths are likely to occur, creating a public health emergency like none we've seen before in this region.

The longest drought in the history of the nation—dubbed The Drought of the Millennium by climate experts—threatens to—

Lexi smacked the button to shut off the radio. Sometimes she wondered why she ever turned on the news anymore. It only stressed her out over things she couldn't do a thing about. It's not like there weren't reminders of the drought and all its effects everywhere she turned. The last thing she needed was an extra layer of doomsaying on top of it all.

She turned onto their street, grateful to be home, where she could shut out all the horrible news and enjoy being with her family. Time to play with Ava for a little bit, then make a nice dinner, sit down and relax. Enjoy the air conditioning. While they still had some.

Lexi stepped inside and stopped short. Jake was sitting at the kitchen table, his head in his hands.

"What's the matter?"

He looked up at her, his face grimmer than she'd ever seen it. "This." He held out a sheet of paper.

She took it and started to read. "Oh." She slumped into a chair, breathless. "Oh my God."

Head bowed, Jake ran his fingers across his scalp as if he wanted to pull out all his hair. "Lexi, we can't go on this way. It isn't working for us here. It's not *going* to work for us here. I can't find a job and we can't sustain all of us on our water allotment. Not with Ava."

Lexi slapped the paper down on the table. "Well, what the hell do you want me to do? Wave a wand and make Ava disappear? You'd like that, wouldn't you? You never wanted her in the first place, and now's your chance to throw it in my face."

"Don't be ridiculous. She's here and she's ours, and we'll take care of her, no matter what. But this is exactly what I was worried about, that having a baby would make it all the harder to stay within our allotment." He gestured toward the paper. "Now it's happened. When we can least afford to pay the fine. And if we don't pay the fine, Water and Power'll get ugly about that real fast."

"My parents—"

"Don't start up about having your parents bail us out. Even if I could stomach that, it doesn't solve the bigger problem. How are we going to make sure we don't blow the allotment a second time? If we do that, these five hundred bucks'll be the least of our worries."

"Don't you think I know that?" Lexi jumped up and slammed her fist on the table. "Don't you think I watch the bills every month? I *know* we've been getting close. I've been trying to keep an eye on our usage."

"Well, it's not enough. Obviously. We were already close, and we went past it because I'm home all the time now. So, I'm not bringing in any pay *and* I'm putting too much pressure on our usage."

Jake stood, hands on hips. "Lexi, this is it. What do I have to do to make you understand? We've got to go somewhere where there are jobs to be had. There is nothing—*nothing*—here. The market was already tight, and now everyone from the steakhouse is out there, too, competing for something that isn't even there."

Lexi pressed her hands to her ears. "I can't even deal with this right now. I just can't. I—I have to go feed the baby."

She fled the kitchen, then stopped outside the nursery to collect herself before going in. No sense in upsetting Ava. It wasn't her fault. Nothing could ever be her fault, she was so sweet and innocent. How the hell could Jake act like she was the cause of all their troubles?

Lexi took a deep breath and went inside. Ava smiled up at her from her crib and waved her tiny fists. She picked her up and held her warm little body tight against her chest. Tears ran down her face as she stifled a sob.

They had to get through this. Somehow. If only Jake weren't so damned stubborn about accepting help. Then it would be so much easier, so much less stress. For all of them. She'd have to find a way to convince him, is all. It was just a little rough spot. Happens to everyone.

Once they got past it, everything would be okay again.

It had to be.

CHAPTER 11

Jake didn't want to think of what the electric bill would look like this month—especially now that his severance was all gone. This latest heatwave was every bit as bad as they'd predicted, maybe even worse. The AC had been running nonstop, day and night. Not like it didn't usually run most of the day during the summer, but now it never once cycled off. Yet it was hardly keeping up. Even with every shade in the place drawn, it was about eighty degrees inside.

Better than it was outside. He'd take eighty over a hundred-and-eight any day. But it was still pretty miserable indoors. He had Ava napping in just her diaper to try to keep her cool, and the poor thing fussed and whined, even with that. There was no chance of taking her outside anywhere. The heat would get her in no time. Jake felt like a mole, trapped beneath the ground, afraid to venture out for fear of being baked alive.

He wiped sweat from his forehead and clicked the remote. Might as well catch the afternoon news before Lexi got home and made him shut it off. She told him between his nagging her to move and the news having only doom and gloom to report, that tuning out was the only way she could keep her sanity. Typical Lexi. She'd rather ignore unpleasant things, hoping they'd somehow disappear on their own.

Jake settled back into the couch. Maybe Lexi had a point. Getting all stressed out over something you couldn't change was a waste of energy. But it was just plain stupid to not act when you *could* change things. He shook his head and tuned into the local news.

Temperatures are expected to drop back down to the upper nineties by later this week, but significant damage has already been done. Power outages are widespread, particularly on the north end of town, where the infrastructure is older. Water and Power is considering using rolling brownouts to try to keep the system from completely collapsing. More details on that plan are expected tomorrow at their daily briefing.

Hospitals are past capacity with heat-related admissions. Every available bed and gurney is occupied right now, with overflow patients out in the hallways. Paramedics are working around the clock to triage calls and provide ER-level care in the field, but there aren't enough of them to cover the entire affected geographic area.

The death toll is high and rising, with five hundred in this county alone over the last several days. Most of the dead are children under four years of age, seniors, and those with pre-existing medical conditions. However, health care providers are starting to see healthy adults succumbing as well.

A spokesperson from the Department of Health said that, of the populations most vulnerable to this heat, those who do survive this heatwave will be more likely to fall victim to heat or other health-related issues in the near future.

Those who've lost loved ones are being asked to consider immediate cremation. There are insufficient facilities to keep bodies properly refrigerated until funerals and burials can be arranged, and this is creating a health hazard of a different kind—

Jake clicked off the television. Enough was enough. Tossing aside the remote, he glanced around the shadowy living room, shuttered tight against the raging heat outside.

And tried not to think of what would happen if they lost power.

CHAPTER 12

*M*eadow Lake's azure water lay before her, inviting her to immerse herself in its beauty. A mild breeze kicked up, cloaking the lake's surface in a million twinkling sunlit diamonds. Puffy white clouds gathered on the horizon, promising a soothing afternoon rain.

Lexi waded into the lake's cool water, deeper and deeper, until it was up to her waist. She dove beneath the surface, holding her breath as long as she could and swimming with strong, smooth strokes out toward the center.

Something dark and shapeless rose up from the lake bed, directly in front of her, reaching for her...

Disoriented, Lexi gasped and snapped to attention. Ava kept feeding like nothing happened. Thank God she didn't drop her while she was out. She leaned back in the rocking chair. Weird dream. Taunting her with something she couldn't have: a refreshing swim in Meadow Lake, her old haunt over on the east side of the county. It had long since fallen victim to the drought, baring its dry bed in surrender. She shivered and tried to shake off the creepy feeling from the dream.

She smoothed Ava's wispy blond hair and waited for her to finish up. Maybe she could slip in a desperately needed block of uninterrupted sleep before Ava woke up hungry again. She must be dead-bone tired to conk out like she just did.

Lexi sniffed, frowned. Must be her imagination. No one would be out grilling at two in the morning. She sniffed again, then opened the window. Something was burning, but what?

She hurried into their bedroom, clutching Ava against her chest. "Jake? Jake! Wake up."

He rolled over, a forearm over his eyes. "Hm, what?"

"I smell smoke."

Jake pushed himself up. "Where, what?"

"Not in the house, somewhere outside."

Jake flung on his robe and they ran for the front door, then stepped outside into the stifling heat. The sky glowed red and angry to the east, and the smell of smoke was unmistakable.

"Oh my God. What is it?" Lexi cringed in the doorway.

"I'll check."

Jake ducked back inside and returned a few moments later, gaping at his cell. "There's an alert from the county. Huge fire up in the hills east of town. They don't know what started it, but it's completely out of control and moving fast." He scrolled and read some more. "And it's coming this way. They're ordering immediate evacuations—"

"Evacuations?"

He scrolled some more, his eyes widening as he read on. "Governor says there's no local water to fight the fire with. Unless they can get some brought in, they'll have to let it burn itself out." He stared down at his cell, shock and disbelief spreading across his face. His voice lowered to a near-whisper. "It says to treat the evacuations as permanent."

"Permanent?" Lexi patted Ava as she started to fuss. "What?"

Jake clutched his cell in both hands. "Says to get out as quickly as possible, take all the essentials you can. Plan on not being able to get back for a long time...or ever."

"That's crazy! Give me that—" Lexi reached for his cell.

Jake yanked it back. "That's what it said, believe me. We better grab what we can and get the hell out. Start loading up the car."

The house rumbled with the sound of low-flying helicopters, one and then another, heading east. Moments later, a voice boomed from a PA system outside. Lexi and Jake peered out the front door. A police car, its flashing lights spreading red and blue alarm through the darkness, crept down the street.

Major fire east of town, heading this way, moving fast. Governor's ordered immediate evacuation of all towns in its path. Do not wait. Take all necessities with you. Repeat...do not wait, evacuate NOW.

Check your cell alerts for details. Repeat: major fire—

The sound trailed off as the car turned the corner.

"Oh my God, Mom and Dad!" Lexi turned to go get her cell.

Jake grabbed her arm. "There's no time!"

Lexi twisted away, jolting Ava into a panicky screeching fit. "I can't leave them. They'll need help packing."

Jake grabbed her shoulders, pulled her close, and locked eyes with her. "Lexi. Listen to me. We only have time to pack what we need—and what Ava needs. We can't head over there and pack them up, too. There is no time."

"You want us to leave them?"

"We can't go help them *and* get out ourselves. They can pack and leave by whatever route works best for them. They're perfectly capable. They're only in their fifties, for God's sake."

"But I can't—"

"You have to! They can take care of themselves. Come on, we've got a lot to do and not much time."

Lexi spun, glancing around the room. "Oh my God. I hope you're right. I hope they'll be okay. This is all too much. I can't even think. I don't know where to start!"

"Baby stuff. Food, water. Grab some clothes. Phones, credit cards, ID. Anything you can't live without that we can fit in the car. Hurry!"

Lexi ran for the nursery. "Sorry, Baby." She plopped Ava in her crib, ignoring her screams of protest, and started stuffing baby supplies into a huge diaper bag as quickly as she could. Her thoughts whirled so fast she couldn't seem to latch onto a single thread at a time. It was all a jumble. Getting Ava and themselves packed up and off to—where? And what about her parents? Would they wind up going off in different directions? How would they all get back together?

And when? Sounded like the fire was huge. And they weren't even *trying* to fight it? It'd blow right through town, with all the brown lawns and dead shrubs around. Tinder dry, and if everyone fled, would the whole town burn down? Would there be anything left to come back to?

Lexi gritted her teeth and jammed more baby stuff into the bag. Can't think like that right now. Better focus and make sure not to forget something important.

"Back in a minute. Hang on."

Ava was screaming so hard she couldn't have heard a word she said anyway. Lexi sprinted through the kitchen and out to the garage with Ava's things. Their SUV stood there in the pool of overhead light, all its doors and the rear hatch wide open. Jake tossed a bag into the cargo, then headed back into the house.

He counted on his hands as he inventoried his progress. "Got my clothes, emergency supplies, sleeping bags, the tent, the camp stove and fuel, computer stuff. Transferred the car seat from your car—"

"We're leaving my car?"

"I don't see us taking two cars, then trying not to get separated out there. It's going to be a madhouse with everyone trying to leave town at once. Better just jam everything we can fit into the SUV. Come on, we still need to raid the kitchen for food and drinks and some cooking stuff." He nodded at her bag of baby supplies. "Good, you've got Ava covered. Get your clothes together, and I'll get started in the kitchen."

Lexi tossed the bag of baby things into the SUV's middle section, just in case she had to get at any of it while they were moving. Still a fair amount of space left. Might as well stuff it full in what little time they had. Better chance of not leaving something important behind.

She stepped back and paused in the kitchen doorway, feeling a little unsteady, unhinged. She leaned against the door jamb, steeling herself. Just get through this. Concentrate on one thing at a time and get through this. Quickly.

Lexi glanced around. Her home. She tried to drink it all in one last time, set it firmly in her mind's eye. Just in case she never saw it again.

No. Can't think like that. We'll get back. May be away a little while, but we'll get back home, and everything will be okay again.

CHAPTER 13

"Quiet her down so I can concentrate!"

Jake glanced from side to side in the predawn murk, itching to put the car into manual mode, gun it, and barrel through everything in his way. Instead, the autodrive had been creeping the car toward the onramp, inch by inch, for the last two hours. He could hardly wait for his chance to get on the freeway and blast out of there. Maddening, how close they were. So close, he could thread his way through all the cars and walk there in a matter of minutes.

Stretched thin, the local police had blocked off the roads they didn't want anyone on, leaving traffic to its own devices everywhere else. Every westbound route was jammed with vehicles of all kinds, their autodrives alternately idling and inching them forward as those inside desperately tried to escape the fire.

The blare of horns filled the air with wave after wave of nerve-shredding racket. Ava picked up on the tension and barely controlled panic; her high-pitched shrieks reverberated inside the SUV like a form of torture. Jake wanted to plug his ears to stop the bombardment of decibels before he gave in and started screaming himself.

The freeway itself was far more congested than he'd ever seen it, but at least it appeared to move at a decent pace after the onramp. He licked his lips and strained his eyes in the darkness. If he could somehow get through this bottleneck, they'd be on their way. But there was nothing. No opening, not even the slightest glimmer of one.

They idled in a sea of vehicles, all at different angles as they jockeyed for an opening, a chance to get on the freeway to go somewhere, anywhere but here. Jake twisted around in his seat. The hills to the east of town burned brighter than even a half hour ago. The fire was coming, and it was coming fast. He hoped things started moving soon, or they'd get to watch their town burn down right behind them...and then be burned alive in their cars.

"I wish we'd gone another way, maybe one ramp up or back or something." Lexi sat twisted in her seat, reaching one hand back to Ava, trying to soothe her without taking her out of her car seat. "We're not moving at all."

"Really? I hadn't noticed." Jake craned his neck, watching, waiting. "I don't know that we'd have done much better. Maybe if we'd taken secondary roads till the next town. Too late for that now."

Lexi pulled out her cell, tapped the screen and held it to her ear. "They're still not picking up." She dropped the phone back in her bag and turned toward the window. "I hope they're getting out in time."

"They'll be okay, Lexi. Probably can't pick up the phone right now, is all. If they're still at the house, they're busy packing, and if they're on the road, they're probably in a mess like this themselves."

"I can't stand this." Lexi twined her fingers in her hair and tugged. "I feel so trapped. Why aren't the cops directing traffic or something?"

"Getting worked up isn't going to help. There aren't enough cops to take care of it all. Hey, why don't you go sit in back with Ava? Calm her down while we're stuck here, then put her back in her seat when we get going."

"There's a ton of crap back there, no room for me to sit next to her!"

"Throw something in front, then. It's not like we're moving right now. Jesus, Lexi."

She shot him a dirty look and made the switch, slamming the door shut and scooping Ava into her arms. Should have thought of that sooner. Ava finally stopped screaming. He felt bad, snapping at Lexi like that, but he had to focus on what he was doing. He didn't dare miss a chance to get on that ramp, get moving at last. For all their sakes.

But moving where? Right now, to be moving west, away from the fire, would be enough. They'd stop for something to eat and figure things out once they got free of the worst of the traffic.

Jake blinked and rubbed his eyes. There. A few car lengths ahead of them, taillights dimmed and flashed and dimmed again as the cars' autodrives reacted to an opening and let up on the brakes. Movement! Like a current flowing within a larger stream, the line of cars in front of him began to advance. Maybe a five-mile-an-hour crawl, but a steady crawl nonetheless. An exponential improvement over the inch-at-a-time torment they'd endured for the last several hours.

"Finally! Looks like it's busting loose."

Lexi gave a little cheer from the back seat. "Okay Ava, here we go."

About twenty minutes later, Jake nosed the SUV onto the freeway and finally felt free to breathe. He settled into his lane, then stretched his neck one way, then the other, to try to work out the burning sensation in his overtight muscles. He never dreamed going thirty miles an hour could feel like he was flying.

On their way at last. To where, he had no idea.

CHAPTER 14

"Look, I'm telling you we can't fight this fire on our own. It's the largest Nebraska's ever seen—by far. We don't have the manpower *or* the equipment, and we sure as hell don't have the water. Oakley, please. You've got to do something."

Jim Percy slumped at his desk in the governor's mansion. He'd holed up there all night since word first came of the fire, working the phone, trying to marshal the resources to save his state from absolute disaster. And coming up empty. This call was his last resort, like crying uncle. He hated being forced to call D.C. and beg the Water Czar for help. And he didn't like the way it was going. Not at all.

He rubbed his throbbing temples, then chewed a couple aspirin and swallowed them dry. As governor, he'd faced crises of every kind, and he'd handled them all pretty damned well— even managing the state through the past few years of record-breaking drought. But this. This was on a scale he couldn't begin to fathom. Made everything else look like child's play. If he didn't get help fast—and lots of it—he could count on the fire spreading through the western half of the state. And taking everything in its path.

A sigh came over the phone. "Sorry. I wish I could help you, but I just can't do it."

Jim thumped his fist on the desk. "Goddammit, Oakley, I've got to get some help here! We need water, and we need air drops to get on this before it's too late. I've tried every other resource I know."

"I can't spare the water. Not for putting out a fire."

"A *fire*? This is no ordinary fire! Everything's so dry, it's spreading faster than anything we've ever seen. It's already taken out a fifty-mile band through the center of the state. And it's building strength, moving faster and faster." Jim choked, coughed. The bitter taste of the aspirin rose up, burning his throat. "People are dying, Oakley! Homes, businesses, farms. Everything is going up and you can't spare some water?"

"No. I can't. The reserves are critically low as it is, and the drought's not ending anytime soon. You'll just have to let it burn out. I'm truly sorry."

"Let it burn out? Are you—"

Click.

"Sonofabitch!"

Hands trembling, Jim slammed down the phone. That was it. He'd played his last card. And lost. Barring a miracle, there was nothing more he could do but stand by, helpless, and watch the tragedy unfold. He stared at the live-streaming helicopter video on his monitor.

A bright-orange belt of fire raged through the center of the state, moving from east to west before his eyes. He looked away. All those people. So many evacuations. The lucky ones who'd gotten out, where had they gone? How many lives, how much property would be lost by the time it was over? What would be left?

And those who didn't get out in time. Jim clapped his hands over his face and sobbed.

Kevin Oakley leapt to his feet and gave his chair a vicious kick. It smashed into the wall and tipped over. He hated his job with every fiber of his being. Every single day he wished he could walk away from it knowing someone else would take over and do it better. He knew full well he just doomed half of Nebraska— and probably more—by denying Governor Percy the water he needed to fight the fire. But he was responsible for the nation's water reserves. He had no choice but to protect what was left.

The drought had been so severe, and so longstanding, that every source of water had been gravely depleted to levels never before seen. Aquifers that had survived previous droughts stood no chance against this one. Lakes, rivers, and streams. All but the very largest were dry as a bone now.

Most of the potable water now came from desalinization plants on the coasts. Some still came from the Great Lakes, and some from the once-mighty Columbia River in the Pacific Northwest. And that water had to be trucked cross-country for distribution in special tanker trucks driven by pairs of armed guards.

All very expensive. Made even more so by the fuel needed to operate the tanker trucks, vehicles that were far too heavy and too old to convert to modern electric power technology. The drought killed the fracking industry several years back, making the country completely dependent on foreign oil, at whatever price those nations wanted to charge. And they knew a seller's market when they saw it.

Kevin righted his chair and dropped down into it. In some ways, his job was simple. Just say *no*. With domestic water reserves as low as they were and no foreign countries willing or able to sell their water at any price, *no* was always the right answer. At least until the drought broke, whenever the hell that might be.

Maybe someday he could spend his time managing and distributing normal water supplies, instead of hoarding every single drop to try to fend off complete catastrophe, an unimaginable death toll. He shook his head. That was just a pipe dream. Even if the drought ended tomorrow—and it showed no signs of doing that—it would take years to restore the reserves to anything approaching normal. *Years.* He'd be retired or dead by then.

He rubbed his eyes and groaned. Meanwhile, he had to guard what little water was left—at all costs. He didn't want to think about what would happen if and when they ran completely out.

But would there come a point when—no matter what he did, no matter how hard he tried—the country would at last run out of water?

The way things were going, it was entirely possible.

CHAPTER 15

Barely past dawn, and the temperature inside the parked SUV was already starting to creep up. Lexi held Ava in her lap, fast asleep after a good, long feeding. She wished Jake would hurry up and get them checked into the motel—even if it did look like a filthy pit of a place. She was tired of being in the car, already tired of nonstop driving with no idea where they were going. She longed for a bed, decent air conditioning, and some rest. Maybe then she'd feel halfway capable of dealing with things. But not now.

Aside from a couple of recharge stops for the car, Jake had driven straight through since they first got on the freeway nearly four hours ago. He'd barely spoken in all that time, like he was lost in his own thoughts and would rather be alone to stew in them. She couldn't find much she wanted to talk about, either. She felt uprooted, lost. And afraid for what would happen to their home, her parents. She couldn't even think past the next freeway sign right now.

Traffic had thinned out some after the first couple of hours, as fellow fire refugees fanned out in different directions to go wherever it was they went. Jake kept going west on I-80, and they decided to stop here in Cheyenne. Find a place to stay, take some time to think of their next move. But it wasn't going too well.

First, they tried the hotels on the main drag. All full. Then they tried using the SUV's nav system to scout out the secondary roads for motels. Same thing. No vacancy. At least, not so far. Lexi glanced out the window at the broken-down hulk of the EZ-Rest Motel. The place could use some paint, a new roof.

Actually, there wasn't much it didn't appear to need, including some serious weed-whacking all over that crumbling asphalt parking lot. Hard to believe it was even in operation, from the looks of it. But it did appear to be open. Jake, stony-faced and determined, strode into the office a few minutes ago to get them a room.

Lexi didn't want to imagine how disgusting the rooms might be, but at this point, she'd risk bedbugs just to clean up a little and get off the road for a while. She couldn't remember ever being in a car for so many hours, or going so many miles. She'd never been to Wyoming before and, so far, nothing about it particularly appealed to her. Even more than she wanted a good nap, she wished they could turn back around and head home, as if this were all a bad joke.

Scowling at the ground, Jake emerged from the office and flung himself into the driver's seat with a groan. Cradling Ava in one arm, Lexi pushed the switch to raise her seat back upright.

"How much did they want for a room?"

He shook his head. "No room."

"Are you kidding? This dump doesn't have one open room?"

"Nope. Some old woman in there at the desk—looked about as worn out as the motel—said they were full and not likely to have an opening for at least a week. I tried arguing, begging, offering her extra money. Nothing worked." He sighed and reached for the starter.

"No. You've been driving long enough. Let me drive."

He turned to her. "You sure? I can go a while longer."

"I'm sure. Ava just ate, so it's a good time for me to take over."

"All right. I wouldn't mind a break."

Lexi settled into the driver's seat, then pressed a couple of buttons to adjust the mirrors and seat to her settings.

"All right, where to now?"

Jake reclined his seat a little and covered his eyes with his forearm. "I really don't know. Just keep going west on I-80 for now, I guess. It has to get better, the farther out we get. More chance of getting a room." He turned toward the window. "At least I hope so."

Lexi started the car and glanced at the dash display before setting off. Everything looked in order, and they still had a decent amount of charge on the fuel cell from the last stop. Too bad she couldn't say the same for herself. Her growling stomach would have to wait. First, they needed to find a room—any room—and get their bearings. Check on what was happening back home. Maybe the news about the fire had all been overblown and they could head back. Could be. The news people always blew stuff way out of proportion to jack up their ratings.

Once she got back on the freeway, she settled in for the drive and checked out the traffic around her. Still thicker than she'd expect in the boondocks of Wyoming. Who lived way out here, anyway? And quite a few Nebraska plates. So they *were* still competing with others who evacuated when they did.

Lexi gasped and white-knuckled the wheel as another car cut in front of them and sped off, going well above the speed limit. She was tempted to take it out of autodrive and go manual, too. She'd get wherever the hell they were going a whole lot faster. But manual was supposed to be reserved for emergency maneuvers or making adjustments in turning or parking that autodrive couldn't do on its own yet. The last thing they needed was a nice, expensive ticket for going manual without good reason.

Clenching her jaw, she forced herself to sit back and let the SUV do its thing. Jake had fallen asleep, so he missed the asshole whizzing by. Rude drivers pissed him off to no end. She glanced in the rear view. Ava slumped in her carrier, oblivious to everything. Thank God they both slept through that. The last thing she needed right now was Jake ranting and Ava fussing.

Up ahead in the distance, she saw the asshole make another boneheaded maneuver. This time he cut in front of a water tanker, barely missing it. Stupid, really stupid. That guy must want to get himself—or someone else—killed. Those tankers were huge, awkward, and prone to jackknifing if forced to make a sudden move. Someone could get hurt, and if the tanker overturned and leaked, a whole lot of precious water could get wasted.

Besides, tanker drivers were always heavily armed, and

they were permitted to use their weapons if anything—defined quite loosely, she'd heard—endangered them or their cargo. That fool was really asking for it, cutting off a water tanker like that. They could probably come up with a reason to shoot him. It happened. Water was so precious that the tankers and their drivers inhabited a legal sphere all their own. Anything was okay as long as it was done in the name of protecting the water supply.

Lexi wondered what kind of hurry that idiot must be in to take risks like that. Maybe he was just an asshole. Plenty of those around. Or maybe he was desperate to get home, or at least to get somewhere safe.

Like they were.

CHAPTER 16

Jake twitched awake, his neck stiff from sleeping lopsided, jammed up against the car window. It took him a couple seconds to remember where he was and why. It took no time at all for him to realize how hungry he was. He sat up and took a quick look around to get his bearings.

He pointed. "Lexi, there's a café up ahead on the right. Pull off for it. Quick, before it's too late. God knows when there'll be another one out here."

"Sure." She slipped into the right lane behind another car, then took the off-ramp. "You sleep okay? You never fall asleep in the car."

"Yeah, guess I needed it." He rubbed the knot in his neck and glanced at the dash display. "Already lunch time? I was out that long?"

"'Fraid so. You and Ava slept right through. Aside from charging stops, I've just been going west like you told me to. You didn't miss anything. Didn't see any hotels while you were out. Not a lot going on along this stretch."

"Anything on the news?"

"I...um...turned off the radio."

"Why'd you do that? There could be an update we should know about."

"Well, as of a couple hours ago, they were still going on and on about how huge and out-of-control the fire is." She shook her head. "I just couldn't listen to any more of that. Didn't think to turn it back on."

"Jeez, Lexi. Well, maybe we can find out what's going on while we get something to eat."

The café looked like a refugee from another era. Little one-story aqua stucco thing with big plate glass windows, a neon sign, and its own little gravel parking lot. Almost like those diners they used to have. Felt like being dropped onto another planet, finding a place like that set in the midst of wide-open sage fields beside the interstate.

A welcome gust of refrigerated air greeted them as they stepped inside, out of reach of the merciless sun hanging in the wide, cloudless Wyoming sky. The place was packed, people all talking at once, their faces turned toward the flat-screen television that dominated the space over the lunch counter.

Jake snagged the last open booth in the corner and helped Lexi set Ava, snugly tucked in her portable carrier, on the seat next to her. He slid in on his side and stretched his legs out under the table. Seemed like they'd been on the run for a lifetime, but it'd been less than twelve hours. Enough time to expect some kind of meaningful update on the fire.

He had the better vantage point for the television from where he sat, so he watched while Lexi fussed with Ava. Some stupid daytime talk show was on. He started to get up to ask them to change the channel when a news bulletin cut in.

Reports continue to trickle in on what authorities are now calling the Western Nebraska Fire Complex. The fire's origin is still under investigation. It's thought that it was started by heat lightening, but arson hasn't yet been ruled out. Regardless of the cause, this has turned into a fire of historic proportions.

The fire began in west-central Nebraska, forming a band traversing the state from north to south. It has quickly spread westward, fueled by parched farm pastures, as well as vast quantities of dead trees and brush. The fire continues to grow in intensity, devouring entire towns in its wake, leaving nothing behind.

Officials say the fire's already done a tremendous amount of damage and taken an untold number of lives. It's going to be a long time before it's out and authorities are able to accurately assess the number of dead, let alone identify them all.

Governor Jim Percy publicly denounced Water Czar Kevin Oakley for refusing to provide water and tanker aircraft capable of delivering that water over the fire. And I quote, "While I understand the need to conserve water supplies for the populace, Oakley's denial of water to fight this horrific fire has already cost us many, many lives and destroyed a major portion of our great state."

Lexi sat wide-eyed, her hand over her mouth, as she heard the news. She grabbed her cell from her bag, frantically tapped the screen and slapped it against her ear. Tears streamed down her face.

"It goes straight to voicemail. Doesn't even ring," she whispered. "Oh God, where could they be?"

Jake reached out and took her hand. "They could be busy. Their phone could be off, saving batteries. Could be anything."

"They'd have called me. They'd have left me a message by now." Lexi sniffed and wiped away tears with the back of one hand. "We should have made sure they got out okay."

"Lexi, you know there was no time. We had to get out of there with Ava when we did, or—"

"Or we'd be dead like them?"

Lexi leapt up and ran to the bathroom. Ava watched her go, then started to wail. Jake went over and tried to quiet her.

A tired-looking, older waitress plodded over to their booth like her feet were killing her. She gestured in the direction Lexi went. "Everything okay here?"

"We'll be all right, thanks."

"Can I get you anything?"

"Yeah, what do you have?"

"Not much." She waved her arm. "It's been like this the past few hours. We're nearly cleaned out. I can get you some mixed vegetables and fish sticks. That's about it."

"Sure, bring a couple orders."

The waitress trudged away like maybe her feet weren't the only thing that hurt. Jake went back to his side of the booth as Lexi returned, her face and eyes red and raw.

"You okay?"

She slid into her seat, head bowed, eyes cast down. "I guess. Maybe. I don't know."

"Ordered some food for us."

"Not hungry."

"Neither of us has eaten since dinner last night. We'll be able to think more clearly if we eat something."

"Whatever. I don't really care right now."

"You *need* to eat. Can't let yourself get run down."

The waitress returned with their food, set the plates down, then limped over to the next table after shooting Lexi a sympathetic look.

Jake nudged Lexi's plate toward her. "Come on. Try to eat something. This is all they had left."

Lexi reached for a fish stick, a blank look on her face, her eyes still red and teary. She chewed it listlessly, as if she weren't even there.

Jake ate his fish stick without tasting it. The look on Lexi's face broke his heart, but there was nothing he could do about it, except make sure they stayed safe for now and landed somewhere soon so they could regroup.

And so they could get some rest. He was too tired to think clearly anymore, and Lexi had been running on pure emotion the entire time. All he knew right now was that returning home was not an option, not after what he just saw on the television news. And they couldn't keep driving forever. They'd have to come up with a plan, and they'd better have their wits about them when they did.

Stupid, rushed decisions always made things worse—and that was the last thing they needed.

CHAPTER 17

Lexi wrinkled her nose as they stepped inside the stuffy motel room. It looked about as old as it smelled, with its harvest-gold and burnt-orange color scheme. Ancient curtains hung askew, harsh mid-afternoon sunlight intruding through the gaps and tears. The carpet wore the stains and cigarette burns of way too many guests. The particleboard dresser and bedside tables looked like beating victims, and the bed sagged beneath its threadbare spread. She didn't want to know what the bathroom looked like, but at least the AC seemed to work.

"Wow. Quite the place." She set Ava's car seat in one of the chairs and made sure Ava couldn't reach far enough to touch anything. She didn't consider herself one of those germaphobes who treated her child like a fragile hothouse plant, but this place was well over the top. Who knew what germs people had left all over that chair—and the rest of the room?

Jake dropped their bags in the corner and rubbed his lower back. "Last room they had. And I can see why. But at least we finally have somewhere to rest up and figure out what to do. Who knew we'd have to drive damned near to Salt Lake to find a room?"

Lexi raised her arms high in the air, then leaned over and stretched down to touch her toes. It felt good just to uncoil her body after so many hours of tense sitting, watching the traffic and worrying about what lay in store for them.

"Yeah. Way too long in the car."

She pulled out her cell and checked her voicemail again, just in case. Nothing. Maybe her parents ran out so fast they forgot their cells. Could happen. Maybe. Better to think that than the alternative.

Jake grabbed the remote, turned the television to an all-news station, and collapsed into a creaky chair. Lexi rearranged the pillows and perched, cross-legged, on the bed. She could feel every spring right through the covers. But it was a bed.

She had to summon every last bit of her nerve to force herself to look at that television screen. If only she could wish this all away, put everything back the way it was. Even just turn the clock back to yesterday, drought and all. At least then they wouldn't be driving around like refugees, wondering when they could go home. *If* they could go home.

Our top story: continuing coverage of the Western Nebraska Fire Complex. The fire has now engulfed most of the western half of the state. Fire officials report zero-percent containment, and no help on the way.

Governor Percy, in a press release moments ago, has now condemned the president for not intervening after Water Czar Kevin Oakley denied his request for water drops. When we reached him for comment, Oakley defended his decision, stating, quote, while I regret the tragedy in Nebraska, the water supply for the country as a whole is my responsibility, and to waste untold amounts of water to fight a fire would be an improper use of such a scarce, vital resource. End quote.

As many as 100,000 people are estimated to have fled the fire since it started at approximately two in the morning, Central Time. Hotels and motels in the escape path are filled to capacity, with many evacuees camping out in their vehicles or in city parks.

Officials in California expressed concern that numerous evacuees may be headed there, thinking water supplies will be plentiful. While California is home to many desalinization plants, the governor points out that the state simply cannot take on that many new residents. Therefore, he has ordered the borders closed to non-residents, effective immediately. Local police and the National Guard have established roadblocks at all the main points of entry.

Lexi sat at attention as sharply as if she'd been hit with a bolt of electricity. "They've closed California? How can they close a whole state? Jake?"

Silence. She glanced over. Jake lay slumped in his chair, chin on chest. Totally out of it. Even Ava was napping. Lexi switched off the television. Enough with the endless stream of bad news. Might as well get some sleep. Maybe after a nap, she'd be able to think straight again. She sure as hell couldn't right now. She'd never felt so overwhelmed and exhausted in all her life.

Lexi curled up on her side and did her best to ignore the stale smell of cigarettes and whatever else that wafted up from the tired, lumpy pillows. A moment later she sat back up, eyes wide. Voices, arguing voices. Just outside their room. She waited, heart pounding, as they passed into the distance and trailed off.

Maybe she should stay awake while Jake slept. Just in case something happened. At least she could lie down while she kept watch, rest her back a little. Her entire body felt stiff and creaky from sitting in the car for so long, all tight and stressed. She rearranged herself on the sagging bed, nestled into the musty pillows, then felt her eyelids close as if on their own volition. Well, maybe just a short nap. After all, the door was locked. They should be safe for now.

As Lexi drifted off to sleep, she wished with all her heart she would wake up in her own bed, in her own home, and realize all this was just a crazy, bad dream.

CHAPTER 18

Kevin Oakley jabbed his touch screen. The web page full of those horrifying satellite shots disappeared from view. If only it were that easy to make this all go away. He rubbed his eyes, wishing he could unsee what the images showed. Unprecedented destruction. Easy enough to predict. Not so easy to prevent. Not with the entire country, coast to coast, tinderbox-dry after twenty years of drought. Mile after mile in every direction, nothing but fuel for a hungry fire. Wasn't a matter of *if*, but of *when*. *When* a massive fire would spark up—no matter the reason—and devour everything in its wake.

The Western Nebraska Fire Complex lived up to its name, already destroying pretty much the entire Nebraska panhandle. The area was so completely charred, it showed up pitch-black on the satellite shots, as if it had been deleted. Which it pretty much had. Even when he zoomed in on the images, he saw nothing but pure blackness. Not even the odd house here and there in the rubble. This firestorm had broken all records. And it wasn't done yet.

The only glimmer of good news was that the fire was fast approaching a massive break line in eastern Wyoming and northeastern Colorado where another major fire had burned last summer. That break line should be wide enough to starve the fire and stop it at last. He hoped so, anyway.

Kevin closed his eyes and bowed his head. Refusing Governor Percy's request for water drops was the hardest thing he'd ever had to do. He knew perfectly well he'd sentenced countless people to their deaths, an untold number of homes and businesses to complete destruction. He'd wanted so badly to grant the request, to save who and what could still be saved. But he couldn't allow himself to do it—or many, many more would die, and the already fragile economy would collapse entirely.

But the worst-case scenario might still happen no matter what he did or did not do. Despite all the rationing that had been put in place, nationwide reserves had dwindled to an alarming level. With a drought this severe and long-lasting, there comes a point where you just can't ration your way out of it. And they'd reached that point a couple of years ago.

Reserves were so far past the critical point that granting Percy's request would have created an immediate nationwide catastrophe. And now it looked like the fire was going to stop on its own anyway. Still, rational as his decision had been, he couldn't bear to think about all the lives lost in the flames, and the wrenching displacement for those who did manage to escape.

Kevin sighed and began drafting an order to send to his regional distribution centers. Now that a wide swath of Nebraska had effectively been wiped off the face of the earth, water rations that would normally go to that area could be reallocated and redistributed accordingly.

A grim silver lining, but a silver lining nonetheless.

Kevin clicked Send, leaned back in his chair, and wished he'd never even been offered the job. Back then, the drought was only in its early stages. It looked like a good challenge, the next step in his career. Something he could manage successfully.

Not something like this. Not something that forced him to choose who lived and who died.

CHAPTER 19

Jake cradled the plastic takeout tray in both hands and savored the aroma as he headed back to their room. Amazing. The coffee and sandwiches actually smelled pretty damned good. Lucky a cheap, run-down motel like this had a breakfast bar at all, let alone one with anything that looked edible. Some hot, filling food and caffeine were just what they needed right now. His stomach growled as he rapped on the motel room door with his elbow.

"Lexi! It's me."

Lexi opened the door, her weary eyes lighting up at the sight of the tray. "Here, let me get those." She took the two styro coffee cups and set them on the scarred wooden table. "What's in the bag?"

"Would you believe warm breakfast sandwiches: sausage, eggs, and cheese. At least that's what they look and smell like. Probably soy or something for the filling. Can't imagine a place like this would spend the money on the real thing." He set the tray down and handed one of the sandwiches to Lexi. "Has Ava eaten?"

"Yep, all done." Lexi tore into her sandwich and slurped some coffee. "Mmmm…this'll hit the spot."

"They had a surprisingly decent spread. There was healthier stuff, too. Cereals, yogurt, that sort of thing. But I figured a big ol' dose of grease and calories would fit the bill much better."

"Damned straight it does. Good choice." Lexi gulped some more coffee. "Coffee's nice and strong, too. Just right. I can't believe we all slept straight through from yesterday afternoon. I'm still groggy."

Jake took a bite of his sandwich. Warm, greasy, and the flavor was not bad at all. Pretty tasty, even. He tried the coffee. "That *is* strong. Good, it'll shake the cobwebs out. I'm thinking we use today to see what's going on, plan and prepare. Spend one more night here to rest up a little, then move on."

"To where?" Lexi froze, a wary look in her eyes.

"Well, let's see."

Jake switched on the laptop and signed in to the motel's Wi-Fi. He pulled up the latest news on the fire, then stopped, his hands trembling over the keyboard. What he saw on the screen looked impossible.

"What is it?" Lexi crumpled up her sandwich wrapper and downed the last of her coffee.

Jake struggled to grasp the magnitude of the destruction that lay before his eyes. "There's nothing left," he whispered.

He slid the laptop across the table, so Lexi could see the satellite map displayed on its screen. "The fire is dying out just over the border, but the entire Panhandle is gone."

Eyes wide, Lexi gasped. "Oh my God, it's just...black." She pulled out her cell, hit speed-dial, and raised it to her ear. After a few moments, she slowly placed the phone on the table in front of her and stared at it.

She spoke as if in a trance. "Still no answer. And no messages."

"Lexi, I'm really sorry."

She looked up at him, her eyes wet with tears. "Maybe they forgot their phones in the rush, you know?"

"Maybe."

Lexi chewed her lip and looked away. "But even if they forgot their phones, you'd think they'd have tried to call from somewhere by now."

Jake put his hand on her shoulder and gave it a gentle squeeze. He couldn't imagine her parents not getting a message through somehow. They must not have made it out. He started to say something, then stopped. Better to let her reach that conclusion herself when she was ready.

Lexi shook her head, hard. "I can't think about it right now. I just can't. There has to be an explanation. They have to be safe somewhere." She pawed at her eyes and sniffed. "So, what do we do now?"

Jake glanced at the satellite image again, the enormity of the destruction still sinking in. "We can't go…east." He couldn't bring himself to say *home*. "And we can't stay here indefinitely."

"Well, what *can* we do?" She folded her arms across her chest.

"Go west. Get to California, closer to the water. They have most of the desalinization plants. We'll be better off there."

"Good luck with that idea. Just after you fell asleep yesterday, I heard on the news they were closing the border, effective immediately. No one gets in."

"No way. They can't do something like that."

"Oh yes they can. And they are. They say they don't have the capacity to take in a bunch of extra people."

"Bullshit. They just want to hog the water for themselves. Besides, California's a huge state. The border's far too long for them to watch every possible way in." Jake gulped some more coffee as he worked the problem over in his mind. "Even if we can't get in, we'll get as close as we can."

He pulled up a map of the western U.S. and zoomed in to search for possible routes. There had to be a way to get there. He ran a finger along the map, piecing together a plan as he went.

"So, we need to get the rest of the way across Utah, and all the way across Nevada. Not all that far as the crow flies. But some of the roads—"

Lexi wrapped her arms around herself as if overtaken by a sudden chill. "What roads are you talking about? Doesn't I-80 take us straight over there?"

"You said they closed the border, right? Well they'll for sure block access from all the major interstates, so I-80's out. We'll need to branch off onto secondary roads and hope they don't have the manpower to watch every single inch of border."

"I don't want to drive around in the middle of nowhere—in the *desert*. It's dangerous! Who knows what's out there?" She stood and started pacing, arms folded and shoulders hunched.

"Look, I can pretty much guarantee we won't get in via I-80. So, it'd be stupid to go that way." He pointed to the map. "If you want to stay on interstate, we'd wind up going through southern Idaho, then way up through northern Oregon. Much longer to go, and they don't have desalinization plants up there. They've been draining the Columbia River for their water. I think there'll be more capacity in California. We just have to find a route that'll let us sneak in."

Lexi stopped pacing and faced him. "Well, what about supplies? And the car won't make it that far on one charge, that's for sure. Probably not a charging station on every corner out in that...wasteland."

"We'll have to run it in gas mode until we get to where there are charging stations. Won't be cheap, but at least it gets decent mileage on gas. We can get some here, then top up at the Nevada border before we hit the back roads. We should be able to make it just fine with a full tank and some extra cans."

"Food?"

"Stock up and take it with us. Lexi, it's not like we'll be on the road for weeks on end. It's six-hundred some-odd miles, probably just one overnight if we play our cards right. We brought camping stuff, and we can sleep in the car, worst case."

Lexi spun around, her back to him, and pressed her hands to her head. "This is completely insane. All of it. I don't want to drive off through no man's land, not knowing where the hell we're going—and with Ava in the car. It's too risky!"

Jake went to her and tried to take her in his arms, but she wrenched herself away from him, sniffling and wiping away tears.

"Lexi. Our home is gone. So are both our jobs." He waved a hand, palm-up. "And we can't stay here. We have to make a new life, settle somewhere. It's going to be a long time before they rebuild from a fire that huge. If ever."

Ava stirred in her carrier, pink fists waving in the air. She glanced around, then her face crumpled and reddened. She started wailing like someone had jabbed her.

Lexi picked her up and held her close, cooing and trying to soothe her. "She's tight as a drum. She must be picking up on what's going on. We can't upset her like this."

"Then we should come up with a plan and work it. Stop

sitting here in limbo, thinking of all kinds of reasons to stay frozen in place. And the sooner, the better." Jake dropped down into one of the wobbly chairs and pulled the laptop toward him. "For all of our sakes."

"Jake, I'm so afraid. I feel like we've lost everything." She swiped away tears with one hand. "And my parents."

"You still have Ava. And me." Jake zoomed in on the map and started to make notes on a scrap of paper. "I'll get us through this, no matter what. Trust me."

He wished he felt as confident as he tried to sound. Lexi was right. They were taking a terrible risk driving through the desert with Ava. If the car broke down. If—

Can't think like that. Can't let Lexi pick up on my fears, either. Just have to plan carefully and get us all through this. There has to be a way.

CHAPTER 20

Lexi slumped on the edge of the sagging bed, her eyes locked on Ava. She'd finally gotten her to go back to sleep in her little carrier, but it'd taken forever this time. No real surprise. They were all suffering through this whole, horrible situation, each in their own way.

Ava was completely off her normal routine, and fussy as hell because of it. Jake was angry because she didn't enthusiastically embrace his insane idea to wander through the desert and hope they could get into California without running into some kind of trouble. So angry, he barely said a word when he left earlier to shop for supplies.

And she'd never, ever felt so vulnerable and overwhelmed. Here she was, sitting alone with Ava in some strange, beat-down motel room. Ripped right out of the life she'd been living only a couple of days ago. No word from her parents, no clue as to their whereabouts. Her home undoubtedly destroyed in the fire. No job to go to, not for either of them. And now Jake was mad at her for feeling this way. As if she could help it! And as if all that wasn't enough to handle, they had Ava to worry about.

Shaking her head, she stood up to stretch a little. Maybe she'd feel better if she moved around some, instead of just sitting there on that awful bed, stewing over things that were all way, way out of her control. She started toward the bathroom, then stopped when she heard a knock at the door.

Lexi groaned and turned. Jake must have forgotten his key, or maybe his hands were too full to open the door himself. She crossed the congested little room in only a few steps, then opened the door a crack.

"Hey, you got some extra space in there? They're out of rooms and we need a place to crash."

Lexi gasped. Two scruffy young guys lurked right outside the door. The closer one leaned toward her for a better look. His eyes were bloodshot, and Lexi smelled booze on his breath. She pivoted and slammed her back against the door, but she wasn't quick enough. She felt him pushing hard, trying to force the door open.

"Let us in—you got room in there! We've been drivin' all night. C'mon!"

Lexi gritted her teeth and pushed back with all her strength. But the door opened a little wider. Desperate for momentum, she strained her leg muscles even harder. The door moved back a little. If only she could get it to click shut. Then it lurched opened a little more than before. They were going to get in! She dug in her heels as hard as she could, but the crappy carpet gave way and bunched beneath her feet. She started sliding, losing ground. The door opened wider still.

"Open up, bitch!"

They kept pounding, pushing, shouting at her. The noises all merged into one menacing, enveloping sound. She couldn't keep this up much longer. They'd get in soon. She had to do something, stop them somehow.

One at a time, Lexi shifted her feet back onto a more stable section of carpet. Her thigh muscles screamed, pushed to their limit. She clamped her jaw and gave another shove, willing the door to close. The carpet tore. Her feet slid a couple inches before she could stop them, leaving her pressed against the door from a lower, more awkward angle. She'd lost too much leverage to keep this up.

Now or never. Had to do it. Before she lost all traction. She bit her lip and gave it everything she had. The door moved back a little, a little more. She couldn't hold on much longer. One more push, the last she had in her. It had to work.

Click.

The door shut. Thank God it was set to lock automatically. Lexi slid down to the floor, arms and legs quivering, as the guys pounded on the door a few more times. Their curses grew fainter as they gave up and walked away.

Too close. That was way too close. Stupid not to make sure it was Jake first. Trembling, Lexi checked the lock once more, put on the chain for good measure, then crawled across the floor to the bed on her hands and knees. She pulled herself up and collapsed on the squealing mattress, completely drained.

Ava started writhing around in her carrier, her face beet-red. She began crying, wailing, and shrieking like never before. Lexi picked her up and felt her forehead. She seemed warm, but it was hard to tell. Her own hand was still sweating from her fight with the door, and she realized she'd forgotten to pack the thermometer. That's all they needed, for Ava to get sick in the middle of nowhere.

Maybe she was being paranoid. *She* was probably the one who was hot, after what just happened. She paced the room, patting and jiggling Ava to try to get her to settle down. Ava's deafening screams shredded her already-jangled nerves.

She didn't want to be here anymore. Didn't want to be torn from her home, alone with a screaming baby. In a piece-of-shit motel room that wasn't even safe. Not with people like that running around. What if they'd gotten in? Did they really just want a place to sleep, or had they been watching, waiting for her to be alone? Maybe they'd been watching the whole time. Would they come back? Did they have guns or knives? What if they waited for Jake and did something to him?

Lexi cowered in the bathroom doorway, clutching Ava and trembling.

Where the hell *was* Jake, anyway?

CHAPTER 21

Jake jammed the plastic gallon bottle of water in with the rest, concealed the stash with a blanket, and stood for a moment, hands on hips. Six gallons. It would have to do. The bottles took up a good chunk of the remaining space in the back of the SUV, and finding six different grocery stores reasonably near their motel had already consumed way too much of the afternoon.

Because of rationing, buying more than a gallon at a time in a single store would have raised questions he didn't want to answer. And they'd better not get pulled over with that much water in the car. A curious cop might suspect they were planning to sell it on the black market and take them in for some harsh questioning. Or worse. He shrugged and closed the SUV's back door. Once they got on those desert back roads, there'd be no cops. Just a whole lot of nothing. Daunting as it was, a whole lot of nothing did have its advantages.

Jake got behind the wheel and hesitated, his finger poised over the Start button, as he did some quick mental calculations. The SUV got spectacular city mileage because of the way the hybrid engine worked. But its highway mileage wasn't so good, and then they'd be out on the open road for several hundred miles before they got back to any real civilization, let alone charging stations. One tank of gas wouldn't get them through all that, better carry some extra on board. He turned on the car and checked the GPS. It showed one of those big-box variety stores not far away. They'd have gas cans. And maybe some other things he should get while he still had the chance.

As he drove the few blocks to the store, Jake tried to imagine everything they might run across on their way through the desert, so he could shop accordingly. It wasn't like they'd be out there for weeks on end, but they'd be stupid not to prepare for whatever the terrain could throw at them. Minor repairs, maybe a few scrapes and cuts, encounters with desert animals, scorpions, and who knew what else—maybe even some desperate people. And they'd be vulnerable, especially with a baby in tow.

Jake stepped inside the store and gaped at the cavernous interior. He normally avoided these places like the plague because of how hard they were to navigate, but the day was fast getting away from him and he couldn't afford to keep running all over town to get everything he needed. He grabbed a cart and sailed past the plumbing, lighting and paint sections, over to automotive. He tossed several plastic gas cans in the cart, then headed for the camping section.

The store carried a dazzling array of just about every type of outdoor equipment imaginable. They already had their tent, sleeping bags, and cooking gear, but they did not have a proper first-aid kit. Better to have one and not need it than to go without. He checked out the selection and grabbed a medium-sized kit, then threw some freeze-dried meals and energy bars in the cart for good measure.

Jake closed his eyes and tried to picture everything they'd packed in their mad rush to evacuate. Between that and what he'd procured today, they probably had what they needed. Even if they didn't, there wasn't room in the SUV for much more, anyway.

He headed down the aisle in search of the checkout area, then found himself in the gun section. The place had quite the selection—all of it behind glass, of course. And it dawned on him. The one thing they didn't have was a way to defend themselves, if it came to that. Who knew what lurked out there in the Nevada desert?

He stepped closer, eyeing the display. Lexi hated guns so much she once told him she'd divorce him on the spot if he ever got one. He didn't especially like them himself, and he had no idea how to use one. Didn't matter. The background check wouldn't be a problem, but the waiting period would take time they didn't have. But he should get something they could use if they had to.

Jake wandered into the hunting section for ideas. The crossbows looked downright menacing, but way too bulky and complicated to be useful in an emergency. Then the knife display caught his eye, though he didn't much care for the idea. A knife would be useless from a distance. Or against a gun. But it was better than nothing. He went up to the glass case for a closer look.

They had everything from little pocket knives that looked almost cute to a model with a wicked blade that looked like something that Rambo character from those old movies would tote around. Some folded and some had fixed blades. One that folded would probably be better. Safer and it would take up less room. Just had to be sure he could get at it and snap it open fast if he needed it. Lexi would not be happy about having a hunting knife around, but they'd be crazy to go off into the unknown with nothing at all for protection.

That one with the four-inch blade seemed like a good choice. Not too big, not too small. And damned scary-looking. He hoped he wouldn't need it at all, but if he did, it'd be nice if just the sight of it would be enough to fend off any trouble.

Jake tried to imagine what it would be like to actually have to use something like that in a life-or-death situation. Could he even do it? Which way should he hold it? If he had to use it to defend against an attacking animal—or human—did it go right in, or did it take a lot of force? He wondered if he should practice on something, just so he'd have some familiarity with the feel of the thing.

Well, that wasn't going to happen. Lexi'd probably have a fit the minute she laid eyes on the thing, so the less she saw of it, the better. Maybe just having a knife like that would be enough, like a sort of good-luck talisman to ward off any real need to use it.

At least he hoped so.

CHAPTER 22

Lexi huddled in the rickety chair, holding Ava snug against her chest, as if that would somehow keep her safe. If only. She couldn't stop staring at the motel-room door, reliving what had happened—over and over—in her mind's eye. That door was so thin, so cheap. Anyone could bust right through it if they really wanted to. That crappy lock wouldn't hold, wouldn't protect her and Ava.

Pure luck she'd been able to fend off those guys. Too close a call, and her own damned fault for opening the door without knowing who was out there. Stupid to forget—even for a moment—she was far, far away from the safety of home. Back where opening the front door to a stranger wasn't likely to lead to a life-or-death situation.

When the hell would Jake get back, anyway? He'd been gone for hours, leaving her and Ava alone and unprotected in this dump. She glanced at her cell on the nightstand. Maybe she should call him. Maybe something had happened to him and she was sitting here, clueless. And with no car. Trapped. No way out. She shivered.

Ava started squirming like she didn't want to be held anymore. Strange. Lexi set her down on the bed and studied her closely. She wasn't taking her bottle as well as usual, as if she wasn't all that hungry. Usually she was voracious. She leaned over for a better look and touched Ava's forehead with the back of her hand. Hard to tell without a thermometer. It was so stuffy in the room, the AC ridiculously underpowered for the job.

Lexi flopped back down in the creaky chair and shook her head. Ava did seem *off* somehow, but she couldn't put her finger on it. Could be the stress of being in a strange place. Or she could be picking up on the tension around her. God knew there was plenty of that. Lexi absently rubbed her taut shoulder. That's probably all it was, just a combination of those things. Who could blame her?

The doorknob jiggled.

Lexi flinched, her entire body instantly tense, back on high alert. *Not again!* She made sure Ava wasn't too close to the edge of the bed and stepped slowly, silently toward the door, her heart pounding. She glanced at the phone and wondered how fast the cops would get there if she called 911.

Snick! The door knob lock released. The door opened a few inches. The security chain snapped tight. Lexi could barely breathe.

"Lexi, open up! It's me."

Lexi flung open the door. "Where have you been?"

Jake stepped in, empty-handed, and shut the door. "What do you mean? I had to go all over town to get everything."

"Well, what did you get? I don't see a damned thing."

"It's all in the car. No sense dragging it all in here, then back out. What's the matter with you?"

Lexi clenched her fists and shouted, "You left Ava and me alone in this godforsaken motel half the damned day." She stamped her foot and burst into tears. "It's not safe here!"

Jake tossed his keys onto the table. "What is your problem?" He waved his arm toward the parking lot outside. "The car's all loaded up. I had to go to a bunch of different stores just to get all the water we'll need. Then I had to go to one of those huge variety stores to get gas cans and other stuff. All that takes time. At least you got to stay in one place, instead of wandering all around town, through traffic and everything."

Lexi flung herself into the chair and buried her face in her hands. "It was horrible."

"What was horrible, sitting here in the air conditioning?" Jake pulled up a chair and collapsed into it. "Jesus, I'm tired."

"The men...they tried to get into the room."

"Men? What men?" Jake jumped up, shoulders tensed.

"I thought it was you and started to open the door, but it

was these two guys. They tried to push their way in."

"What the hell? Where'd they go?" Jake glanced from side to side as if he expected them to jump out of the closet.

"They left. I barely got the door shut in time."

Jake rushed over, took her in his arms, and held her tight. "Oh my God. I'm so sorry. Are you okay? Did you call the cops?"

"No, I didn't think it would help. They went away as soon as I got the door shut. I thought it was them again just now. Or some other creeps."

He stroked her hair and spoke in a low, soothing tone. "I'm so sorry that happened and I wasn't here to protect you. Don't worry. We'll get out of this place tomorrow morning, head for California. Back roads through Nevada, just like we planned."

"Jake, I'm scared."

"We'll be okay. I promise. I got us some protection."

Lexi pulled away and looked him in the eye. "You didn't get a gun? You know how I feel about them, especially with Ava around."

"No, not a gun. A hunting knife. Not ideal, but it's something."

Ava let out a wail. Lexi picked her up and tried to soothe her, but Ava only cried harder.

"So, this is what we've come to. Fugitives, armed with a god-damned hunting knife, wandering around aimlessly. My God, this is just too much. I can't stand it anymore!"

"Lexi, if I could magically make everything the way it was, I would. In a heartbeat. But there's no turning back. You saw the satellite shots. I swear we'll get through this somehow, make a new life for ourselves. I'll make sure of it."

Lexi held Ava against her shoulder and patted her on the back until her cries dropped a few decibels. "I know you can't perform miracles. It's just so...hard to deal with all this. Hey, I'm really sorry I snapped at you. It's been a horrible day, and Ava's been cranky as hell. Her appetite sucks, and she won't settle down no matter what I do."

Jake held out his arms. "Here. Let me hold her for a while. Take a shower, relax a little. You'll feel better, then I'll go get us some food and bring it to the room, okay?"

Lexi handed Ava over. "Thank you. That *would* be nice."

She stepped into the bathroom, shut the door, and leaned back against it. The paper-thin walls didn't keep Ava's crying out entirely, but it was an improvement. She stepped over to the shower and checked it out. Streaks of rust stained the tiles and tub. Thin, threadbare towels drooped over a rack that hung from loose screws. A laminated sheet of paper tacked to the wall announced in bright-red, bold letters:

AUTOMATED GOVERNOR IN USE!!! 5-MINUTE SHOWERS!!!

NO RESETS ALLOWED—PLAN ACCORDINGLY!!!

Lexi sighed. At least there was a fresh bar of soap and it was an actual shower. Not pretty, not extravagant, but better than nothing.

Might as well make the most of her five minutes of showering pleasure—probably the last bit of quasi-luxury to be had for the foreseeable future. There'd be no showers at all, rusty or otherwise, out in the goddamned desert.

Lexi hoped a lack of indoor plumbing was the worst thing that awaited them out there. She slipped out of her clothes, turned on the water, and shivered as much more horrible possibilities paraded through her mind.

CHAPTER 23

Jake stretched, propped himself up on an elbow, and eyed the dust-covered alarm clock on the equally dusty nightstand beside him. Six in the morning already. A couple of hours later than he'd intended to get up and going. With nothing but desert and low-three-figure temps ahead of them, the earlier they got on the road, the better. He twisted around to check on Lexi. Still sound asleep. He hated to wake her. Ava had kept them both up most of the night, fussing and carrying on. They were all stressed, unmoored from life as they'd known it, at least for now. They could all use a good, long rest, a chance to recover. But that wasn't going to happen today.

He rolled onto his back and stared up at the dingy, pock-marked ceiling, doubts and worries racing through his mind. Were they really as prepared as they needed to be? He wished he could be sure. He'd tried to think of all the possibilities, of anything and everything that could happen. But something was bound to pop up that they hadn't planned for. Something always did. And when it did, would they be able to handle it? Hell, they hadn't even decided where they planned to end up, other than somewhere in California. And even that vague goal was likely out of reach if they hit a roadblock at the border.

He nudged Lexi. "Hey, time to leave this posh resort and push on."

She groaned and swatted at him. "Leave me alone. I just fell asleep. What time is it?"

"Six."

"Can't we sleep a little longer? Check-out's not till eleven."

"Sorry, we're headed for wide-open desert. All sun, no

shade. I want to get in as many miles as I can before the worst of the heat kicks in."

Lexi threw off her covers, pushed herself up, and slouched on the edge of the bed, her back to him. "I guess you're right, but I wish we didn't have to wake Ava up already. Not after all we went through getting her to sleep."

"I know. It was a tough night for all of us. With any luck, it won't be more than a couple days before we can settle in somewhere. We'll all feel better then."

Lexi turned and shot him a dirty look. "It's all just that easy, is it? Just move on like nothing happened." She picked up her cell from the nightstand and peered at it, then shook her head and set it back down. "Still nothing from my parents...or *anyone* from back home."

Jake moved close, took her in his arms, and spoke softly in her ear. "I didn't mean it that way. I know this is harder for you than it is for me. But it's the only thing we can do right now. You saw what the fire did. It'll take a long time to sort out where everybody went. They could be safe somewhere."

"I hope so." Lexi shrugged out of his embrace, then went over and stood beside the chair where Ava lay sleeping in her carrier. "But they should have called by now."

She was right. Her parents certainly *would* have called by now, no matter what they had to do to get to a phone. Many times over, most likely. If they were alive.

"Lexi...Lexi, wake up. We're passing the Bonneville Salt Flats. Check 'em out."

Lexi mumbled something as she awoke, then craned her neck for a better look. "Wow. I've seen pictures, but it's not the same as seeing them for real. They're blindingly bright." She shielded her eyes from the glare. "Do we have time to stop?"

"The pullover looks pretty crowded. Anyway, I'd rather push on. It's a hundred and eight out there right now."

Lexi waved her hand, then rubbed her eyes and yawned. "Oh God no. Never mind. I have no interest in baking my brains."

Jake glanced at the dash display. Engine temp still looked

good, even with the AC blasting inside the car. Awful lot of dead cars along the side of the road through this stretch, probably with overheating problems. He didn't want to join them. Some had handmade signs on their windshields and looked like they'd been there a while.

"How's cell reception through here?"

"Why?" Lexi gave him a nervous look and dug into her bag.

"Just curious." Jake pointed at another dead car as they passed by it. "Lot of cars sitting out there. Curious why they haven't been towed: if there're no tows available or if they couldn't even make the call and had to walk it."

"Still some good bars." She clutched the phone like a lifeline.

"I expect we'll lose signal not long after we get off the freeway. Anything you want to do while you have reception, better do soon."

Lexi stared down at her cell. "Great."

Jake reached over and squeezed her hand. "We'll be okay. I love you and Ava more than anything, and I'm going to do everything humanly possible to get us all back on track."

"Look out!"

Jake grabbed the wheel with both hands and swerved to avoid the idiot who sped up from behind and cut in front of him. "Bastard! Middle of nowhere and he has to drive like that."

Ava began screaming like someone had just slapped her. Lexi twisted around in her seat and tried to comfort her.

"Do you need me to pull over, so you can get back there?"

"Yeah, would you? She looks mad as hell. Probably could do with a feeding."

Jake glanced at the GPS display. "Looks like a rest stop in only a few miles. I'll stop there."

"Good. I could use a bathroom break, too."

"I'd rather have you in front with me, but maybe it'd be best if you rode back there with her, at least for a while. Might keep her calmer."

"She's usually the calmest baby on the planet. I don't understand why she's so easily irritated all of a sudden." Lexi stifled a yawn. "Sounds like a good idea, though. And if she quiets down, maybe I can take a little nap with her."

"You do that. I'll need a break later, and then you'll be fresh and can take over driving for a while."

Maybe. Once they hit the secondary roads, it'd likely take both of them to navigate so they didn't waste time and gas taking a wrong turn. Probably wouldn't be able to afford the luxury of having one of them sleep while the other drove. Too many unknowns, and even a small mistake could be costly out there in the Nevada desert.

Jake rubbed at a painful knot in the side of his neck. It'd cut their daily driving hours—and progress—down if they couldn't switch off like he'd initially assumed. But it was the smarter way to go. Might keep them from getting into a tricky or dangerous situation. He drew a deep breath and shifted around in his seat to get more comfortable for the long road ahead.

Better take it all one step at a time. Stay sharp, stay focused. Avoid trouble at all costs. Lexi was teetering on the edge already, worrying about her parents and caring for Ava. And that incident back at the motel. Lexi was still pretty shaken by that, he could tell. Who could blame her? He couldn't let anything like that happen again. He had to do the thinking for both of them, and with the baby along, he had to be ten times as careful about everything.

No matter what, he had to control the situation and protect his family. Make smart decisions, be strong for them all, and get them to a safe place as quickly as he could. He'd promised them, and he would keep his word.

He hoped to God he could pull it off, because he could never forgive himself if something happened to Lexi or Ava.

CHAPTER 24

"You sure we have enough gas to get where we're going? Wherever that is."

Lexi wrinkled her nose at the faint gasoline odor wafting through the car as they sped along westbound I-80. Jake had driven them to several different stations in Wendover to fill up their gas cans. Just a precaution, he'd told her. He didn't want it to be obvious they planned to drive off the main highway. Didn't want anyone following them, thinking maybe they could somehow take advantage of them.

She was glad he was thinking ahead like that. Sort of. It also made her realize all that could go wrong, how much danger they might put themselves into. Now the thought of being out there in the desert, alone and vulnerable, terrified her. So many things could happen.

"Should be plenty, even assuming the worst MPG this thing is rated for. Besides, we couldn't fit any more in if we tried. It's all pretty jammed up back there."

"Wish we had somewhere to strap it outside. Smells."

"That should go away soon. They're all sealed tight. I made sure. The smell's coming from a couple of drops I got on one of the cans when I was filling it. I don't like the idea of carrying it all inside the car either, but it's best we don't have our stash displayed for the world to see."

"Oh, I suppose." Lexi stared off into the distance, the scenery blurring into itself as they whizzed by. "Do you really think we need to worry about people...bothering us?"

"Probably not. We might not even meet up with anybody at all, the way I'm planning to go. But I'd rather be overprepared than underprepared."

Lexi pointed. "Look. There's the Nevada border. The Silver State, huh. And a new time zone."

"And West Wendover is right there, just across the border. That's where we'll leave I-80. Go south for a bit, then head west to cross into California through a less populated area. Hopefully that way we won't run into any patrols or roadblocks."

Lexi twisted in her seat to look behind them. The *Welcome to Utah* sign faded quickly into the distance. She turned back around and took in the view. Probably the last bit of civilization for a while, such as it was. Gas-and-charging stations and second-tier casinos, all jammed up cheek-to-jowl against the border. Last eastbound haven for gamblers before hitting Utah. The place had a despairing, ugly air about it. But at least it was populated. She still didn't like the idea of heading out into the middle of nowhere. Not one bit.

Desert chaparral replaced West Wendover's desperate glitz as they headed south off the interstate. It didn't take long before it looked like they'd landed on another planet. Nothing but dry sand in all directions, heat ripples rising and dancing in the air. Her fear growing, Lexi snatched up her cell and watched the bars recede as fast as West Wendover.

"We're losing reception. Down to one bar already."

"I figured that would happen."

"Are you sure we're doing the right thing? Why can't we stay on the freeway a while longer? Take the side roads once we get closer to California." Lexi glanced from side to side. Nothing but desolation. "It would be so much safer than wandering around in this."

"Because I'm worried if too many other people have the same idea, we'll end up stuck in a bunch of traffic and have to backtrack to get around. I think we have a much better shot at getting through unnoticed if we take the less-traveled route."

"But we're all alone and running out of cell service. Anything could happen, and we won't be able to call for help."

"Lexi, it's not like we'll be going for days and days like this. It's about five hundred miles as the crow flies. We can do it with one overnight—two, worst case—depending how fast the roads are, and how much they twist around. The car's not that old, and we had it serviced recently enough. We'll be fine."

"There goes the last bar. No service." Lexi put her cell down in her lap, face-down, the sight of the *No Service* symbol filling her with terror.

"Chill, would you? We'll be okay. I need you to keep an eye on the GPS for me."

"Chill. Yeah, look at the dash. Says it's a hundred and ten out there now."

"That's exactly why I wanted to get on the road earlier, to avoid the worst of the heat as much as we could. I checked the fluids when we stopped for the gas. We're all topped up."

Lexi folded her arms across her chest, gazed out at the barren landscape, and shook her head. "I really don't like this."

"We'll get through it, okay? Now help me out here. Which way at the fork up ahead? I'd say to the right, so we start heading west."

Lexi fiddled with the GPS. "Yeah, the left fork does swing east. But I can't find a name for the one you want to turn on."

"Well, it's on the GPS and goes the direction we want. That's what matters."

A few miles after the fork, they came upon a beat-up old sedan stranded at the side of the road, its hood up. One man bent beneath the hood, only his lower body visible. The other, a shaggy-looking guy in tattered jeans and no shirt, lolled against the car. He signaled them to stop as they drew near. Jake sped up, his jaw clenched.

"Oh my God, they're stuck out there!" Lexi checked her cell. Still no service. "How are they going to get help?"

"I don't know, but we're not stopping. They might have been okay, but for all we know, it could be a set-up. Can't take that chance."

"What if *we* break down out there and no one stops?"

"Let's hope that doesn't happen. If it does, we'd better be ready to figure it out ourselves. I'd be surprised if anyone stopped to help—and the whole point of taking the route we're taking is to avoid running into anyone anyway."

Lexi twisted around in her seat. The shirtless guy was standing in the middle of the road back there, giving them the finger.

His mouth was open wide, shouting at them, though they were already too far away to hear him. She shivered and turned back around.

Something about the way the sun glinted off his dark glasses creeped her out, like there could be anything behind them. Or nothing at all.

CHAPTER 25

Jake eyed the dashboard display. One hundred and twelve freakin' degrees out there now. And it looked it. No relief in sight. No trees, no shade. Just scrubby sage here and there, barely clinging to life in the baking desert basin. Not long after they'd turned off I-80, they'd passed a few broken-down shacks and what used to be homes in a couple of abandoned developments, surrounded by the parched remains of landscaping. Built back when people could afford the water to dare to live in the desert.

A gas station sign atop a tall pole beckoned ahead in the distance, swimming in the heat haze like a mirage. The tank was about three-quarters full. Maybe they could top it up there and conserve their hoard of gas. A bathroom break would be nice, too.

"Where are we?" Lexi stirred awake from a restless nap in the passenger's seat.

"There's a gas station up ahead."

Lexi squinted into the glare. "It looks lonely out there."

"I'm sure it is. First one I've seen since we turned off the main drag. Looks like one of those old-fashioned, gas-only type places, too. What little infrastructure there is out here's likely too spread out for charging stations to be of much use."

Minutes later, Jake pulled up to the pump and shut off the engine. "Well, this looks like a bust."

A thick layer of grit covered the pumps, their analog displays cracked and yellowed, their paint desert-bludgeoned into a dull rust-red. A sign beside the building displayed obviously out-of-date gas prices. Grime covered what glass remained in the busted-out windows. The door stood half open, its wood warped, paint peeling. Broken glass littered the ground all over the place.

"It's creepy, like something out of that old series, Twilight Zone. I expect a zombie to stagger out of the office any minute." Lexi rubbed her arms. "It's making my skin crawl."

"Might be a good idea to see if the bathrooms still work, anyway. You go first. I'll stay with Ava."

Jake got out of the car to stretch a little while he waited for Lexi. The heat was merciless, even in the dappled shade of the bullet-ridden metal awning that sheltered the pumps. The emptiness and near-silence were unnerving. Nothing but sand, glaring in the bright sunlight, surrounded the gas station. The only sound was a hot breeze whistling through the broken panes of glass.

Screaming, Lexi burst out of the bathroom and sprinted back to the car, mindless of the oppressive heat.

"What happened? What's the matter?"

Lexi strung her words together between gasps. "Horrible... waiting in there...scorpions! Bunch of 'em...all over the floor... nasty!" She shook her head. "Not going back in there...no way."

Jake chuckled. "I've never seen you run quite so fast."

"It's not funny! It's not—" Lexi dissolved into giggles, her shoulders jiggling. "Probably should have expected it, from the looks of this place." She wiped tears from the corners of her eyes. "I'll just go behind the damned building."

Lexi was right. It did look like something straight out of a horror movie. It wasn't the end of the world, though. They had enough gas with them to make it to California as long as they were careful. He'd made sure of that—and was glad of it. If this was the best they could do along this stretch of road, the pickings would be even worse along some of the other, even less well-traveled, roads he had planned.

Lexi came back around the building, wiped sweat from her forehead, and leaned against the car, fanning herself. "Okay, your turn. Let me warn you, it's pretty nasty back there. We're not the first ones to think of going there instead of in the bathrooms."

"Okay, I'll brave it. Get out any snacks you want, long as we're stopped. I'll have whatever you're having."

Jake picked his way toward the rear of the building, avoiding the larger shards of broken glass as best he could. He took care of business as quickly as possible in the relentless heat. The place was disgusting. Graphic graffiti—violent and vicious—covered the back wall from top to bottom. Odd, with no one around, the taggers kept to the back and didn't just cover the entire building. Who the hell would catch them at it out here?

A plume of dust rose in the distance as Jake came back around to the front. The first car they'd seen in quite a while. It broke free of the dust cloud as it drew closer. Some old clunker, weaving back and forth and going way too fast. Must be drunk or high, driving like that.

"Get back in the car, Lexi. Now."

"Huh?" Lexi was bent over, digging around in the ice chest for something. "What's the matter?" She glanced up, then shut the SUV's back compartment.

"I don't like the look of that. Get in."

Jake jumped in, started the car, and gunned it the instant Lexi shut her door. The tires squealed and the rear end shimmied as he turned onto the road and sped away. He glanced in the rear view, hoping that car stopped at the gas station. Might be whoever kept up that graffiti. And if it was, he didn't want any sort of encounter with them. Not way out here with no cops, no cell reception.

Lexi twisted in her seat for a better look. "They're still back there, driving like idiots. Maybe we should've just let them pass by and go on."

"I was worried they'd stop at the gas station and hassle us somehow. I don't like the way they're driving. Might be high or drunk, looking for trouble."

"They could just be screwing around. It's not like they're doing it in heavy traffic."

"Could be. But I don't want to take the chance it's more than that." Jake glanced in the rear view again. "Shit. They didn't pull over at the gas station. They're catching up to us."

"Oh my God." Lexi cowered in her seat and whimpered.

Jake struggled to stay calm—or at least look it. If he showed fear, Lexi'd panic and he couldn't deal with her hysterics right now. The car pulled up behind him, close enough he could read the plate. The glare made it hard to tell for sure, but it looked like a bunch of guys in there.

The car pulled even closer, only a couple of feet from their rear bumper. Its front fenders were bent and mangled, giving it the look of a car with nothing left to lose. Jake gave it more gas, just enough to put a little more space between them and still keep control. He hoped he wasn't encouraging the driver by reacting. Lexi cringed in her seat, sniffling and shaking.

The car swerved into the other lane, its tires kicking up sand along the far shoulder. Jake held his breath as it drew even with them, speeding along on the wrong side of the road. He kept his head facing forward, sneaking a peak from the corner of his eye.

The passenger window rolled down. Jake's heart pounded. A crazed-looking young guy hung out the window, his mouth open wide, laughing. He gave them the finger, then dropped back in his seat and took another hit off what appeared to be an oversized joint. The car lurched ahead and cut in front of them, its rear bumper loose and flopping.

Lexi screamed and hid her eyes. Jake stomped the brake, the tires skidding in sand near the edge of the road before coming to a stop. The derelict car accelerated, then made a sudden turn onto a dirt road up ahead, disappearing in a cloud of dust.

Lexi sobbed, her hand pressed to her chest. "Let's go back to I-80. It *has* to be safer than this."

Jake rested his forehead on the steering wheel and caught his breath. "They were just messing with us. It's over now."

Lexi screamed as he pulled back onto the road. "No! Let's go back!"

"Calm down, I've got it under control."

"I don't want to be out here, Jake! There could be more like them. They could turn back around. It's too dangerous!"

"Settle down, you'll wake Ava. We'll be okay. Besides, we'll waste too much time and gas going back now. We have to keep going."

Lexi folded her arms tight across her chest and turned away from him. "You'd damned well better be right. I don't like the way this is going at all. I want to go back. Before it's too late."

"I'm right, you'll see. It'll be fine."

He hoped he was right.

CHAPTER 26

Lexi tore off her sunglasses to get at her itching, burning eyes, then thought better of it and put them back on. If only she could run some cool, clean water over her eyes. Better yet, *ice* water. That's what they needed. Pawing at them only made them hurt worse. Between the constant glare and the fine grains of sand that snuck in through the car's AC, the insides of her eyelids felt like sandpaper, constantly grinding on her eyeballs. Sighing, she pressed her hands on the SUV's side body and took a stretch.

Three days. Hard to believe it had been only three days since the fire forced them from their home in the middle of the night. Seemed like way longer than that, almost as if they'd always been on the road. And this first day of desert driving seemed like a week all by itself. At least the worst of the heat was over for the day, now that the sun dipped low in the west.

But that meant they had to face the night soon, alone in the middle of the Nevada desert. Lexi glanced around. The empty terrain looked endless, like there was nothing at all beyond it. Like no matter what they did, they would never be able to drive out of it and into anything approaching a normal life, ever again. Suddenly chilled, Lexi wrapped her arms around herself. *Can't think like that. It's just desert—it isn't sentient, for crissake.* She shook her head as if to clear out the foreboding thoughts.

The landscape out here was devoid of everything, including real campgrounds, so Jake had chosen this spot to stop for the night. Empty in the middle of empty. Flat, well off the road, and free of chaparral. Should be easy to set up their tent, anyway. Lexi wandered around while Jake dug out the camping gear. She poked at a pile of dark ashes with the toe of her shoe.

"Someone's been here before," she shouted back at Jake.

"Not surprising. May not be much traffic out here, but it's not like no one ever comes through, I imagine." He joined her and set down the gear. "Oh good. No holes in the ground."

"Holes?" Lexi jumped back, half-expecting something to pop out of the ground and attack them.

"You know, for desert things. Critters are less likely to make their homes where the ground tends to get disturbed." Jake slipped the tent out of its bag. "Here, help me set up. Then we can eat something and feed Ava."

Lexi crossed her arms over her chest and hugged herself. "I'm not so sure now."

Jake unfurled the tent footprint and spread it out on the ground. "What's the problem? Come on, I want to get set up before we lose the light."

"I don't like it here."

He stood up, hands on hips. "What would you suggest? We don't have time to hunt for another spot before it gets dark. Why go somewhere with a bunch of cactus and scrub to clear when we have this?"

Lexi strained to see into the distance. "That's exactly it. People have used this site before."

"So?"

She turned to him. "What if someone else shows up later tonight, wanting to camp here? If we're all set up, we're stuck. We can't just pick up and go if there's trouble. If we stay in the car, we can just take off if we have to."

Jake frowned and stared at the ground, thought a moment. "Good point. Whoever stopped might be okay. But if they're not..." He stooped to pick up the tent footprint, started folding it up. "You're right. We sleep in the car. But let's have something to eat first."

He took the camping gear back to the SUV and returned with some Clif bars.

"Here, two for you and two for me. Gourmet dinner." He tried a smile.

"Thanks." Stomach growling, Lexi ripped open her bar and bit off an enormous chunk.

Jake devoured his first bar, then tore into his second one. "I didn't realize I was so hungry. These things are lifesavers."

Lexi licked a stray smear of chocolate from her finger, then pretty much inhaled her second bar. Dinner was over almost as fast as it started. They hadn't even sat down, and she didn't remember tasting any of it. Her stomach seemed shocked into silence by the sudden blast of calories.

"Here, I'll take those." Jake crumpled all the wrappers into a ball and returned to the SUV to tuck them away.

Lexi went to the car and got a bottle ready, then took Ava from her car seat, perched on a nearby rock, and started trying to feed her. Right there in the middle of the damned desert, like they were some pack of drifters or something. Unbelievable. The temperature was finally comfortable enough to get Ava out in the fresh air for a while.

She watched Jake as he sauntered along the edge of the road, working out the kinks after doing the bulk of the day's driving. His shadow grew longer in the setting sun with every step.

Lexi wished he'd hurry back. He wasn't that far away, but there was something so horribly isolating about the terrain that he might as well be miles away, clear out of sight. She glanced at the road behind her, both hoping and fearing to see a car approach. Anything could happen to them out here, and they were on their own to take care of themselves.

She held Ava's bottle in place with one hand, then pulled her cell from her pocket and snuck another glance at the bars. Nothing. Nothing at all. Jake told her to quit looking, at least until they got closer to a major road. He said she was only making it worse for herself, checking so often. She slipped it back into her pocket. Maybe he was right. The No Signal symbol just hammered home how alone they were.

But which was worse? Being alone or having someone show up? Those guys earlier had just been messing with them, but if someone really wanted to hurt them or take advantage of them, it would be so easy out here where there was no one to see, no one to help. No 911 to call.

Ava pushed her bottle away and started to whine. Lexi stroked her forehead, tried to soothe her. She seemed unusually warm, but maybe it was the desert air, heavy with heat even at sunset. Her appetite still wasn't what it usually was. Had to be the heat and being strapped in her car carrier for hours on end. Lexi hoped they found somewhere to settle in soon. But no matter what Jake said, no place they could find would ever feel like home to her. Not truly. Nothing could replace what the fire had taken away. Ever.

Lexi returned to the car, changed Ava, and tucked her into her car seat for the night. Poor baby, having to sleep in that contraption instead of her nice comfy crib. Yet another thing stolen by that damned fire. She flexed her low back and gazed at the passenger seat—her own makeshift bed. They'd all have an uncomfortable night, but they could move fast if they had to. She hoped she was being needlessly paranoid.

Jake ambled up to the car, wiping his forehead. "Ready to turn in? I want to get an early start tomorrow while it's cooler."

"Sure, I'm tired enough to sleep. Have a good walk?"

"Yeah. Just had to move around some."

They got into the car, reclined the front seats as far as they would go, and settled in for the night as best they could. The last of the sun disappeared behind a mountain, leaving behind a burgundy glow in the western sky. A few stars revealed themselves. At last, though still warm, it no longer felt like they were trapped in a furnace.

"Jake?"

"Yeah?"

"I'm scared. I'm really, really scared."

He reached over and squeezed her hand. "Trust me. It may take a little time, but everything's going to work out."

"I hope so."

Lexi gazed out at the sky through the dusty windshield. The stars never seemed so far away. Neither did safety, security—and home.

CHAPTER 27

*L*ate again. Jake leaned up against the driver's side door, fidgeting in the growing heat as he waited for Lexi to get a move on. He glanced to his left and scowled. The sun was fully up now, painting the eastern sky salmon pink. And once again, they were behind schedule, at least to his thinking. So much for being on the road before dawn, to travel in the relative cool as long as they could.

When he tried to wake her earlier, Lexi complained she hadn't slept all night, had only just fallen asleep, and refused to budge. He felt bad for her, so he let her sleep a while longer. But now she was moving like she was still asleep, taking forever to do the simplest things.

And the sun was up there, gathering strength, beginning to beat down on them already.

"C'mon, Lexi. Let's go." He turned and drummed his fingers on the hood of the car.

Lexi called out from the back seat. "I'm still trying to get Ava to take her bottle. She's acting like she's not hungry. That can't be. I haven't fed her since before we turned in last night."

"Well, try again later. Or stay in back with her and keep trying. Whatever. But we really need to get going. I want to make the border, so we can get a room tonight instead of sleeping in the car again."

"I'll stay in back. She's got to eat."

"Fine." Jake took a quick walk around the car, made sure everything looked as it should before starting off. Doors all shut. Back gate closed. Nothing left behind. Everything looked in order, except the SUV was so thickly coated with dust, its actual color was completely concealed.

He got in and started the car. Dash gauge said eighty degrees already. Way cooler than it'd be in only a couple of hours, though. He studied the GPS, made some mental calculations. They'd likely have to keep going a bit after dark to do it, but they could still make the border tonight. Long day of driving to endure, but it'd be worth it to find a place to stay.

Driving through all this desolation made him nervous, more so than he cared to admit. He'd planned everything out so quickly, he felt sure he must have missed something. He had no idea what, or whether it would matter. But the possibilities haunted him. And sharing his worries with Lexi was out of the question. She was way out of her element, driving through the desert so far from home, with no set destination in mind. He had to keep up a façade of absolute confidence for her sake.

Jake maneuvered the SUV out of the sand and back onto the road. Heat ripples already rose from the black asphalt. He inclined his head from side to side, trying to work out a kink in his neck from sleeping crumpled up in the driver's seat. Hindsight was wonderful. They could have slept in their tent with proper pads and gear last night and been far more comfortable. No one had showed up, let alone anyone dangerous. Lexi was right, though. If someone had—

Ava let out the most ear-shattering screech she'd ever mustered, even after getting a shot at the doctor's office. Then she started to cry and sob like the world was coming to an end. Lexi tried to shush her, to no avail.

Jake gritted his teeth against the stabbing pain in his ears. "What's bugging her now?"

"I don't know. She spit up a couple of minutes ago."

"Her routine's been turned inside out. That's probably what's upsetting her. She's usually pretty laid back."

"I hope that's all it is. I've never seen her like this—and refusing to eat, too. Jake, I'm worried."

"All the more reason to make the border tonight, find a motel. We'll all sleep better."

A loud buzz went off, triggering another scream from Ava.

"Oh, shit!" Jake punched the steering wheel with his fist.

"What is it?"

"Flat." He steered the car off the road, onto a sandy clearing, and cut the engine. "Just what we needed."

"Oh my God, what'll we do?" Lexi's voice, tinged with panic, rose above Ava's cries.

"Stay inside and take care of her. I'll handle it."

"Are you sure?"

"Yeah. May have to dig around in the back to get at everything. If I have trouble jacking it, I might ask you to get out."

"All right." Lexi sounded close to tears.

"Don't freak out, okay? It's just a flat. I'll take care of it."

Cursing quietly, Jake took a deep breath and forced himself to face the task at hand. Mid-morning and it already felt like a blast furnace out there. Ideal conditions to have to wrestle with a flat tire. He took a walk around the car. None of the tires looked flat. Maybe the alarm was malfunctioning. That would be nice. He leaned down for a closer look, one tire at a time.

The hissing told him what he needed to know. The rear passenger tire was losing air—and fast. He opened the back gate and groaned. They'd managed to jam in everything they thought they could possibly need, but now it all had to come out, so he could get at the tire-changing gear. Nice design.

Lexi leaned over the back seat. "What are you doing?"

"Everything I need is under all our stuff."

"I can help."

"No, no. Just stay put. You finally got Ava calmed down. No sense upsetting her."

Jake worked quickly, yet methodically, to clear out all their crap and arrange it on the ground. That way he could reload fast once he was done with the tire. He rummaged around in the tool compartment and tossed the jack and tire iron down next to the flat. Pausing first to wipe sweat from his forehead before it got in his eyes, he lowered the spare from under the car and set it out by the tools.

Squatting low, he popped off the wheel cover, then positioned the jack and pumped it a couple of times to snug it in place. Sweat trickled down his back as he slid the lug wrench over the first nut and gave it a shove. Nothing. Not even the slightest movement. This was going to be fun.

Maybe momentum would be his friend. He stood, then gave the thing a good stomp. And missed. He landed in a heap in the hot sand, sharp pain shooting through his ankle. The rest of the lug nuts better not be this stubborn.

Jake tried another nut, cocked back his arm, and gave the lug wrench a good smack to convince it to go on the first try. His hand slipped and smashed onto the ground.

"Son of a *bitch!*" Blood oozed from his index finger knuckle where he scraped it on the wrench and then ground it into the sand. He dusted it off and sucked the flesh until the bleeding slowed.

"What happened?" Lexi popped out of the car, eyes wide.

"Nothing. I slipped. Go back inside, let me finish up."

"Oh my God, you're bleeding!"

"Yeah. I'm bleeding, all right."

His jaw set, Jake tried to ignore her—as well as the pain in his hand and ankle—while he kept working. He had to get the job done, or they'd be stuck out here. And if that happened, they were as good as dead. He worked the wrench furiously, sweat stinging his eyes. Finally, he got the rest of the nuts off, even the one that required the special key. That left only the first stubborn bastard. He aimed carefully and stomped the wrench with his other foot. This time it budged, just a little. He worked it until it came the rest of the way off, then lined up all the nuts together, out of the way.

"Here." Lexi held up the first aid kit. "That needs to be cleaned and bandaged. You'll get an infection."

"Let me finish up first. I'll just get it dirty again."

"Can I help?"

"No, this is the heavy part."

Jake pumped up the jack, pulled off the bad tire, muscled the spare into place, then lowered the car a little. Blood dripped onto the sand from his knuckle as he positioned and tightened the bolts. At last, he popped the wheel cover back on, released the jack, and stood, his sweat-soaked clothes pasted to his body. Jesus, what he wouldn't do for a cold shower.

Lexi leaned against the car, her face white. "I need to sit

down. I feel a little woozy." She plunked down in the sand, eyes closed and head bowed, and set the first aid kit aside.

Lexi never could stand the sight of blood. He'd just have to take care of it himself. Jake grabbed the kit, took out the hydrogen peroxide, and bit his lip. The cut on his knuckle was a little deeper than he thought. Almost bad enough for stitches. Hopefully not quite that bad, though. Not like there was an urgent care on the next corner—not out here in nowhereland. And it hurt like hell already. The peroxide would be a real treat.

He held his breath and sloshed peroxide over the wound. It bubbled and burned like a sonofabitch, red-streaked foam dripping onto the sand. He gingerly wiped it down with some gauze, then grit his teeth and gave it another shot.

"Are you done? I can't look, or I'll get sick."

"Almost."

He dabbed at the wound with some fresh gauze and gave it a close look. The bleeding had slowed to an ooze. Nice job. He squeezed some antibiotic ointment onto the knuckle, positioned a couple of clean gauze pads over the mess and taped them down firmly. His injured hand throbbed and ached in the baking sun. If only he had some ice to put on it. But that wasn't going to happen. What little they had left in the cooler had surely melted by now.

"All done. It's safe to look now."

Wincing, Jake shoved the bad tire into position and cranked it up into its storage bay beneath the car. He'd try to find the puncture some other time. Right now, he just wanted to get back on the road and under way. He bundled up the jack and tools and tossed them back into their compartment under the cargo cover.

"Can you help load everything else back in?"

"Sure." Lexi pushed herself up and got to work.

"Thanks."

"Does it hurt bad?"

"Not too bad," Jake lied. Better take some ibuprofen, keep the swelling down. If it got to hurting much worse, it'd be hard to hold the steering wheel.

He checked his watch. More than two hours wasted. On top

of a late start. Excellent. He squinted into the sun. And fighting with that flat in the heat had drained him, big time. No time to rest, though. They had to keep moving. And now they had no spare tire. Not a comforting thought. He flexed his injured hand. Damn, it hurt. And his ankle was none too happy with him right now, either.

Better not worry Lexi. She had enough on her mind, with Ava and all. He hoped they could still make it to a town tonight, somewhere they could clean up, get some real dinner, and try to have a decent night's sleep for a change.

But that didn't look too likely now.

CHAPTER 28

Jake slapped the steering wheel with his uninjured hand, jolting Lexi out of her half-trance.

"Sorry, Lexi. That flat blew our schedule out the window today, and I'm way too tired to drive any more. Especially after dark. My eyes feel like someone shredded them and stuffed them back in their sockets. Can't imagine how much worse they'd be without sunglasses."

Lexi massaged her throbbing temples and averted her gaze as the setting sun took aim at their faces. If only she could dig her fingers in behind her eyes, where it hurt the most. The last thing she wanted was to spend a second night out in this god-forsaken place, uncomfortable as hell and exposed to whatever might come their way. But she, too, was worn out from the long, hot day on the road—and Ava's constant fussiness.

"I can't drive any more today, either. My head's about to explode and I don't trust myself to navigate this terrain in the dark anyway. Guess we don't have much choice." She sighed and pointed. "Up ahead there looks like as good a spot as any to stop."

Jake pulled over, cut the engine, and rested his head on the steering wheel. "I thought the road would be faster, too. But we've been fighting a headwind the whole way on top of everything." He turned to her. "Sorry. I know you wanted to take the interstate, but I still think this'll pay off when we try to cross into California."

"It'd better, after all this. We probably wouldn't have gotten the flat in the first place if we'd taken the interstate. And so you wouldn't have hurt your hand. How's it doing, anyway?"

"Oh, it's fine. No big deal."

"Fine? Really? Look at it! The gauze is all bloody. We should change it and make sure it's stopped bleeding. You could get a nasty infection if it isn't kept clean."

He leaned back in his seat and ran his good hand through his hair, pushing it back off his face. "I'll take care of it while you feed Ava, okay? Then we can have something to eat and turn in."

"All right. Probably better you do it, anyway. I'm afraid to even look at it. I don't think I'll ever get used to the sight of blood."

Lexi squirmed in her seat, trying to get into a position where no part of her was crunched or twisted—and finding it impossible even though she was dead-bone tired. Jake had fallen asleep almost as soon as he reclined his seat. Hours ago. She envied him. He could sleep anywhere, any time. And he could handle any situation that came his way without freaking out. She envied him that, too.

The tire pressure alarm went off and he just went right out there and tackled that flat, with the sun beating down on him the entire time. No panic, no hesitation. Just went out and got the job done, regardless of the conditions. And now he had that nasty cut on his knuckle. He said it wasn't bothering him, but she'd stolen a quick glance at it while he had the bandages off. It was deep. It was ugly. And it was red-rimmed already. She hoped it wasn't getting infected.

So now they had no spare tire and they had no idea how badly the other tire was damaged. What if they got another flat before they made it to civilization? Lexi gazed out into the interminable darkness and shivered. They'd die out there in that fucking wasteland, that's what. They had a decent store of food, water, and gas with them. But if their SUV was disabled, their stash wouldn't be enough to save them. Without the protection of the car's AC, it wouldn't take long to bake their brains. What a lovely way to die.

And Ava's appetite was worse than ever. She was barely taking her bottle at all now. Lexi offered her plain water earlier just to keep her hydrated, and she barely took that. Lexi bit her lip. What could the problem be? It scared her, not knowing how to get Ava back on track and having no one she could ask for advice, no doctor she could take her to. She was always such an easygoing baby. But she must have reached her limit with all this driving around in the bright, hot sun. The sooner they found a place to stay—even temporarily—the better.

Lexi watched a shooting star zip across the sky and disappear beyond the horizon. It made her think of home, so far away. What was it like in their town right now? Was their house even standing? Were her parents alive? What about all their friends, their co-workers? Would they ever be able to go back? Jake's idea of relocating closer to a reliable water supply was entirely logical. Just like him. Mr. Logical. But nowhere else could ever be home for her. Not really.

All she could think of was how much they'd lost. She couldn't even begin to visualize their future. Just a darkness as deep as the midnight sky lurking outside her window.

CHAPTER 29

Jake switched on the car's power and scowled at the GPS screen. He zoomed in, then out, then back in again, trying to find just the right road. Damned sun was up already, casting its malevolent glare over everything in its path and making it that much harder to read the GPS. Days sure seemed like months out here in Nowheresville, Nevada. He'd be glad to trade it for California. Any part of California would do.

He pointed at a narrow, twisting line on the screen. "Check this out. If we take that road there, we'll make it to the border tonight, head up into some mountains. It'll be cooler, if nothing else."

"*What* road? I don't see any road."

He zoomed in some more and let his finger hover over the display. "That one. A few miles from here, it branches off from the road we're on. See? Then it crosses the border right over there."

Lexi flopped back in her seat and finger-combed her dusty, tangled hair as she turned away from him to gaze out the window. "It's even less of a road than the one we're on. I don't know. Can't we stay on this one?"

He zoomed the display back out and pointed. "Look. If we stay on the road we're on, it takes a big left right there. Goes way around, gets to the border much farther south. This other road is actually more direct to where we need to be."

Lexi shrugged and stared down into her lap. "Okay, if you think it'll be faster. I've had enough of this damned desert. No cell reception." She turned again to look out the passenger-side window and sighed. "No nothing."

Jake started the car and cranked up the AC. "Okay, let's go."

The sooner they got out of this frying pan and into California, the better. Ava wasn't handling it well at all; her appetite had been off since they'd left Nebraska. They were all grimy, exhausted, and in desperate need of a shower, a decent meal, and a proper bed. And he didn't like what he saw when he changed his bandage this morning. The skin along the cut on his knuckle had turned puffy, red. And it hurt like hell to flex his hand. Probably not bad enough to justify a trip to the ER, but the wound could use better care—and a cleaner environment—than he could give it right now. He didn't dare tell Lexi about it, though. Better to keep his worries to himself and not upset her any more than she already was. At least his ankle had quit hurting. Good thing he hadn't damaged that, too.

Up ahead on the right, a makeshift sign lay propped against a stumpy barrel cactus. A simple red arrow, painted on a weathered piece of plywood, all buckled and cracked. Must be the road they wanted. Without the sign, he would have missed it and had to waste time and gas circling back. Nice of someone to put it there. He glanced at the GPS to confirm, then turned off the asphalt onto the loose gravel road.

Dust kicked up right away, enveloping the SUV in a cloud so thick he could barely see to navigate. Jake turned on the wipers to clear the windshield. It helped. A little. Gravel crunched beneath the tires. This road may be more direct, but it was going to be much slower going than the paved main road. He wondered if they'd made the right choice on balance, whether they would make the border tonight after all. Well, if they didn't, it wouldn't be for lack of trying. He'd make sure of that.

He longed for a motel room and a bed like never before. Even though they'd been switching off driving now and then, and this was only the beginning of their third day crossing through the desert, he felt done in, like he could lie down and sleep straight through a full day. Maybe more.

But the driving was only part of what was wearing him down. The rest was a nagging fear of the unknown and what might still go wrong, plus having to be constantly on guard to keep Lexi from panicking over all the things they couldn't control. He glanced over at her. She'd fallen asleep, her head resting against the window. Ava had been a handful again most of the night, keeping them both up for hours. He was glad Lexi was getting some sleep, such as it was, crumpled up in the car like that. The sight of her made him want all the more to get them to a decent place for the night.

Shoulders tensed, he hunched forward and squinted into the dust cloud, straining to see past the hood of the car. This was going to be one long, hard day if the damned dust didn't let up. And no way would Lexi switch off with him in this. She couldn't stand to drive in poor visibility. In a hard rain where the wipers couldn't keep up, she'd pull over right away and stay put until the rain slowed. He laughed to himself. A hard rain. When was the last time *that* was a problem?

Jake slammed on the brakes, jarring Lexi awake. Ava started crying and sputtering from the back seat.

"What is it? Where are we?" Lexi sat straight up, glanced from side to side, and shouted to be heard over Ava. "What's going on?"

"I thought I saw something up ahead. Didn't want to hit it."

"How can you see *anything* in this?"

"Road's turned to gravel."

Jake kept his foot on the brake, hoping no one rammed them from behind while he waited for the dust to settle. He was sure he saw something up ahead, but what? A bend in the road with some cactus? An animal?

The dust finally thinned enough to reveal a grisly sight. About ten yards up ahead, a van and a sedan lay twisted and tangled together on their sides, blocking the road. Looked like a head-on collision. Mangled bits of metal lay strewn about. Impossible to tell if it was fresh or old.

"Oh my God!" Lexi covered her face with her hands.

Jake put it in Park, hopped out of the car, and hastened toward the wreckage. The sun was so strong, it felt like running through the inside of a furnace. If there was anyone still inside those cars, they were likely dead from their injuries or the heat. Or both. And if they weren't dead, they'd need help badly. Probably more than he could give them with just some water and their little first aid kit.

As he drew closer, he identified one of the mangled vehicles. A late-model sedan, the kind with an engine too powerful for its own good. Jake imagined what likely happened. Probably someone hotdogging it on the gravel road, going way too fast for the visibility, and assuming they had the road all to themselves. Never saw it coming. Panting and sweating, he squatted down next to the shattered windshield and bent to look inside.

Lexi's shrill scream startled him. He jumped up too quickly, slipped on some loose gravel, and fell hard onto the searing hot ground. Two men in ragged clothes emerged from behind the overturned van, one brandishing a tire iron and one swinging a baseball bat. Jake caught only a quick glimpse of them before pushing himself to his feet and racing back toward Lexi.

The gravel shifted, taking his right foot out from under him. He fell face-first onto the ground, breaking his fall with his hands. Sharp pain shot through his injured knuckle. Gravel crunched behind him as the men closed the gap. He turned, started pushing himself up. The guy with the bat took a swing at his head. The bat *whooshed* by his ear. He kicked up, catching the creep's shin, knocking him over, right into the path of the guy with the tire iron. They tangled up and both went down, yelling and cursing.

Jake sprinted the rest of the way to the car and flung himself in before the attackers could catch up to him. He stomped on the accelerator so hard he kicked up a spray of gravel before the tires caught. He cut the wheel to the left, fishtailing in the loose sand, then blasted around the wreckage and down the road.

He was going way too fast for gravel—fast enough to stay just ahead of his dust cloud. He could see ahead and to the side pretty well, but behind him, that wall of dust blocked his view. He locked his eyes on the road and his hands on the wheel, desperate to put as much distance as possible between them and those men. His injured knuckle throbbed in time with his pounding heart. Adrenaline shot through him like live wires.

"I think I hear something," Lexi shouted as she cocked her head, listening.

Jake strained to hear, then opened the window a crack. Dust

billowed in, coating the dash. A droning sound. "Watch behind us. I'm going to make a move."

He made as sharp a right turn as he dared in the treacherous sand and gravel. He hoped it was enough to get around their dust cloud and give Lexi a view, however brief.

"See anything?"

"They're on motorcycles!" Lexi clung to the grab handle above her door and shrieked. "Oh my God, they're coming after us!"

"Hang on."

Jake shut out Lexi's and Ava's screams as he steered back onto the center of the road and gunned it. He had to focus, take in the situation, and make the right move. Or they'd all die.

He glanced around. Nothing. Nowhere to hide. Nowhere to turn off for help. What if those guys had guns? Wouldn't they have used them already? He hoped so—he had no protection against gunfire. Few options at all, for that matter, to protect them from crazies like that. He was on his own to somehow get to safety. Nothing else he could do but haul ass and hope those fuckers wiped out or gave up.

He barreled down the road in white-knuckled terror for another twenty minutes or so, hearing nothing, seeing nothing but what was in front of him. He took a sharp left at the far end of a group of low sand dunes, then spun around and braked hard. He nosed the car out a little at a time until he could just see around the dunes. He tapped his fingers on the steering wheel, willing the dust he'd kicked up to settle, to let him see.

At last the dust dispersed. The road was clear. No other approaching dust clouds. Nothing as far as he could see. They must have given up, turned back to wait for another victim.

"Where'd they go?" Lexi's trembling voice cut in.

"I don't know, but if they were still chasing us, we'd see their dust."

Lexi released her death grip on the grab handle, clapped her hands to her face, and sobbed.

Jake reached over and rubbed her shoulder. "It's okay. It's over. Everything's all right now."

She glared at him, tears cutting tracks through the grime on her face. "They could have killed you. Could have killed all of us!" She twisted around in her seat and *shushed* at Ava until her cries dwindled to sobs.

"I know, I know. But we got past them." He eased the car back onto the road. "Better keep going so it stays that way."

Jake tried to ignore the throbbing pain in his injured knuckle as he clutched the wheel—hard—to stop his hands from trembling. He had to look calm, like it wasn't that big a deal. For Lexi's sake. She looked like she was on her last nerve as it was.

Truth be told, he wasn't doing much better than she was. He didn't want to think of what could have happened back there. Too many ugly possibilities. He pushed aside the gruesome images that tried to force their way into his mind. No, he had to be sure nothing like that happened again.

He accelerated, paying close attention to the SUV's handling. He had to push it as hard as he could without taking it too far and losing control on the gravel. An exhausting, white-knuckle way to drive, but worth it to get to that damned border as fast as possible. Only then could he relax. When they were safe.

CHAPTER 30

Lexi stared out the window at the interminable desert land-scape as Jake sped along in silence, jaw muscles rippling. No point in trying to talk to him while he was so focused. Maybe she should try to take a nap. Ava finally screamed herself to sleep a couple of hours ago, not long after that whole terrifying incident with those motorcycle creeps. But she'd been way too quiet the last few miles. Lexi unbuckled her seat belt and turned around to check on her. Ava writhed in her carrier, her face a bluish shade of white.

"Stop the car—something's wrong with Ava!"

"What's the matter?" Jake hit the brakes and skidded off the road in a cloud of dust.

"I don't know! I think she's having trouble breathing."

Lexi jumped out of the car and yanked open the rear door. Hands trembling, she fumbled with the fasteners, finally freeing Ava from her car seat. She scooped her up, then realized she had no idea what to do next. Ava struggled silently in her arms, her eyes wide with panic.

Jake took one look, then ran to the other side of the car and hastily cleared off the back seat.

"Put her here. Get her out of the sun."

Lexi rushed to the other side of the car and laid Ava down on the seat as carefully as if she feared breaking her into a million pieces. The poor little girl waved her tiny arms and legs, twisted around as if she were in some kind of pain. Then she opened her mouth wide in a what looked like a silent scream. And her color seemed to be getting worse.

"Oh my God, what's *wrong* with her?" Lexi shifted her

weight from foot to foot. She had to do something, couldn't just stand there. But what? She couldn't call for help. They were nowhere near anything. And she had no idea what was going on, what to do about it.

Jake leaned over and pressed the back of his good hand against Ava's forehead, her arms, her legs. "She seems a little hot, but it's hard to tell. I don't like how she's breathing."

"Her little chest...the way it's moving. It's like she's barely getting any air!"

Jake pried open Ava's mouth and peered inside. "Could she have gotten hold of something and swallowed it?"

"Who knows with all the shit back there with her? How should *I* know? I can't watch her every single minute!" Teetering on the edge of pure, blind panic, Lexi clenched her fists and pressed them to her cheeks.

Jake rummaged around in the back of the SUV, then came back with the first-aid kit. "Maybe something stung her."

"But where? I don't see anything. What're you going to do?"

"Antihistamine. See if I can get some down her. I had a dog get stung once. Worked great. Took down the swelling really fast."

"But she's only a baby! How do you know how much to give her?"

"I'll only give her a little. Get me a bottle and some water."

Lexi plucked one of Ava's bottles from the diaper bag, sloshed some bottled water in, and handed it to Jake. At least he had some idea of what to do. But what if it didn't work? Her brain felt paralyzed with panic. She glanced around. The barren desert terrain mocked her, made her feel insignificant. And incredibly helpless.

Jake broke open a capsule, sprinkled some powder into the water, then capped and shook it. "Okay, Ava. Drink this down. Just a little bit." He gently tried to coax her to drink, but she struggled, turning away and refusing to take the bottle.

"Let me try."

Lexi grabbed the bottle and tried to get Ava to take it. Ava twisted her head away, balled up her fists, then suddenly stretched all her limbs out straight and rigid. Was she in pain?

Was she having a seizure? Trembling, Lexi dropped the bottle on the seat.

"Did she get any of it?"

"No! We have to get help. Come on, let's go." Lexi cleared a spot for herself and jumped into the back seat. She clutched Ava to her chest. "Hurry!"

Jake ducked his head inside the car. "Lexi, there's nowhere to go for help. We're hours away from anything."

"I told you not to go on these shit roads, away from cell reception. Away from everything! At least get us back on that more major road. Someone might come by."

"We can't turn around. Too risky—that trap might still be there. All we can do is get her as stable as possible and keep going. Try to get her to take the medicine."

"Come on, Ava. You've got to take this." Lexi picked up the bottle and froze. "Jake, she's turning blue!"

"Jesus. Give her to me."

"What're you going to do?"

"Make it so she can breathe. Better not watch."

Lexi held Ava tight. "How?"

"Trach. Give her to me. *Now.* No time to waste."

Jake snatched Ava away. She flopped in his arms, limp as a rag doll. "Move her car seat over here. Either that or you hold her still for me."

Lexi slammed the carrier down on the bench seat between her and Jake, then covered her eyes and sobbed. "I can't watch, I just can't do it."

"Then don't. I need to concentrate."

"Isn't there any other way—"

"Wish there were."

Lexi wanted to clap her hands to her ears, to be anywhere but there, hearing Jake trying to operate on their little girl. But she couldn't *not* listen. She cringed in her seat, shaking violently. Every little sound seemed magnified against the hot, heavy silence of the desert around them.

Jake didn't say a word while he worked. She heard him digging through the first aid kit, then ripping paper, probably opening a pack of gauze. She heard snipping, then a very brief sound. The sound of something wet, something tearing. She held her breath, swallowed bile—and tried not to picture what Jake was doing to Ava.

"She's breathing again."

Lexi opened her eyes and peeked through her fingers, as if that would make it easier to look at what Jake had done. She recoiled and swallowed more bile. It was even worse than she'd imagined. The entire front of Ava's little T-shirt was soaked with blood. A bloody square of gauze with a hole cut in the middle was taped to her tender neck.

"Oh, Jake! There's so much blood—and she's still bleeding."

Jake doused a pair of scissors with hydrogen peroxide. Blood and foam dribbled onto the sand next to the car. "I know. The gauze should help it clot soon." His hand shook as he wiped sweat from his forehead.

Lexi swallowed hard and studied at Ava's face, trying not to look at all the blood—and trying hard not to throw up or pass out. Her color was a little better already and her chest was rising and falling more like it should. But she looked dazed, like she was neither awake nor asleep.

"Why does she look like that?"

Jake was filling a baby bottle with plain water. "I don't know. Probably traumatized. I hope that's all it is. Here." He handed her the bottle. "We've got to get some fluids in her soon as she's conscious. As much as we can. She was probably dehydrated from the heat already, and the bleeding's making it worse."

"Jake…her pupils." Lexi could barely breathe. Ava's eyes looked black, like a cheaply made doll. The pupils were so wide.

Jake leaned down for a better look, then waved his fingers close to Ava's face. No reaction. He gently touched a fingertip to her eyeball. No response. Hand trembling, he pressed a finger to the side of her neck. And again. He stood, covered his face with his hands, and unleashed a heart-wrenching sob.

"Jake!" Lexi unstrapped Ava from her carrier and picked her up. "Ava!" She was completely limp, arms and legs lifeless.

Lexi laid her baby down in her lap, her hands flitting around like butterflies afraid to land. The bleeding had stopped. Ava lay absolutely still. Not breathing. Not anything.

This didn't happen. It couldn't have happened. Ava was just unconscious. That was it. She'd lost a lot of blood and was tired. She'd come to in a few minutes, drink some water, and be fine.

"Lexi."

Lexi glanced at her shoulder, where Jake's hand, wet with tears, rested. "What?"

"We can't stay here."

"Ava needs to rest a little first. The road's bumpy. I don't want her getting jostled around right now."

"Lexi…she's gone. And we can't stay here."

"No, she's just—"

"She's gone, Lexi. I wish I could change that, but I can't." He swiped tears from his eyes. "We can't." He choked on the words.

Lexi hugged Ava close. "She just needs to rest. She'll be okay."

Sobbing, Jake shook his head and closed the door. Without another word, he got into the driver's seat and pulled back onto the road.

"I told you she needs to rest! Stop the car!"

Jake didn't answer, kept driving. Bastard. Lexi held Ava's limp little body tight, willing her to wake up. If she could get her to drink some water, she could start replenishing all that blood she lost.

Lexi settled back in her seat. Maybe it was just as well Jake was pushing on. The sooner they got out of this damned desert and to some town, the better. Then they could get Ava to a doctor. Make sure she got whatever treatment she needed to start feeling better.

CHAPTER 31

If only he could drive fast enough and far enough to leave behind everything that had happened—all the loss, all the pain and grief. But driving wasn't the solution. And starting over was an illusion. Now more than ever, there would be no starting over for them. Just a change of scenery. Nothing more.

Jake rubbed his eyes and tried to focus on the road ahead through the dust and glare. Lexi hadn't said one word since they'd left the spot where it happened. She just sat back there, rocking Ava in her lap. He wondered if she meant what she said or if it was just her emotions talking. Did she really think Ava was still alive? And if she did…then what was he going to do?

He'd done what he could for Ava, what he thought would help her. But it wasn't enough. Worse, he couldn't help thinking he may even have killed her, or at least hastened her death. He'd never know the truth, and the question would torment him the rest of his life. All he knew for sure was he couldn't save his own baby girl, and now they were driving around in the desert with her little body in the car. He couldn't begin to wrap his head around that. If only he could retreat into not believing it had happened. At least for a while.

He glanced at the GPS. Not far from the border now, as the crow flew. They'd hit small towns at best in such a remote corner of California. Just like he planned, to better their chances of slipping across the border without being noticed or stopped. But his brilliant plan had a downside. There'd likely be fewer services in small towns. He sighed. People die in small towns, too. There *had* to be someone around who could help them take proper care of Ava's body.

Now he had to make yet another choice—and he was sick to death of making choices, weighing consequences at every turn. And living with those consequences. He shook his head and scowled at the GPS. It showed the road forking not far up ahead. Which way to go? The rightmost path went through some low hills. He much preferred level terrain, better traction on this crappy road surface. But that road looked like the shorter route overall. Jake swung right at the fork. Anything to get this trip over with sooner.

He set his jaw. Hard to believe any road could be in rougher shape than the one they'd just been on, but this one was. Rutted and grooved, like some violent storm had rolled through at some point, cutting sharp gullies through the gravel and sand. Jake had to put the SUV into four-wheel mode and pick his way over some exposed rocks. Sweat trickled down his forehead, down his sides beneath his shirt, despite the blasting AC inside the car. Looked like no one had driven this way in quite some time. They were even more on their own than before. Better not run into trouble out here.

Jake clutched the wheel in a relentless death grip. Sharp cramps stabbed his hands. His injured knuckle burned and throbbed. He tried to set aside the pain, focus on negotiating the road ahead of him. He didn't dare relax his grip, not even for an instant. Driving through this mess required his full attention, else he could damage the car or get it stuck. And there'd be no way they could free themselves. That jack wouldn't hold in this sloppy gravel. They'd die out here.

He stole a quick glance in the rear view. Lexi just sat there, shoulders slumped, staring down at Ava. Maybe reality was sinking in, and she was processing what had happened in her own way.

He'd give anything to turn back the clock, make different choices. They had to evacuate to escape the fire, no question. But they didn't have to take this crazy, stupid journey to some promised land that he made up in his head out of hopes and wishes.

It sounded supremely logical to him at the time. If they had to leave their home, why not move where there were better water sources? It made perfect sense. But if they'd just stopped and settled down at the first opportunity, wherever that turned out to be, Ava would be alive right now. She might not have gotten sick in the first place. And even if she had, they would have been near doctors, a hospital.

She wouldn't have died. And Lexi wouldn't be sitting back there, holding their dead child, awash in unimaginable pain. So much destruction, all because of the stupid, overconfident choices he made.

He knew it in his heart. It was all his fault, and he'd have to live with that forever. He could still see Ava in his mind's eye, lips tinged blue, the scissors poised over her fragile neck. Then the blood, when he plunged in the blade. So much blood. But it did help her breathe, if only for a few minutes. He forced the images down and away. He couldn't deal with that while he tried to avoid fresh disaster on this gruesome excuse for a road.

Jake followed a curve around a row of sand dunes. Any other time, he'd find beauty in the formations, want to photograph them, capture the moment before the sand shifted to a new shape. But right now, the dunes felt like the enemy, blocking his view of the horizon, of the road to California and their final destination, whatever the hell it was.

He rounded the last dune. And stopped. Another dune hiding behind it had migrated right onto the roadway, completely blocking the way forward with a ten-foot-high wall of sand. He glanced at the GPS, the dune, then back again, desperate to find a way around the blockage so they could still make the border. He felt boxed-in, trapped. Defeated.

The GPS revealed no easy solution. To bypass the blockage, they'd have to leave the road entirely and hope they didn't get bogged down in deep, loose sand before they could pick up the road again. And there might well be some other blockage farther on, given the condition of the road so far. Jake shook his head and let his shoulders sag. Too risky. They'd get stuck for sure. So much for the shorter route.

No choice except to turn around, backtrack through all the gullies and rocks he'd just navigated, then take the left fork, the longer route. And hope there wasn't some other blockage awaiting them on *that* road. At least it looked more level. If it was in better shape, it'd be a faster road than this one, anyway. Still, they'd lost a lot of time, and they were going to lose even more now.

Sighing, he checked the gas gauge. Might as well top the tank before they got going again. He glanced in the rear view. Still clutching Ava, Lexi stared out the window, her face expressionless. He wondered what was going through her mind.

Jake plodded to the back of the car, opened the rear compartment, and surveyed his stash of gas. It had better be enough. They'd used some of it since they left Wendover, and he had no idea when they'd come across another gas station, let alone a charging station. He picked up one gas can. Nearly empty. He dumped it into the tank, then grabbed two full ones and dumped them in.

He got back in and started the car. The tank stood at half-full. They had a bit more gas in back, but not a lot. Should be enough to get them out of this hell and into California—if they didn't hit another dead end somewhere along the way.

That other fork better be passable. It was their only way out of this damned desert now. They couldn't go back to the main road without passing by that staged accident. Couldn't risk running into that trap again. Might not be so lucky a second time. Besides, even if they could get through there safely, they probably didn't have enough gas to make it all the way back to West Wendover.

And they couldn't keep driving around with their little girl's dead body in the car.

CHAPTER 32

"Why're we stopping?" It hurt to speak, to force the words out of her parched throat. And it felt unnatural for the car to stop moving. It seemed as if they'd always been driving—as if they always *would* be driving. She didn't want to stop. Better to stay suspended in this weird limbo than face whatever the future held for them now. Now that everything good had been destroyed.

Lexi listlessly gazed out the dusty window. The landscape looked the same as ever. For all she knew, they could be right back at the makeshift campsite where they'd spent their first night in the desert. Back when Ava was alive. Seemed like weeks ago, but they only started driving through Nevada the day before yesterday. How could that even be? She swiped a tear from her face.

Jake turned around in his seat and spoke softly. "Lexi." He bit his lip and looked away, then back at her. "We need to…take care of Ava."

"What…what are you saying?"

"I'm really sorry, but doubling back from that blocked road delayed us badly. I think we could still make the border tonight, but it'd be well after dark. Too late to find someplace to have her properly taken care of—and I'm not sure I trust this road enough to try to drive it at night anyway. We have to…take care of her…here."

Sobbing, Lexi clutched Ava's cool, lifeless body close. "I don't want to leave her out here like some…animal."

"Lexi, we can't keep her."

"Don't you think I know that? Jesus, Jake! It's just…I *hate* it out here. I don't want to be here. I don't want *her* to be out here. I want to be home. I want Ava back."

Jake reached out and wiped a tear off her cheek. "Me too, Lexi. I wish I could change things back the way they were, I really do." He sighed. "But I can't."

He got out of the car without another word and rooted through the SUV's back compartment. Lexi watched as he wandered around with the folding shovel in one hand, poking the toe of his shoe in the sand here and there until he settled on a spot. Then he began digging, his eyes cast downward, never looking up or around. *He's really going to do it.* Lexi sobbed as the sand piled higher and higher beside Ava's grave. The higher it got, the sooner she'd have to say goodbye.

She gently laid Ava down in her lap. She wished she could remember her alive and healthy, but she could already tell this horrible last image would always remain with her. The bluish skin, the dried blood caked all over her neck and T-shirt. Her lifeless eyes, the pupils dilated so wide that looking into her eyes was like looking into oblivion itself.

Lexi'd never felt so alone, so broken. Nothing would ever be the same. She couldn't imagine recovering from this. Not ever. She watched Jake digging, digging. He wanted a fresh start. Well, he had one now. No fresher start than when you've lost everything.

Wiping sweat from his forehead, he set down the shovel and plodded toward the car. Lexi clutched Ava close one last time, her little body stiff, cold. Unresponsive. Jake opened the door and held out his arms, silent.

"I'll take her myself."

Lexi got out and willed herself to keep it together as she marched to the open grave with Ava in her arms. Despite the rippling heat, she shivered as she gazed down. A simple hole in the ground, surrounded by low scrub and prickly cacti and God knew what horrible creatures that came in the dark of night. A terrible and lonely place to leave her only little girl, like something unwanted. She shook her head. Not like there was much choice. Jake was right about one thing. Who knew when they'd get to a place where they could have her taken care of properly, with the dignity and respect she deserved?

She knelt in the sand and gently lowered Ava into the ground. Late-day sun cast a warm, pinkish-orange light and long shadows. Night would come soon. She pushed herself up and ran back to the car for Ava's favorite blanket. Of course, it didn't really matter, but she couldn't bear to think of putting Ava down without that blanket. She never slept without it.

Lexi knelt back down, covered Ava with the blanket, and carefully tucked its soft, satin-bound edges beneath her, just as she always did at bedtime. Just as Ava liked it best.

"Sleep well, baby."

She leaned over, kissed Ava one last time, then stood and dusted off the sand. "Go ahead and bury her now. It's what you've always wanted." She turned and started for the car.

Jake flung down the shovel. "What?"

Lexi kept walking, didn't look back. "You never wanted her. Never wanted a baby. So now you have your wish."

Jake caught up with her, grabbed her by the shoulders, and spun her around to face him. "That is not true. Okay, I didn't think we were ready. But when I saw her for the first time—"

"Yeah, right. You saw her for the first time and knew there was no turning back, that's all!"

Jake let go of her, turned away with his arms folded across his chest. "Jesus, Lexi. How do you think I feel right now? I cut into our little girl to try to save her, and it didn't matter. All I did was hurt her and make her bleed. For nothing." He clapped his hands to his face and sobbed.

Tears streaming down her face, Lexi snatched up the shovel and stomped toward the grave.

"Wait...let me..." Jake came up beside her, knelt in the sand, and leaned over to kiss Ava. "Goodbye, Ava." He pushed himself up and stood, silent.

Ignoring him, Lexi took one last look at Ava. Then gently, so gently, she began shoveling.

When she was done, she patted down the sand until it formed a smooth, graceful mound, then sat next to the grave, cross-legged, and stared at it. *That's it.* Ava had only been in their lives for a few months, and now she was gone. Buried in the middle of nowhere, where they could probably never find her little grave again, even if they tried. Lexi ran her fingers along the sand, as if trying to comfort her little girl. Jake sat down next to her, head bowed.

They sat that way, neither one speaking, until the sun dropped beneath the horizon and a chill crept into the air.

CHAPTER 33

Jake awoke to a relentless stabbing pain behind his eyes. His injured knuckle throbbed and burned as he lay crumpled up in the reclined driver's seat, eyes shut tight against the rising sun. An overwhelming feeling of hopelessness and loss weighed him down like a physical thing. Then he remembered why.

Ava.

He opened his eyes and turned toward the passenger seat. Empty. He must have been completely done in, sleeping right through the night and not even hearing Lexi get out. He pushed himself up, heart hammering. If he didn't hear that, what else didn't he hear? Way out here, anything could happen. Dangerous to sleep that soundly until they were somewhere safe. He shook his head. *Safe.* As if he'd done such a great job already. He certainly hadn't kept Ava safe.

He glanced out the window. Where the hell was she? He got out and hurried to the other side of the car for a better look around. And stopped.

Still as a statue, Lexi knelt in the sand, staring down at Ava's grave. She had her arms wrapped around herself as if she were cold. God knew how long she'd been there.

Jake wanted to go to her, to comfort her. To grieve with her. But there was something about how she held herself, how she was looking at that grave, that made him think he'd be intruding if he did. It was almost as if she were trying to communicate something to Ava one last time before they left her alone out there forever.

He loved Ava like he never imagined he could love a child,

but still, he didn't have the bond with her that Lexi had. And now he never would.

The sun rose higher, gathering strength, once again punishing everything in its path with its killing rays. Jake climbed back into the SUV, switched on the power, and checked the GPS. It wasn't that much farther to the California border. They could have made it last night—but not until well after dark. He was right about that much, anyway. It would have been too late to wander around looking for something like an undertaker, or wherever it was you took your dead child in a strange place.

Jake switched off the GPS and hung his head. Lexi was right. He hadn't wanted a baby, not yet. But it wasn't as if he intended to lead some aimless, irresponsible waste of a life. It was just that a baby was, to his mind, the ultimate responsibility. Irreversible. He wanted to be completely sure before he took that step.

He'd finally given in to Lexi's constant harping, against his better judgment, and in a time of epic drought and uncertainty. And he *did* love Ava the moment he first laid eyes on her. But Lexi never let him forget how hard he fought against having her in the first place. She'd always believe he secretly didn't want Ava, didn't love her. She probably also believed that maybe, just maybe, he'd somehow contributed to her death. And he'd never be able to prove to her she was wrong. Especially since he couldn't even prove it to himself.

Judging by the things she said last night and from the way she was looking at that grave, Lexi would never forgive him for burying Ava where they'd never, ever be able to visit her again. Where she'd be at the mercy of the elements, like something discarded. Not like someone who was loved.

Jake slammed his fist on the steering wheel, then bit back a cry of pain. He clutched his injured knuckle with his other hand. It felt hot, damp. Probably bleeding again. *Stupid.* Just like this whole plan. He'd thought—he'd really *believed*—he was using the forced evacuation to improve their lives. Better access to water. Better jobs. Less stringent water usage enforcement. It had gotten like a police state where they lived. The slightest misstep, and you'd get a stiff fine, penalty, even jail time. That was no place to raise their little girl.

Brilliant plan. Just fucking brilliant. Too bad it cost them their child. And likely more, much more.

Lexi opened the door and got in, head bowed. "Let's go." She sounded defeated, exhausted.

"You sure? We don't have to rush if—"

Lexi glared at him. "It's not like I can bring her back if I sit there long enough!" She stared down at her lap. "If only I could."

"Lexi, I am so sorry. If I could change anything, I would. Believe me."

She turned away. "Shut the fuck up. You've done enough. Just go."

Several hours later, they came up on a small, battered, bullet-ridden wooden sign that simply said "California". *Finally.* Jake glanced at Lexi. She had her head turned away from him, her arms folded across her chest. He decided to cross the border in silence, keep moving until they arrived at a stopping point.

At least one thing worked out as he planned. No one was guarding the border out this way. In fact, it looked just as lonely and empty up ahead as it did behind them, except, mercifully, the road was now paved. They were right not to push to find somewhere to take Ava last night. There was nothing in sight here at the border anyway.

Jake glanced at the GPS. Nothing right here, but they were finally within striking distance of some decent-sized towns if they kept to this road. He tried to ease the muscle in his right shoulder, knotted from sleeping all cramped up in the car last night.

Beeeep!

"What is it?" Lexi bolted upright.

"Tire alarm." *Please God, let it be a false alarm.*

Jake cut the wheel and pulled off the road, into the sand. He shut off the engine and made his way around the SUV, holding his breath. And there it was. The right rear, hissing out the last of its air as he watched it pancake in the sand. *That's it. Game over.* If it's leaking that fast, no way could he just pump it up every few miles and limp into the first town he found with some sort of service station. And no good spare, either. They were screwed. Well and truly screwed. They hadn't seen one other car since their encounter with those thugs. And it didn't look like this road got a lot of action. No one was going to pick them up and take them to town.

Sighing, he got back in the car. "Right rear's flat. Undrivable. Any cell reception here?"

Lexi fumbled in her bag, pulled out her cell and turned it on. They waited in silence for it to boot up and answer the question. She shook her head and put the phone away.

"Nope."

"Shit. Okay." Jake turned the GPS back on and zoomed in. "I hope this thing's right. Shows a town a couple more miles down the road. Doesn't look like much, but it's something. Better than sitting out here, hoping someone happens by."

"Can't you fix it?" Lexi waved her arm toward the cargo area. "You bought everything there was to buy before we left Utah. Don't you have something to fix it with?"

"No. I figured if we got a flat, we'd just put on the spare. Didn't count on getting more than one."

Lexi grabbed her hair in her fists and growled through clenched teeth. "Jesus. Just when I thought it couldn't get any worse. We might as well just fucking die out here!"

"Lexi, get a grip. Looks like there's a small town only a couple of miles away. Could be a lot worse. Like if this happened two hours ago." He started to get out of the car. "I'm going to fill a canteen with water and go. Want to come with me or stay with the car?"

Lexi shook her head. "I don't want to bake out here all alone with no way to get hold of you." She paused, her hand on the door handle. "You sure we can't just keep driving on it? If you go slow enough, control shouldn't be a problem, right?"

"Yeah, but driving on it will wreck it completely. At least right now, there's a chance it can be fixed."

"Figures." Lexi groaned and opened her door. "How stupid of me to think we could catch a break somehow. Let's go. Might as well get this over with, so we can move on to the next disaster that awaits us."

CHAPTER 34

"Slow the hell down, alright?" Lexi bent over to get the pebble out of her shoe. Goddamned thing had been jabbing the sole of her foot for the last ten minutes, while Jake strode along through the furnace-blast heat like he was late for an appointment.

He stopped, turned, and rested his hands on his hips while he waited for her. "You okay?"

"Just something in my shoe."

Lexi stood, readjusted her fanny pack, and trudged on until she caught up with Jake. So far, California wasn't one bit cooler than the damned Nevada desert. It even looked pretty much the same. In fact, if she hadn't seen the crappy little sign with her own eyes, she wouldn't have believed they'd crossed into another state. So much for Jake's fantasy of the paradise that awaited them in California.

She longed to be back inside the car—with the AC on full-blast. Better than walking through this baking hell. She squinted into the sun, sweat stinging her eyes. Looked like something up ahead, so the GPS hadn't lied about that. Whether it was what they needed was another story. It'd better be. She couldn't imagine walking much farther with the sun beating down on her skull. If there was nothing else for miles and miles, they might as well lie down and die and be done with it all. Or fuck it and run the car on the flat tire, all the way to L.A. if they had to.

Jake nudged her toward the middle of the road and pointed. "Look out. Snake over there."

Lexi glanced where Jake pointed. A snake, the color of dark sand and about as big around as her bicep, slithered off into some sage scrub and disappeared like he'd never been there. Goosebumps covered her sweat-drenched arms. If there was one snake, there had to be more. And look how fast they could move when they wanted to. Maybe that's why she hadn't noticed any before. All those horrible things that lived in the desert. Scorpions, tarantulas. They had to be out there, waiting in force. Way more than the few she'd seen earlier on. She stared down at the ground before her as she walked, ready to spring out of the way of any venomous thing that might cross her path.

"Are you sure we wouldn't be better off just driving the car as is?"

"Only as a last resort. I don't want to risk wrecking the tire. Look, it's not much farther."

Lexi took a swig of warm water from her canteen, grimaced at the metallic aftertaste, and forced herself to keep going, to get through this. One step at a time. Don't think about the heat. Or the snakes. Or anything else. Just walk. Just walk and try not to think about *anything*.

Because there was nothing she *could* think about right now that wouldn't throw her into a meltdown she might never come out of. Can't go there. Not now. Not until she was somewhere safe, somewhere she'd have the space and time to process everything that had happened. And to think about how to put her life back together.

After the longest, most miserable hour of walking ever, they came up to the town, such as it was. Nothing but a collection of parched-looking old wooden structures at the side of the road.

She stopped. "Looks deserted. Terrific." She kicked at the sand with one shoe. "After all this."

"Let's get a closer look. Probably more behind those. At least I hope so."

"You hope so."

Muttering, Lexi shook her head and followed Jake. This had been a complete waste of time and energy. They should have just driven on. The hell with the tire. What damned difference did it make? Was there really any point anymore? Ava was lying in a shallow grave in some wasteland, and they were pushing on as if they had a reason to live. She sure couldn't think of one right now.

They came up to the first of the structures and peered inside through a broken window. Heaps of rat shit in every corner. A stained, torn mattress in the middle of the floor. They moved on to the second of the structures. More of the same, only this time with scattered piles of filthy rags and empty cigarette packs.

Jake sighed and led them to the last of the old buildings that fronted the road. Much larger than the rest, it featured a rickety metal awning and a worn wooden bench out front, like it used to be a gas station back in another century. Several lopsided shacks stood farther back off the road. They looked even less promising.

As they approached, the front door flew open and banged back against the wall. A white-haired old man with a bushy gray beard sprang out and leveled his shotgun at them.

"What the fuck you doin' here? Get out!"

Jake held up his hands. "Whoa, whoa. We got a flat up the road."

Squinting, the man eyed them each in turn, shotgun still at the ready. "How do I know you're not here to rob me?"

Hands raised, Lexi cleared her throat. She could feel the gun pointed at her, almost like it was touching her. "It's true. Spare's flat, too."

Scowling, the man maintained his shooting stance. Rail-thin and tanned nut-brown, he wore nothing but a pair of grubby, torn jeans.

"Ain't no vacation resorts out this way. The only ones who come by here, come by because they got reasons why they don't want to be seen. So, what's your reason?"

Lexi and Jake exchanged glances. Jake gave her a slight nod, then began, "We had to evacuate—fast—from a huge fire in Nebraska. We were trying to get to California."

The shotgun twitched. "California's a long way from Nebraska. You couldn't have landed someplace else?"

Lexi dropped her arms and took a step forward. "Look, mister. I wish we *had* stopped somewhere else, but we're here and we need help. We just want to get on our way, not cause any trouble." This was really the last straw, to be looking down a shotgun in the middle of some ghost town shithole. "If you want to shoot us, get it over with. I don't want to be here anyway."

The man lowered his shotgun and relaxed his stance. "I'm sorry, lady. Not many people come through this way, and the ones who do would just as soon shoot me and take what little I have. Got to be cautious." He held out a calloused hand. "Name's Ray."

Heart hammering, Lexi croaked, "I'm Lexi, this is Jake."

Jake reached out, shook his hand. "Pleased to meet you, Ray."

"C'mon, c'mon out of the sun. Let's sit down here in the shade." Ray set aside his shotgun and plunked his wiry frame onto the weathered wooden bench by the front door.

Lexi sank down onto the bench next to Jake, relieved to be off her feet and in some shade at last. Even better not to be staring down the barrel of a shotgun. But she couldn't quite trust the guy's sudden change of tune. Maybe *he* was the one who liked to trap people who came through. Like a spider waiting for flies.

CHAPTER 35

Ray tipped his head and smiled at Lexi, exposing an eclectic set of worn, yellowed teeth. His eyes, faded cornflower blue with a whitish cataract haze in the pupils, seemed to light up when he looked at her.

As he watched the desert rat's sudden transformation from raging hermit to welcoming host, Jake wondered how often anyone dared stop here, let alone stick around to chat. Probably not very often. A raised—and likely loaded—shotgun tended to quell the urge to linger. It certainly scared the shit out of *him*.

But Lexi! He couldn't believe what she just did. Like she suddenly became someone else entirely. He'd been trying to think of a way to get them out of the line of fire, then she walks right into it and defuses the situation. Lexi was a lot of things, but never fearless, let alone reckless. Her ploy had worked, but what a crazy risk she took. She could have gotten them both killed.

The old guy sure seemed to take to her. Undoubtedly the only reason he put down the gun. Couldn't blame him for coming out loaded for bear like he had, though. Out here alone like he was, vulnerable. But to what? Didn't look like he had much worth taking.

Ray nodded and swept open his arms. "This here used to be a gas station, but business dropped off so bad it made no sense to bother keeping it up. Sold the pumps for scrap metal a few years ago. But I kept all my tools inside the garage back there. I can probably fix your tire. Unless it's real bad, in the sidewall or something."

Lexi leaned toward him, her most irresistible smile plastered on her face. "Could you maybe fix both tires? It's really scary driving around without a good spare."

"Sure. 'Less it's really wrecked, like I said."

"Thanks, we'd really appreciate it." Jake was getting antsy sitting there watching Lexi chatting up shotgun-man like it was the most normal thing in the world. Her sudden change was starting to worry him. He'd much rather pay the guy, get the tires fixed, and move on. But maybe they could learn something useful about the area if they drew him out a little first. "So, you live out here alone?"

Ray stretched out his legs, leaned back on the bench, and absently tugged at his beard. "Yeah. Been out here maybe ten, eleven years now. Never did like city life. Too goddamned many people. So, I opened up the gas station."

Lexi glanced around, rubbing her upper arms as if she were chilled. "I can't imagine living out here alone."

Ray winked at her, one corner of his mouth curling up. "Oh, I like it fine. I do repairs, charge enough to get by."

"But what do you do about food and supplies?" Lexi inclined her head.

Ray sighed out a long breath and rubbed his knees, the denim there as faded as his eyes. "I don't need much, just for myself. Got an old truck out back. Every so often, I drive into town, stock up on gas and food." He pointed. "It's a couple of hours down the main road there. I've got power and a well. A little water goes a long way for me, but I keep a tank back there, too. Hidden away so it doesn't attract the wrong kind."

"A couple of hours? Is there somewhere to stay there?" Jake would kill for any place with a shower and a bed, whatever it cost. And an end to this hellish road trip.

"They got a motel there, yeah. But it's not a big town. I don't know how much room they have. You're welcome to stay here if you want, but I don't have a spare bed or anything. You'd have to camp or sleep in your car."

"Thanks, but we'd really like to get to a motel tonight, stay in a room for a change." Jake stood up, hoping to move the process along.

Ray gave Lexi another lecherous wink. "Can't say's I blame ya for that." He grinned his yellow-toothed grin.

Lexi winked back.

Jake wanted to get out of there more than anything. Get Lexi somewhere she could decompress. The more he watched her, the more he worried she might need some kind of professional help.

CHAPTER 36

"Just a couple miles back up the road, you say?" Ray slid in behind the wheel of his trusty pickup and slammed the door shut, disappointed to see Jake plunk himself down in the middle of the bench seat. That Lexi would have been much nicer to look at.

"Yeah, not very far. Unless you're walking." Lexi tried to shut her door, but she couldn't budge it on the first try with those skinny arms of hers. She tugged at it a few times with both hands, hinges squealing in protest, and finally got it to close.

"Alrighty. Can't tow with this. We'll just bring back the tires, and I'll work on 'em in my garage." Ray started the old truck. It came to life with a cough and a rumble.

As he turned onto the road, he checked out the young couple from the corner of his eye. They kept looking at each other, then looking away. Something seemed unsettled between them. Something more than just a long, hot road trip and tire trouble. Maybe it had to do with being forced out of their home by the fire. Seemed deeper than that, though.

He made a U-turn and pulled up behind their disabled SUV. Nice rig. Nebraska plates. So, they were likely telling him the truth about why they were passing through this way. And they seemed harmless enough, unlike some of the scum that snuck around on the back roads around here—the kind he had to always be on guard for.

But still. He couldn't shake the feeling there was something they weren't telling him. And it was something big, something important to them, judging from their body language. Not really his problem, though, long as they weren't out to kill him or rob him.

"Any fancy locks on that wheel, or can I just go for it?"

"There's one lug nut you have to use this special key on. I'll get it." Jake motioned to Lexi and, after another brief struggle with the door, they got out.

Ray climbed out, walked over to the flat tire, and squatted down for a closer look. Nothing obvious showing, anyway. Could just be a pinhole from a cactus needle. Lot of flats out here from those. Easy fix if it was. He went to the back of his truck to get his tire iron and jack and paused. Jake was having a helluva time digging through all the crap they had jammed into the back of that SUV. He started tossing stuff out onto the sand, and Lexi kept trying to stack everything neatly, as if that was really important to her for some reason.

Lot of stuff for just two people, even for a road trip all the way from Nebraska. Lexi snatched up a bag and clutched it to her chest like it was full of gold or something. All pink and girly. Like something you'd put baby stuff in. She turned away and walked to the other side of the SUV.

"Got it." Jake triumphantly held up a small vinyl pouch.

Ray knelt down in the sand and set to work. There was a story here, but he wasn't going to ask. He wouldn't like someone prying into *his* business—well-intentioned or not—and he believed in treating others as he wanted to be treated. Life went a whole lot smoother that way.

Grunting, he gave a final tug. The wheel slipped off its bolts and flopped down in the sand. He dusted off his hands and stood.

"Okay, get the other one and let's chuck 'em in the back of the truck."

"Sure thing." Jake sprang into action, turning the crank to lower the spare from beneath the rear of the SUV. He rolled it to the back of the truck, heaved it into the bed, then went back and started jamming all their crap back into the rig.

Lexi reappeared from the far side of the SUV, dabbing at her eyes. She carefully placed the pink bag in the back on top of the rest of their stuff and closed the liftgate, then followed Jake back to the truck, head bowed.

Ray settled into the well-worn driver's seat and almost asked her if she was okay, then thought better of it. *Let it be.* He threw the truck into gear and headed back.

"You all just have a seat out here and relax. I'll let you know what I find."

Ray rolled the two tires into his shop and turned on the light. He started with the one that had still been on the car, peering at the tread. Flat as hell, but nothing obvious stood out. He pumped it up some, then uncovered his test tank, immersed the tire in the water, and watched it closely. At last, he spotted a stream of tiny bubbles seeping from a spot in the tread. Toward the sidewall, but not close enough or big enough to be a problem to repair. He marked the spot with a white grease pencil and set the tire aside.

He stood the second tire upright and searched for the puncture. Something glinted in the light. He leaned in for a better look. A nail. Good-sized one at that. And right up against the sidewall. Bad deal. Not too big to plug, but the fix might not hold—and the sidewall could give out. He marked the spot with his grease pencil and set to work on the repairs.

Ray rolled the tires back out front, tossed them into the bed of his truck, and wiped off his hands with a shop rag.

"All done. Pinhole in the spare you had on there. Easy fix. Probably from a cactus needle. But the other one, that's a problem. Big-ass nail right by the sidewall. I patched it, so you can use it in an emergency—but only at low speed and for as few miles as possible. Anything more and you risk the sidewall blowing out on you. Replace that one as soon as you can."

Jake stood. "Thanks. What do we owe you?"

Ray caught a look at Lexi—and her red eyes. He waved his hand. "Don't worry about it." He glanced at the mid-afternoon sun. "Let's get you back on the road so you have time to find a place to stay tonight."

"Good luck, y'all. Nice meeting you."

Ray waved back at the young couple and watched them get into their SUV. Turning away, he wiped sweat from his face with a forearm, then tossed his tools into the bed of his pickup.

As they drove off in a cloud of dust, Ray wondered just what had happened to them. Did they really uproot themselves like this just because of that fire, or was there something more? Or had something happened to them along the way?

He'd never know. Shaking his head, he started his truck and headed back to his place. He felt bad for that Lexi. Whatever it was, though, all he could do to help was fix their tires. Wished he could've done more, but he had nothing else to offer.

He slowed the truck to let a snake cross the road, then drove on, glad he kept his life free of complications.

CHAPTER 37

Lexi watched Ray's outpost fade into the distance behind them. It looked lonely and beaten down, out there by itself. Like it was the only thing left on this damned, barren planet. She turned back around and stared into her lap. Strange how a place like that could feel like an oasis out in this cruel desert.

"That was nice of him."

Lexi raised her head, startled. "What?"

"That guy, Ray. To fix the tires for free like that."

"Oh. Yeah. It was."

"From what he said, sounds like we can get a room in town tonight." He turned to her. "Get a break from driving and…take some time to…you know…come to terms with things."

"Come to terms? How am I ever supposed to *come to terms* with what happened? With Ava lying out there in the desert like some—" She waved her hand and turned away. "Please. I can't even talk about it."

"I know, Lexi. Believe me, I know. If there were anything I could do to change what happened—to bring her back—I'd do it in a heartbeat. But I can't." His voice cracked.

Lexi stared out the window as Jake fell silent. She couldn't even think of how to exist right now, let alone find the energy and courage to pick up and go on. He made it sound so simple. Maybe for him, it was. Maybe it was what he really wanted all along. No baby to tie him down. Well, now he had what he wanted.

At least the terrain was finally changing. And good riddance. She never wanted to see desert again. Now the interminable sand and scrub brush were giving way to trees as the road wound through a mountain pass. But the trees looked tortured, dead or nearly so. What should have been gorgeous green pines was a sea of russet, dried needles ready to erupt into flames. Proving that nothing and nowhere had been spared by the drought. Jake's dream of finding a better place to live was just that. A stupid, costly dream.

And they still had no clue as to their final destination. Where would they end up—and would it be any better than what they left behind? They might even find themselves worse off. Jake couldn't have been the first one to get the bright idea of moving closer to a water source. What if there really was no more room? What if people were downright hostile to yet more outsiders trying to push their way in?

Even if they found a decent place to live, how could they go on together after what happened to Ava? No matter how much he tried to convince her otherwise, she knew Jake never wanted kids. Not really. She didn't think he'd do anything on purpose to hurt Ava, but subconsciously? Maybe. She glanced at him, driving along like nothing happened. How could he even do that much right now? He seemed so...unaffected. Like it was just something that happened one day, instead of the horrible, life-altering tragedy it was.

Just as they rounded another curve, Jake stomped on the brakes. The SUV skidded to a stop a few feet from a downed pine tree that lay clear across the road. Lexi clapped her hand to her head. Just when they were finally out of the desert and on a decent, paved road. The shit never ended.

Jake groaned. "Crap. Going to have to hack through that with the ax. I didn't think to pack a saw."

"Great. So now we're stuck."

"Like I was supposed to know this was here? Jesus, Lexi."

Jake got out, slamming the door behind him, then dug through the cargo area for the ax. He plodded over to the tree and stared down at it for a moment, then swung the ax high overhead and brought it down. Again and again. Wood chips flew in the air as he hacked and hacked. At that rate, they'd be there until the end of time.

Lexi glanced at the road behind them as Ray's words came

back to haunt her. A man like that, not afraid of living alone in the desert, with all its hazards. But even he feared people. The kind who used these empty roads to sneak around, the kind who'd kill you just to take whatever you had. Lexi rubbed her arms and shivered. They were completely exposed to whatever or whoever might come along. Nowhere to go. Nothing to defend themselves with.

She turned back around, watching Jake, willing him to hurry up and finish so they could get the hell out of there. But the tree was good-sized. He wasn't making fast progress with just that stupid little camp ax. She stared at the stand of trees by the roadside. What might be hiding in there? Animals? People? She flashed back to the ambush they encountered back in the desert.

Someone could have knocked that tree over to set a trap. Trembling, Lexi glanced around the inside of the car. Was there anything she could use to defend herself if it came to that, even something makeshift? Not a goddamned thing she could see. She thrust her hand into her bag, pulled out her cell, and turned it on. At least it didn't display the No Signal symbol anymore. Barely. The signal consisted of one pathetic, flickering bar. She shut off the phone and tossed it back into her bag.

Lexi opened the glove compartment to see if maybe there was something in there she could use in a pinch. She spotted the knife Jake had bought, looking almost innocent in its leather case. She touched it, hesitated, then picked it up for a closer look.

She unsnapped the fastener that held the case closed and slipped the knife out, then weighed it in her hand. It wasn't huge, but it had some heft to it. Definitely not some cheap toy. She slid her thumb onto the release button, then slowly unfolded the knife, revealing a two-inch-wide serrated metal blade extending from the black handle. The sight of it glinting in the sunlight startled her so badly she nearly dropped the thing in her lap. She quickly folded the knife back up and put it back in its case, then tossed it into the glove compartment and slammed it shut.

The knife was just an inanimate object, yet it looked deadly and threatening, like a coiled, silent snake. She wished Jake hadn't bought it—but at the same time, she was glad he did. She just hoped they wouldn't have to use it.

Unable to shake the weird feeling she got from looking at the knife, Lexi stayed rooted in her seat, every muscle tensed, watching behind them, watching Jake, watching the trees for movement, for any sign of someone or something hiding in there. If she got out and left the relative safety of the car, could she help him finish up faster? No, they only had the one ax. She'd just have to wait for him to finish. Seemed like he'd been out there hacking away for days.

Jake straightened up and rubbed his lower back, the ax dangling at his side. After a brief break, he positioned himself over the trunk and hacked at it lengthwise until a piece finally split off. He reached down and tossed it into the dried weeds at the side of the road.

Lexi leaned forward in her seat, shoulders taut, teeth clenched, as he dropped the ax, bent down, and pushed another piece of the trunk, a few inches at a time, until he got it to the very edge of the road. *Come on, come on. We've got to get out of here.* He straightened again, took a big breath, then bent down and gave it a good shove. This time it rolled over, down into the gully.

At last, he wiped away sweat and trudged back to the car as if the battle with the tree had sapped his last remaining energy. Blood seeped through the bandage on his hand. He tossed the ax into the back seat and got in.

"It's going to be tight," he panted, "but I just can't do any more."

He started the car and eased it toward the gap he'd hacked into the downed trunk. Lexi bit her lip. *Too tight!* Jake edged the driver's-side wheels into the gully. The SUV tilted to the left. Lexi felt sick. What if they flipped over? The car jiggled as the right-front wheel went over the bits of wood still partly blocking the gap. Jake kept on going, his jaw set. They jiggled again as the right rear wheel went over the same wood. Then he steered the driver's-side wheels back onto the road and hit the gas.

Lexi pushed herself back in her seat, closed her eyes, and let herself breathe again. *God, what next?*

CHAPTER 38

Jake rounded another hairpin curve, ascending farther and farther into a wasteland of dead and dying pines. Goddamned drought hadn't even spared the forest way up here. Such beauty, ruined. At least a desert was *supposed* to look bleak and dry. But really, what did he expect? The drought had destroyed everything else in its path. Why'd he ever think he could just drive his way out of it? What a deluded idiot he'd been to think they'd find some untouched nirvana waiting just for them.

He wondered what lay ahead for them both. And what lay ahead for their relationship after what happened with Ava. He chewed his lip. God, it was all over so fast. He hadn't had time to think, barely any time to act. And he'd never know if he did the right thing, the only thing—or exactly the wrong thing.

Had he killed his own child?

That question would torment him the rest of his life. And Lexi's.

Did she blame him for what happened? Probably. And she had every right to. After all, it was his fault, one way or another. He'd taken them all on this disastrous road trip as part of his half-baked plan to change their lives for the better. He'd changed their lives, all right. That much was certain.

He stole a quick glance at Lexi. She just sat there, staring off into the distance, her hands fidgeting in her lap as if of their own volition. So much remained unsaid between them that the air inside the car felt heavy, electric with tension and anger. They needed to get out of this weird limbo, face each other, and say everything that needed to be said. No matter how much it hurt. But that wasn't going to happen while they were still in the middle of nowhere like this, driving. Endlessly driving.

The next bend in the road took them over a summit. From there, the road wound its way down into the valley below. Off in the distance, Highway 395 cut across the parched, brown land. A medium-sized town stood maybe halfway between them and 395. Must be the town Ray told them about. Finally, they could find a room and get off the road, at least for a while.

Jake descended toward the town as quickly as he dared on the twisting road. The interior of their SUV had begun to feel like a prison—and not just physically. His mind felt trapped, incapable of thinking anymore, except in the same tired and painful circles.

Nearly an hour later, he pulled up in front of a motel on the main road. It was one of those older places, an L-shaped, single-story, concrete-block building. He turned into the driveway and parked in front of the office. An obese man sagged in a chair outside one of the rooms, smoking a cigarette. Beat-up old cars populated the parking lot. A palace, it was not, but it would do.

Lexi stirred as if she were waking from a nap and took a look at the place. She said nothing.

"Be right back."

Jake got out of the car to go check in. Might be a nicer place down the road. Or not. Better grab what he could, at least for tonight. It was only mid-afternoon, but he didn't much feel like driving anymore today. Matter of fact, he didn't much feel like driving anymore *ever*.

He stepped inside the office. A small plastic fan sat atop the abandoned front desk, stirring the sweltering air around, but cooling nothing. He tried to ignore how run-down the place looked: the stained threadbare carpeting, the overflowing ash tray on the desk, the filmy plate-glass windows letting in rays of vengeful sunlight.

"Hello? Anyone back there?"

"Just a minute!"

Jake stood at the desk, wiped beads of sweat from his hair-line as he waited. A couple of minutes later, he heard a muffled sound, like a toilet flushing in another room.

An old man with a deeply lined face hobbled out from the

back room and glared at him. "What do you want?"

"A room. For two, my wife and me."

The man shrugged. "No rooms left."

Jake glanced through the smudged window. A couple of the rooms had no cars parked outside. "You're telling me you're full?"

The man planted his arthritis-gnarled hands on the desk and leaned forward, his breath hot and foul. "That's what I'm telling you."

"Look. We've been driving for days. We'll take a single for one night if that's all we can get. Just a bed and a shower, 'sall we need." Jake pulled out his wallet. Maybe the guy was angling for more money. At this point, he hardly cared. Money was the least of his problems.

The man took a step back and set his hands on his hips. "Did you see a vacancy sign? No. You didn't. Because there isn't one. I haven't rented a room by the night for the better part of a year now. Long-term renters only. Lot less trouble. And I'm full up."

Jake sighed and bowed his head. "All right. Can you tell me where we can get a room in town?"

"Can't speak for other towns, but I can tell you, you won't find anything here. Everybody's been moving to California. Just because we have a coastline and those saltwater processing plants, they think we're the land of cheap water here. Well, we're not. That's why I rent to nothing but long-term residents now. Overflow from the bigger population zones. Not enough housing for all the idiots who've moved here, so I figured their idiocy was my business opportunity. Me and all the other motel owners out this way." He held out his hands, palms out. "So, you might as well push on, though I don't know you'll have any better luck anywhere else."

"Thanks a lot." Jake turned and stumbled out the door. This shithole of a town wasn't even on the main highway. If there were no open motels way out here, where *would* they find a room?

The moment he got back into the car and shut the door, Lexi snapped at him. "Well? Which room did they give you?"

"None of them. They're full."

"Oh, bullshit!" She pointed to a room at the end where a tattered curtain hung askew in the window. "That one looks empty. No one's parked there, and I doubt people call and make reservations in advance for a dump like this."

"He said he's full. It's all long-term residents now."

"Then let's go somewhere else. Not like this place is any prize. It can't be the only motel in town. For chrissake, Jake."

Jake sighed and told her what the motel owner had said. "Now I'm not sure where we're going to find a place. Or when."

CHAPTER 39

Lexi stared at Jake, trying to take in what he just said. She couldn't possibly have heard him right. This piece-of-shit place was full and there was *nothing* else in town? Maybe nothing else *anywhere*? This couldn't be. It just couldn't be. It was like some sick joke on top of everything else that had happened.

"So, are you saying we're stuck living in the car like homeless people? Is that what you're telling me?"

Jake rubbed his forehead and stared down into his lap. "If this guy is right, and telling the truth—"

"Why are we just finding this out now? And why are we finding it out *here*?"

"I didn't see anything about this in the news, not on the radio or the Internet. How else would we have found out?"

"Well, California made a big deal about closing its borders to new people. Maybe we should've taken the hint."

Jake's face reddened. "I thought they were closing the borders to prevent this kind of thing from happening—not that it had already happened."

"Well, I guess we're too damned late. Great. We manage to sneak through the border without getting caught, but now we have no place to go!" Lexi slammed both her fists on the dashboard. "Brilliant!"

"I'll figure something out. I will."

"Yeah, you've done such a great job so far. We have no idea what's become of our home or my parents. Off we go with a baby in the car, no backup plan, no nothing. And here we are. Ava's dead and we have nowhere to go. My God, it doesn't get any better than that!"

"Lexi—" Jake reached for her.

She slapped his hand away. "Leave me alone. You've done enough. I can't stand being in here another minute."

Lexi flung the car door wide open and jumped out. She staggered a little at first, her legs stiff from sitting in the car too long, then took off running as fast as she could go. The hell with the heat. Anything to put some distance between herself and the damned car. And Jake. And everything.

She rounded the edge of the motel property and sprinted down the sidewalk on the main drag, grateful no one else was out on the street in the stifling heat. It felt good to run, even with no destination in mind. To take some kind of action, no matter how futile, instead of sitting in that car for hour after hour and hoping something would come along to take away her pain.

If only she could run backward, turn everything back the way it was before the fire. Hard to believe it had only been a matter of days since they fled their home. It felt like she'd lived and lost a lifetime's worth in that short time.

After only a couple of blocks, sweat streamed down her face, stinging her eyes. Her clothes lay plastered against her skin. The hot air felt like a wall, something solid and sentient, determined to stop her. She gulped lungfuls of air, struggled to keep going. She couldn't let it stop her. She had to fight her way through it, to overcome it. Anything to stop feeling so helpless and defeated.

"Lexi, stop." Panting, Jake caught up to her and grabbed her arm.

She spun to face him and wrenched her arm away. "What the hell do we do now? Tell me that," she said through clenched teeth. She folded her arms and glared at him. "Got any bright ideas?"

Lexi jumped out of the car before Jake could react. He reached out and called to her, but it was already too late. She took off running without so much as a backward glance, her sneakers slapping the pavement. Jake hesitated, wondering how far she intended to go, what she thought she'd accomplish—other than giving herself a heat stroke. If only it were as simple as running off somewhere. He wished they *could* just run, leave all this behind, and somehow find themselves in a better place.

She rounded the corner, out of his line of sight. Jake sighed, got out and locked up the car, then broke into a fast trot. As soon as he turned the corner, he spotted her up ahead. The heat seemed to be slowing her pace some. Gasping and panting, he ran faster to catch up, then reached out for her.

"Lexi, stop."

Spewing angry words, she pulled away from him and stood there with her arms folded and a defiant expression on her face. He'd never seen her look at him like that before. So cold and hard. Not that he didn't deserve it for all the costly mistakes he'd made.

"C'mon, Lexi." Jake reached out to her again.

She slapped at him. "Why? Why should I come with you?" Her face crumpled, fighting back tears. She swiped at her eyes and tried to stand firm.

"Let's go back to the car." Jake gently put his arm around her. "Cool off a little, have some water."

Head down, Lexi shuffled along beside him as if all her strength had suddenly drained away. "What are we going to do? We can't live like this. I can't."

"I'm so sorry, Lexi. I'd give anything to undo all my mistakes. I should have planned way better than I did. But even if I had, I couldn't have predicted… everything that happened. No way to know Ava would get sick."

Lexi pressed a hand to her forehead. "She never got sick. Ever. She was always so healthy. I don't know what happened." She sobbed. "And now I'll never know."

Jake helped her into the car, then got in and moved to a parking spot on the street so they could have a little space and time to themselves without any trouble from the cranky motel owner.

He shut off the engine and faced her. "I can't bring Ava back, but I'm going to do everything in my power to set everything else right, to make this work."

Lexi turned away, shoulders hitching as she sobbed. "Good luck with that."

Jake started to answer, then stopped. Better let her have her space and not push her. At least she was back in the car with him. That would have to do for now. Besides, he had no idea *how* he could ever make things right, just that he'd have to find a way, no matter how hard it was or how long it took.

He pulled out his cell and checked for a signal. Finally, not just a signal but a halfway decent one. He searched for a local news feed. They hadn't had much news for the last couple of days, just some broader reports they picked up here and there on the radio. Nothing that would have warned them about what to expect once they got to California.

Jake felt sick as he skimmed the feed. The motel owner wasn't lying or exaggerating.

An excessive influx of people had caused overcrowding every bit as bad as he'd described. Even worse near the more desirable locations. Hotel rooms were practically a thing of the past. Even the big chains had converted most of their rooms to longer-term units and were charging as much as the market would bear to those with lower-wage jobs. Real apartments, condos, and rental homes went for sky-high rates. Only the most affluent could afford them.

No matter how hard he tried, Jake couldn't think of a single thing he'd done right. They should have stopped as soon as they were outside the wildfire zone. Coming out to California was an even bigger mistake than he realized. He slammed the cell down in his lap.

CHAPTER 40

Lexi winced as Jake threw down his phone. "Now what?"

Jake shook his head. "It's true, what the motel guy said."

"Well, what are we going to do?"

"I don't know yet. Let me think."

Lexi stared into her lap. This nightmare was never going to end. They should just restock all their supplies and turn right the fuck around. Better yet, take I-80 outbound and put as much distance between them and California as fast as they could. Head back toward Nebraska and stop as soon as they found someplace reasonably acceptable. Give up on California. She never even wanted to hear the word again.

Jake was back on his cell, trying to find some good news somewhere, no doubt. Well, good luck with that. She glanced around. What a dumpy little town. Looked like the kind of place where all the refuse would land anyway. Should have been a pretty little haven, with those mountains as a backdrop. But even the mountains here looked like a lost cause, all rust brown with dead pines.

Something caught her eye in the rear view. A beat-up old van pulled to the curb a few yards behind them. It looked as scummy as the kind of people who'd probably taken over this town. One headlight smashed, bumper twisted and hanging sideways, like they'd hit something with it and didn't care enough—or have the money—to repair it. The van was covered with road dust, its paint faded and peeling in places. Looked like it'd been in a few accidents over its sorry life.

Other than the van, the town looked fairly deserted. Hardly any traffic to speak of, even on the main drag. No one out walking, but that wasn't unusual in the never-ending heat wave that accompanied the drought.

Both of the van's front doors opened and two men got out. They looked about as derelict as the van, with their tattered, stained clothes and ratty, dirty-looking hair and beards. They held their arms behind them and kept glancing around as if they were looking for something. Then, as if they'd traded a secret signal, they strode toward the SUV in unison.

"Jake—"

He tore himself away from his cell's display. "What?"

"Behind us!"

The two men stopped behind their SUV to peer into its cargo section.

"Here. Call 911. Now!" Jake slapped his cell into her hand as he twisted around for a better look.

Lexi fumbled with the phone. Her hands shook so badly she hit all the wrong numbers. She stole a quick glance back when she heard the SUV's rear gate swing open. One man was already rummaging around in their stuff while the other strode up to the driver's side door. Frantic, she tried again, struggling to make her fingers work.

Without warning, the man yanked open the driver's door and yelled, "Get out!"

"Wait! Don't!" Jake raised his hands.

The man pointed an enormous handgun in Jake's face and wrenched him out of the car with his other hand before he had a chance to react. Lexi screamed and dropped the phone.

Arms up, Jake stood, his eyes trained on the gun. "What do you want?" His voice shook and his face grew pale.

"Whatever you have, asshole." He steadied the gun with both hands. "What've they got back there?" he shouted to his partner.

The gunman smiled, revealing rotted teeth and ravaged gums. Meth mouth. A habit to feed. And he might even be high now, desperate and crazed. Lexi froze, barely able to breathe.

"Mostly just clothes and shit," he yelled. "But they do have a nice stash of water."

"Grab it, then. Hurry up."

"Look, that's all we have." Jake kept his arms up. "We can give you some of it, okay?"

"Shut the fuck up."

The man swiftly jammed the gun's muzzle against Jake's temple. And fired. Jake's head exploded in a shower of red. His body fell to the ground. Just like that. Like in some movie. Lexi screamed. *No...Jake—*

"Nobody fuckin' argues with me." The man shot another round into Jake's still body, then leaned over and spat.

The other man ran up and pointed at Jake's body. "Dammit, Marco, not in broad daylight!"

Lexi heard the men start arguing, but didn't waste time trying to make out the words. She had seconds to flee, or she'd be next. She grabbed the side of the steering wheel and launched herself over the center console and into the driver's seat.

While the men were still distracted, she slammed the door shut, hit the Start button, and gunned it down the main drag. She kept one eye on the road, one eye on the rear view. One of the men crouched, aimed, and shot. She ducked. The bullet zinged off the car's body. She straightened up and glanced back again. They'd gotten into their van and were coming after her.

Lexi kept up her speed, hoping no one came out of a side street without warning. No way could she stop in time. She looked again. Stuff from the back of the car tumbled onto the street behind her, forcing the van to swerve from side to side as it pursued her. She hit the button to close the back gate before she lost everything back there.

A sign for a turnoff loomed up ahead. She took it, glancing back once more as she turned. No sign of the van. Where'd it go? Had they given up on her or had they taken some side street to come around and trap her? She didn't know, couldn't know. All she could do right now was keep her foot on the gas and hope they'd gone back to whatever hole they came from—and try not to think of Jake lying on the pavement dead back there.

CHAPTER 41

Thunk!

The SUV lurched and jostled as Lexi took the bumpy dirt road way too fast. Couldn't slow down, not for an instant. Thinking wasn't an option. Not yet. Right now, she focused only on maxing the distance between herself and those men—and what they did to Jake. Move. Keep moving.

She glanced in the rear view, straining to see through the dust kicked up by the SUV. No one there. No sign of anyone since she took the turnoff from town maybe a half an hour ago. They'd have caught up to her by now if they intended to, wouldn't they? She hoped she was right.

Now she had no clue where she was or where she was headed. She'd barely had time to escape. Just had to take the first way out that presented itself. Best she could tell, this was some old forest service road—one that was rarely used, judging from the tall clumps of dried weeds running along its center.

Her knuckles ached from gripping the steering wheel so hard. She peeled one hand off the wheel and flexed some circulation back into it, then the other. She couldn't begin to process what happened. Not right now. And she had no idea how she'd managed to respond so quickly, running on nothing but adrenaline, to get herself out of danger. At least for now.

Lexi slowed down, then maneuvered the SUV behind a stand of dying pine trees where she couldn't be seen from the road—just in case—and shut off the engine. She leaned her head on the steering wheel and drew in a deep breath. Her arms and legs felt like they had no muscles, only bone. Heavy, heavy bone.

Maybe she should call the police. She grabbed Jake's cell

from the passenger seat where she dropped it. No signal. She tossed it aside. What could the police do anyway? She didn't get that good a look at the men. Besides, nothing anyone could do would bring Jake back. So, what did anything else matter?

It all happened so fast. Too fast. One minute she and Jake were alone, trying to figure out what to do, then those men showed up. Blink. Now she'd lost Jake. Just like that. No chance to save him, no chance to say good-bye. No chance for anything.

Now she was truly alone in the world. Everyone she'd loved, gone. No one to rely on but herself. She pushed that frightening thought aside. If she dwelled on it right now, she'd drown in her own terror. Better to deal with one small, tangible thing at a time. Forward progress in baby steps was better than no progress at all. Better take inventory. Start there.

Lexi opened the driver's side door and forced herself out. Hot, dry, dusty air weighed her down, threatened to push her right back into the car. She fought the temptation to let it. Trembling, she rested one hand on the door jamb while she tried to steady her legs. A crease in the passenger door caught her eye. The bullet they fired as she got away. Could have been dead right now if it had come through the window instead. She shook her head and went around to the back to see what she had left.

She opened the cargo gate and peered inside. Most of the clothes they'd brought—and Ava's little baby bag—were gone. The gas cans were still there, though they were mostly empty now. About half the water was gone. Whether the men took it, or it fell out on the street before she had a chance to shut the back gate, she didn't know. Didn't matter anyway. She slammed the door shut. At least she still had *some* water.

She felt a little dizzy. And tired. So tired. She got back in on the driver's side, shut and locked the door and reclined the seat as far as it would go. She lay there, shivering in the late-afternoon heat, thoughts churning through her mind too fast to grasp or control. Horrible images. Jake, the gun pressed to his head. Jake, his head shattered by the bullet, falling to the ground. Jake and Ava. Ava and Jake. Losing one of them was unthinkable. Losing both of them was unbearable.

Maybe she should have let the gunman finish her, too. It would have been so much easier than this.

Lexi stood in the front yard of her house. Dawn was just breaking, the sun painting the sky all pink and orange. It was cool, cool like it hadn't been in so long. Dew sparkled on the grass like tiny jewels. Beads of it lay on the leaves of the shrubs by the house, transforming them into a gorgeous, glittering display. She reached out, touched one. The water clung to her finger. She touched it to her lips. So fresh and sweet. Somehow, the world had renewed itself. Everything was right again.

Inside the house, Ava was crying. She must be hungry. Lexi stepped up and reached for the doorknob, tried to open the door. Locked. She patted her pockets. No keys. She didn't want to wake Jake, but she had to get inside to feed Ava. She knocked on the door. Nothing, just Ava crying. She knocked harder. Jake! Jake, let me in!

Why didn't he answer?

Ava's cries grew louder, changed tone. Now she sounded absolutely terrified. Lexi pounded on the door and screamed for Jake to open it. She grabbed the doorknob again, then snatched her hand away. It was hot! She took a couple of steps back, confused. An orangish light showed through the curtains. She frowned and glanced behind her. Was the sky reflecting in the glass?

Hungry orange and yellow flames devoured the curtains, surged higher and higher. The windows exploded, showering her with glass. Enormous flames opened great holes in the roof and reached for the sky.

She could no longer hear Ava's cries.

Lexi lurched upright, screaming. Disoriented in the darkness, she tipped sideways and smacked against the car door. For an instant, she didn't know where she was or why. Then she remembered. The forest road. Her terrifying escape. Jake. She clung to the steering wheel like a lifeline.

Nothing but pitch blackness out there, so dark it seemed to be closing in, trapping the car in its void. No one to hear her scream. No one to help her. She fumbled for the buttons, turned on the car's accessories and headlights. Nothing out there but trees. At least in the path of the beams. She checked the time. Midnight. Somehow, she'd fallen asleep for hours, drenched in her own sweat.

Lexi squinted and strained her eyes to see if there was anything or anyone lurking in the trees at the edge of the headlight beams. Nothing that she could see, but outside that pool of light, there could be anything.

She made sure the car was locked, then sat in the dim glow of the instrument panel, struggling to get her bearings and decide what to do. That horrible nightmare had jolted her wide awake. She felt like she should do *something*, but what? She wanted to move on, to be anywhere but out here all alone and vulnerable. But it was so late and so dark, and she had no idea which way she should go. If she just took off driving, she might get herself completely and irretrievably lost. Better to stay put until it was light again.

Reluctantly, she switched off the lights and allowed the darkness to swallow her again. The last thing she needed was to strand herself out here with a dead battery.

Lexi shivered, the sweat running cold on her skin, as she stared out into the impenetrable darkness and prayed for dawn.

CHAPTER 42

Lexi awoke from a fitful sleep, confused and racked with pain. Her left arm lay trapped beneath her, dead asleep, and she'd somehow contorted her shoulder into an agonizing, awkward position. Wincing, she pushed herself up with her right arm and raised the seat back. Early morning light flooded the interior of the car, already warming it. Another stifling-hot day awaited.

A pervasive sense of dread settled on her, threatened to suffocate her. Like that lingering feeling that comes after an intense nightmare. *If only.* She combed her fingers through her dirty, tangled hair, pushed it back from her face, and let out a long, trembling sigh.

She was parched, hungry, and bone-weary, but none of that seemed to matter now. She'd lost everything. Absolutely everything. Stripped away, just like that. She had nowhere to go and no one to go there with. She shook her head, her hair falling back over her face. If only they'd stayed close to Nebraska, never taken this ridiculous leap of faith, hoping for a new life.

She had a new life now, all right. Starting from zero. Make that *less than zero*.

Lexi leaned back in her seat and stared at the roof of the car as she weighed her choices. One choice was obvious. Give in. Let go. Didn't cost money. Didn't require her to figure anything out. Or struggle. Or fight. She licked her chapped lips. Simple, really. And the heat would speed things along. Not like she had anyone left who cared if she lived or died—or any kind of future to look forward to. None that she could see, anyway.

She yawned and stretched, shaking the last of the pins and

needles from her left arm. If only she'd been able to do more with her life. She regretted that. She and Jake were still just starting out. Who knew what their lives would have held, what they would have accomplished together if all this hadn't happened? And poor Ava. She never had a chance at all.

Never had a chance.

A sudden rage sparked within her, then burst into an all-consuming flame. Lexi sat up, fists clenched. That goddamned drought! It set off the entire chain of events that destroyed their lives. The drought took everything from them. All the children they would never have. Their home. Her parents, their friends. Their jobs.

Ava.

Jake.

Everything.

Because of the drought, here she was, hiding out alone in the forest like some fugitive, thinking about what a waste her life had been.

Tears streaming down her face, she beat the steering wheel with her fists and glared at the rays of sun filtering through the dying trees.

"Fuck you! You don't get to take everything from me! I won't let you!" She sobbed. "It's not fair...it's not fair."

Lexi swallowed the last bite of an energy bar, sipped more water, then set her bottle in the cup holder. She took a deep breath and started the car. New life begins *now*. Her nothing-left-to-lose life. She stared at the GPS to get her bearings. She'd fled so fast she had no idea which way she'd gone, or how far. Just that she had somehow escaped with her life.

Looked like she had about twenty miles of rough, twisting forest road to backtrack on before she'd hit the town. She ran her finger along the route on the GPS display. No way would she go back there, no matter what. If she skirted the edge of town, there was a road that would take her to another similarly sized town, the next one over. She had enough food and water for now. Not like she had anyone else to feed.

But fuel was an issue. The gauge was hovering closer to the

E than she'd like, and they'd gone through their stash of gas on the road through Nevada. Jake had planned to get more gas and plug in the fuel cell once they got a room. She glanced again at the GPS and did some quick math in her head. She should have enough. Just.

Lexi shifted into Drive and started back the way she came. She kept a close eye on the GPS as she went, wary of taking any wrong turns. Didn't have the gas for any false starts. She left the radio off. She wanted focus—not distraction—right now. Even if it made the car seem even emptier than it was. She had to get used to being alone. Had to embrace it, run with it.

Because it was all she had now.

CHAPTER 43

Lexi shuddered as she turned onto the secondary road, skirting the edge of that horrible town on her way to somewhere else. Anywhere else. No way could she drive through that place again. That street where they'd shot Jake down like a dog. She'd never get that image out of her mind. Ever. And she sure as hell couldn't risk running into those men again—or anyone else like them.

But what happened to Jake…afterwards? Had anyone taken care of his body? Impossible to find out now. Better to just move on, get as far away as she could. Nothing she could do would make a damned bit of difference anyway.

She grabbed her water bottle and raised it to her lips. Empty. She'd filled it before starting off that morning, but she'd already driven for several hours—much longer than it should have taken to get this far. Should have been a simple thing to backtrack her way out, but somehow, she made a costly wrong turn somewhere along the twisty forest road. Even with the GPS, she'd gotten so turned around and confused, she couldn't believe she made it out at all.

Hand trembling, she set the water bottle back in the cup holder. Her stomach growled. She wouldn't mind some food, either. Something other than a power bar, for a change. As long as she lived, they'd remind her of their doomed trip across the Nevada desert. Water and power bars. Power bars and water. With the occasional freeze-dried packet of flavorless hiker food thrown in. Like the modern equivalent of jerky, or whatever explorers used to carry with them on trips into the great unknown.

She glanced at the GPS. The next town wasn't much farther now. And the road before her was smooth and straight and pleasant enough to drive on, especially compared to that forest road and all the other treacherous roads they'd been on since leaving I-80. Yet it looked misplaced there, in the middle of the high desert, with no roadside amenities along it. And so empty. She hadn't seen a single car going either way along it so far.

Something didn't feel right. She pressed harder on the accelerator. Instead of speeding up, the engine coughed and chugged. The fuel light came on some miles back, but she thought they built some margin into that, so it came on before it was really running on fumes. Just for situations like this.

The engine gave an extended cough and sputtered out. Heart pounding, Lexi cut the wheel, coasting onto the shoulder just in time, before she ran out of momentum. She propped her forehead on the steering wheel, fighting off a wave of dizziness. Stupid! If she hadn't taken that wrong turn in the woods, she'd have had enough gas to make it.

Not a damned thing out here, as far as she could see from where she sat. Not so much as a billboard. Just a ribbon of road cutting through high-desert scrub. No one was going to come by and stop. Not soon enough, anyway. The GPS said it was only about three miles to the edge of town. Only. She should have been more careful in the forest. This wouldn't have happened. It was her own damned fault.

And mistakes can kill—as she knew all too well.

No more mistakes. Lexi took a deep breath as she tried to organize her thoughts, to think things through before screwing up again. But precious few choices presented themselves. Middle of the day, the hottest possible time. Too fucking bad. She'd have to tough it out. Couldn't just sit there and bake in the car. She flung open the door and pushed herself out, forcing her body to obey her newfound determination.

The cargo compartment was still a mess from those assholes rummaging through it. Jaws clenched, she grabbed one of the empty gas cans. It would be too heavy for her to carry full, but she wouldn't need much gas to drive the rest of the way into town. Then she could fill up the car and all the cans.

She locked up the car. No sense taking any chances on someone coming along and pilfering what little she had left. She paused, one hand on her fanny pack, then opened the passenger door and reached into the glove compartment. She slipped the sheathed knife into her fanny pack and locked the car up again. Might as well have some protection on her.

She started off down the road in the direction of town, the merciless sun hammering her, punishing her for each and every one of her stupid mistakes.

Three miles. That wasn't the way to think about it. Not if she wanted to live. Because if she thought about it that way, she'd sit down at the side of the road and never get back up. One step at a time. Keep going one step at a time, and there'd come a step that would get her there. Don't think about how long it was going to take. Just fucking do it.

Now she knew what it felt like to be one of those characters in the movies, trudging through the desert, seeing mirages reflecting nothing more than misplaced hope. Up ahead stood a run-down little gas station and C-store at the edge of what appeared to be not much of a town. Steps away. She could make it now. She pushed on, praying the place was open and operating.

And that it wasn't a cruel mirage.

She glanced at her watch. She'd been putting one hot, tired foot in front of the other for the better part of two hours, doing her best to ignore her thirst and the relentless heat that crushed her like a great weight. Amazing what you can do when you trick your own mind.

She plodded up to the door and went inside. A current of semi-cool air listlessly flowed toward her. Still, a welcome improvement from being outside with the sun pounding her from high overhead. A short, blond, youngish man in overalls came in from the garage, wiping his hands on a shop rag.

"Can I help you?"

Lexi's knees nearly buckled with exhaustion and relief. Finally, someone who could help, at least on some level. She felt like she'd been alone in the wilderness for months, not just overnight.

She held up her gas can. "I need some gas. Ran out a few miles outside of town."

His eyebrows lifted. "You walked here in that heat?"

"Like I had a choice?"

He chuckled. "Stupid comment. Of course you didn't."

"I need food and water, too." She glanced around at the aisles of snacks and supplies. Small store, small selection, but it would do.

"Tell you what. I need to wrap up this repair, then I can lock the place up and take you back to your car. Might take about an hour, maybe a little less. Then you can drive it back here and load up with whatever you need."

"Well—"

"Really, I'd be happy to do it. Crazy—and dangerous—to let you walk all the way back in that heat." He waved his arm toward the garage. "Just need to finish this. Promised the customer, you know. You help yourself to whatever you need in the meantime, okay?"

"Okay, thanks."

"Good, good. Name's Don, what's yours?"

"Lexi."

"Pleased to meet you, Lexi. I'll wrap this up as quick as I can." He nodded and disappeared into the garage.

Lexi went outside to put some gas in her can, then set it on the floor by the counter inside the store. She scoped out the offerings as she grabbed a bag of chips and a bottle of water, then plunked down in one of the cheap plastic chairs that lined a makeshift waiting room.

She tore open the chips and devoured them so fast she had no idea how they tasted. Didn't matter. Just something to fill the void in her stomach. Then she chugged down a good pint of the water and wiped her mouth. She leaned back in the uncomfortable plastic chair.

Dinky, tired old place. So old, she didn't see a charging station around. Good fit for a tiny, tired town clinging to life in the high desert. She wondered if the guy was the owner or just the mechanic. Either way, no one was watching the counter and the till. Anyone could come in, load up on stuff, and bolt before he could get out from under whatever car he was working on. Maybe he didn't much care.

"All right. I'm done now. Let me lock up and we'll get you back to your car." Don tossed aside his greasy shop rag and pulled a ring of keys from his pocket.

Lexi pointed at her gas can and took another long swig from the water bottle. "Don't you want me to pay you for this gas and stuff now?"

"You're going to drive back here to fill up, aren't you? We can worry about it then, how's that?"

"Fine, thanks. Yeah, I'll load up on snacks and drinks then, too."

"Sounds like a plan." Smiling, Don took her gas can and locked the front door behind them. "Truck's out back."

She followed him to a broken asphalt pad behind the gas station. Dried weeds stood tall in the plentiful cracks. She hoisted herself into the passenger side of his pickup while he set her gas can in the back bed.

He slid in and started the engine. "So, what brings you out this way?"

Lexi hesitated, afraid to answer. If she did, it all might flow out, completely uncontrolled. To a stranger. A nice one, but still.

"S'okay if you don't want to tell me. I was just making conversation." Don eased the truck onto the street. "This way?"

"Yeah."

Moments later, they pulled up behind Lexi's SUV. Don got the gas can and emptied it into the tank while Lexi stood by, feeling grateful for the help, but embarrassed for needing it. How stupid to run out of gas. She should have made it on what she had. If only she'd been more careful on that forest road.

If only a lot of things.

Don tapped the last few drops from the can. "That's it. Now you can come back and fill 'er up under your own steam."

Lexi met him back at the gas station minutes later. They stood by the pump, watching in awkward silence as the meter ticked on.

"It's getting kind of late in the day. Do you have somewhere to stay?"

Lexi glanced away and tucked her hair behind her ears. "No, not really. I hadn't figured that out yet. Is there a motel here?"

"Not in this town. We only had one little ma and pa motel to start with, but it's converted into apartments now. And the kind of people living there…well, they're not the type a woman alone would want to be anywhere near."

"Where's the next town, then?"

"It's a ways off, and they may or may not have a room. I'm not sure." He studied her. "If you'll excuse my saying so, looks to me like it's been a while since you had a decent place to stay."

Lexi took a step back, unsure of where the conversation was leading. "Well—"

Don held his hands up and shook his head. "Sorry, I didn't mean that how it sounded. I'm not judging, and I won't pry. I only want to help if I can. My little studio apartment won't work. Way too small. But you can stay here. In the office. You'd have the whole place to yourself. There's a cot, a bathroom. It's nothing terrific, but it's shelter, it locks up, so it's as safe as you're likely to get around here."

Lexi weighed his offer. She really didn't have the energy left to push on right now. It sure would be nice to not have to worry about hunting for someplace to stay for the night—and maybe not finding anything anyway. Even a cot would feel like heaven compared to sleeping in the car again.

"Thanks, that'd be great."

"Glad to help. I'll get everything all set for you. Help yourself to whatever you want in the store for dinner. There's a microwave for heating stuff up. Like I said, the Hilton it ain't, but it's the best you'll get in this town."

Lexi watched as Don hustled off to do whatever preparations he saw fit. She bit her lip and forced herself not to cry, to simply feel grateful for an unexpected kind deed.

CHAPTER 44

Lexi pressed a big red button and watched the service bay door rumble its way down, then shut tight against the concrete floor with a clang of finality. That's it. Sealed in for the night, all safe and sound. Don had told her to park her car inside, then close up behind it. He chose his words carefully and tried not to scare her, but his message was clear: she'd be better off if no one realized she was there. This town was no place for a lone woman.

Arms folded, she leaned back against her car and checked the place out. A gas station it may be, but it was the most shelter she'd had for the night in what seemed like forever. Don was right. It ain't no Hilton. But right now, it felt damned near luxurious. She shook her head and allowed herself a brief chuckle, until her stomach brought her back to reality with a long, insistent growl.

She wandered into the C-store to cobble together a meal. Don said she could have whatever she wanted. On the house. What a nice guy he turned out to be. He seemed to sense that she needed shelter, yet also needed her space. As kind as he'd been, she welcomed the solitude. She couldn't imagine making conversation right now. Not with him, not with anyone.

She browsed the selections in the display cases. The fridge offered a row of wilted, bare-bones cold sandwiches, undoubtedly made with that nasty agri-tech stuff that passed for lunch meat these days. She wrinkled her nose. Nothing looked appealing. Maybe she'd have better luck in the frozen section. She trudged over to the freezer and smiled. A mother lode of single-serving pizzas of all kinds. Even if the pepperoni and cheese were agri-tech, the spices and fake flavorings would make up for it. She shoved a couple of them in the microwave, then fidgeted while she watched the timer count down ever so slowly.

Lexi hauled her steaming-hot pizzas, some napkins, and a couple of cold beers back into the office and set up her dinner between the stacks of paperwork that cluttered the beat-up metal desk. She dropped down into the chair and inhaled deeply. Cheap frozen pizza never smelled so good. She wolfed them both down and finished the first beer in no time flat. Leaning back in the creaky chair, she took a leisurely sip from her second beer and let the alcohol's warm rush put a little distance between her and her problems.

Setting aside her beer, she ventured into the bathroom and stared at herself in the smudged mirror. She reached out and touched the reflection with her fingertips. Was that haunted, haggard person really her? Her eyes looked like she'd aged years, not days. Like an apparition. She withdrew her hand and averted her eyes.

She'd kill for a real, full-length shower about now. She gave a short, bitter chuckle. If only it were that easy to wash away the grime, the pain...everything that had happened. She'd stand under blazing-hot water until her skin turned red and wrinkled. But long showers like that were a thing of the past, thanks to the drought. Better to just be grateful for tonight's shelter and indoor plumbing. And hot food instead of a damned energy bar.

Lexi ran the water to let it warm up a little, then put the rubber stopper in the chipped, rust-stained porcelain sink and let it fill. She stepped out of her clothes and washed herself off as best she could with wet paper towels, then dipped her head under the faucet and shampooed with liquid hand soap. She rinsed out the soap, finger-combed her hair, and dried herself off with more paper towels. Better. Not great, but better. She put on her clothes, started back toward the office, then froze.

"Hey! Anybody in there?" A young male voice, coming from the front of the C-store.

Whoever he was, he was banging on the front door now. She clenched her jaw. Stupid! Should have turned out the store lights after getting her food. Holding her breath, she tiptoed over and peered around the doorway to the main store area, staying low so she wouldn't be noticed.

A couple of guys in their late teens, maybe early twenties, stood outside the C-store's glass front. They looked pretty sketchy with their wild hair and frayed clothes. Judging by the way one of them was swaying, they might have already had a few. She ducked back inside the office, heart pounding, hoping they'd just leave and not try to break in.

They pounded and shouted for a few more nerve-wracking minutes, then there was a loud bang, like one of them kicked the front door. Then silence.

Lexi finally let herself breathe again, then took a quick peek. Gone. Thank God. She hustled out to the front counter and switched off the store lights, then retreated to the office and stared up at the large, tattered map of California tacked to the wall. Someone had circled the town with a blotch of black ink. She studied the roads leading out of town. Which way to go?

No point in going back the way she came. Maybe just keep going pretty much west and see what happened? Impossible to decide anything by looking at the damned map. All the towns looked the same. Just names on a piece of paper. No clue as to which would be good—or even safe—to spend a night in, let alone to stay.

She slapped the map, turned away, and shook her head. Maybe the best thing was to head for a major highway. Better chance of cell reception than on these secondary roads out here. Then she could do some research, come up with some kind of coherent plan.

Lexi plunked down on the cot. Its springs screeched in protest. The bare mattress was thin, worn, and yellowed with age. But at least it was an actual mattress. She could finally stretch out and have a chance at a halfway-decent night's sleep. Maybe after that she could think better, figure out what to do next. Right now, her mind was way too overloaded to function.

She switched off the light and lay down. Her body felt so heavy, so drained, like she couldn't get back up if she wanted to. She closed her eyes and breathed deeply. But instead of soothing her, allowing her to rest at last, the darkness and silence let loose a flood inside her mind. Mental images—horrible images—rose up to torment her. Ava's cold, blue lips. Jake's life stolen in a blaze of crimson spatter. Desert. Desert everywhere. Dry, eternally dry and glowing with red-orange flames.

Lexi curled up in a ball, hands pressed to her eyes, and sobbed as the images played inside her mind like some kind of torture, forcing her to relive all of it. So much had happened, one tragedy after another. No chance to grieve, to let it all out, until now. Her entire body quaked with each sob, like it would shake apart before she was done. And she didn't care if it did.

Finally, throat sore and eyes burning, Lexi sniffed, then wiped the tears from her face with the back of one arm and rolled onto her back. Maybe this was what it felt like to have no more tears left. Empty, but strangely renewed. The awful images gone from her mind. At least for now.

Headlights blazed across the wall, wrenching her back to the here and now. She lay there, eyes wide in the darkness, as she mentally ticked off all the doors she had locked when Don left her there. Could she have missed one?

She got up and crept to the office door, crouching there in the darkness as she gazed out the store's front bay windows. A pickup truck stood in the light from the awning over the pumps. She swallowed and pressed a hand to her chest. Just someone pumping gas. After several minutes, the truck drove off.

Lexi grabbed the flashlight from its wall cradle and made her way through the building, checking every possible entrance point. All locked. She was as safe as she was going to get. She returned to the office and sighed. Better just calm down. Might be more self-serve people stopping by all through the night.

She turned on the office lights, then sat down on the cot and stared at her fanny pack for a moment before unzipping it, as if she were afraid to look at what was inside. She pulled out the knife Jake bought, then slipped it out of its leather sheath and ran her finger along the shiny black handle before opening the blade. She examined the knife from various angles, its cold steel blade glinting in the light from the overhead fluorescents.

Strange how the thing felt in her hand. Frightening, yet

comforting at the same time. Like it would save her life if she needed it to. But could she really use it if it came to that? She wrapped her fingers around the handle, hefted it. Then thrust her arm forward, jabbing the blade into an imaginary assailant.

Maybe. Maybe she could.

She folded the blade back down and slipped the knife into its sheath, then slid her fanny pack beneath the cot, with the knife resting on top. Just in case.

Lexi turned off the overhead lights and lay back down on the cot, the flashlight at her side. She reached down and brushed her fingers against the knife once more before closing her eyes and at last drifting off to sleep.

CHAPTER 45

Startled out of a sound sleep, Lexi nearly toppled off the cot. She clung to its edge, muscles taut, heart pounding in her throat as she glanced around the room, bathed in morning light. Coiled like a snake, she listened intently while she tried to think of how to defend herself from whatever just woke her up.

"Lexi? You still in there? It's just me—Don." His voice came from the front of the store. He sounded hesitant, a little shy.

Relieved, she cleared her throat, amazed how quickly the adrenaline rush had turned her mouth cotton-dry. "I'm in here," she choked out.

Don poked his head in. "Were you comfortable enough? I hope you slept okay. That cot's not exactly luxurious."

Lexi sat up, caught her breath. "Yeah, thanks. It worked out well. Had some dinner, cleaned up a little. I really appreciate you letting me stay here."

He smiled. "No problem. I wish I could have offered you something more suitable."

She waved her hand. "No worries. This was just what I needed."

"You can stay another night if you want. It's no problem. Or if you need longer."

"Thanks, Don. That's really kind of you." She quickly tucked the knife into her fanny pack before he could spot it, then stood and started gathering her things. "But I really need to get back on the road."

"Okay, well, if you need anything else, let me know. I'm going to go get things ready to open up now."

"Sure."

Lexi watched him go. Seemed like a nice young guy. Probably glad to have some company. Maybe she should take him up on his offer. It would be nice to hang out and rest for a couple of days before pressing on into the unknown. She shook her head. No. This wasn't the place for her. Time to get going, before she fell victim to inertia and lost her will to go out and find a new home, a new life of her own—whatever that might look like.

A short time later, she waved goodbye to Don and pulled out onto the street, ready for the journey with full gas cans, a good supply of water and a stash of nonperishable foods and snacks. No more back roads for her. Only major highways from now on. Fastest way to get to wherever the hell she was going to end up. And far better cell reception. She never did like traveling without reception, with no way to make even an emergency call. And she needed the data reception to help her decide on a specific destination. Might as well try for somewhere in California, rather than admit it was all for nothing and turn back for whatever was left of Nebraska.

She stepped on the gas and put Don and his little town behind her.

Lexi took a sip of water, set her bottle back in the holder, then glanced in the rearview mirror. She hadn't noticed the motorcycle cop before. How long had he been behind her? She eased off the gas a little, hoping she could trim a few miles per hour without looking obvious about it. But if he was after her for speeding, he'd surely had plenty of opportunity to pull her over already. What was he up to?

She gripped the steering wheel with both hands, her neck and shoulders rigid. Even when she'd been speeding, she hadn't been *that* far over the limit—had she? She wasn't driving recklessly, just trying to get some miles under her belt before it was time to stop for the night. She'd never been pulled over in her life, and she didn't want to start now. Her heart beat staccato in her chest.

She checked the mirror again. Still there. Her eyes shifted to the dash. Right at the speed limit. Other cars had blown right past her on the highway since she noticed him following her. Why wouldn't he go away, follow somebody else? She was tempted to turn off somewhere just to get him off her back. But what if he followed her off the exit? She checked the GPS, looking for the next major turnoff. Then she spotted the flashing red and blue lights.

Lexi pulled to the shoulder, stopped the car, and rolled down her window. Her heart pounded so hard she could barely breathe. The trooper stalked up to her window, eyes hidden behind sunglasses black as hell.

"License and registration, please."

Hands trembling, she rummaged through the glove box for the registration, finally found it, then set it on the passenger seat. It was as if she could feel the burn of his eyes on her the entire time she was hunting for the paper. Then she reached into her fanny pack for her wallet. She let out a little gasp when her fingers brushed against the knife. She hoped the cop didn't notice—or worse, see the damned thing. All she needed was for him to think she was armed and about to try something. She fished out her license, then handed it and the registration to him.

He glanced at them, fingering the edges as if making sure they were real, then directed his dark glasses toward her. "Where are you headed, ma'am?"

Lexi searched for a good answer and came up short. Way short. Why the hell did he care, anyway? If he thought she was going too fast, why not just say so and give her the damned ticket? Then he could go on and pick off some other victims. Make his quota and then some, most likely.

He waited for an answer, his mouth a thin, straight line below those awful sunglasses. She could almost imagine him tapping his tall, black-leather boot on the pavement.

She swallowed hard and gave it her best shot. "I'm heading north until I can pick up the next westbound highway."

Still clutching her papers, the cop folded his arms and planted his feet. "Visiting someone?"

"Um, no."

"Here for vacation, then?"

"Not really."

"Then what are you doing here? Business?"

"No. Officer."

"Okay, ma'am. I'll get to the point. You have Nebraska plates, a Nebraska license, and you're not here for something specific and temporary. Are you not aware that California has outlawed long-term stays for non-residents?"

Lexi hung her head. The less said, the better. He had her there. She knew perfectly well they'd blocked the borders, but it'd been about the last thing on her mind under the circumstances. Maybe she should have thought about that and just high-tailed it out instead of wandering through California, hoping to land somewhere before some other horrible thing happened.

"Ma'am? All the major entry points are blocked. How'd you get in?"

"I...we—" Lexi fought down tears.

The cop just stood there, those sunglasses pointed right at her like the face of some hideous robot.

The words started to spill, like poison draining from an infected wound. "We had to evacuate. Huge fire was coming. We left in a hurry, just looking for somewhere safe to go. Ava—our baby—died in the desert. We got through near some little town on the Nevada border, way south of I-80. We were trying to find a motel and they shot him!" She covered her face with her hands and sobbed.

"Shot who, ma'am?" The cop leaned down.

"My husband!" She choked. "Couple guys tried to rob us. Jake tried to stop them, and they shot him. Couple of days ago."

"Did you report it to the local police?"

"No. I was afraid they'd shoot me, too. I took off as fast as I could go. They followed me at first, then I turned onto some forest road and lost them." She wiped tears from her face.

"Ma'am, I'm very sorry. If you want to file a report, I'll make sure it gets to the right place. They might still be able to apprehend them."

She waved her hand. "It won't bring him back. I don't even want to think about it. I keep seeing his face, all the blood."

LISA VON BIELA

The cop hesitated as if he were considering something. "I'm under orders to arrest anyone in the state illegally."

"Oh my God." Lexi froze. *Not jail!*

He held out her papers. "Here. You've been through enough. I'm not going to arrest you. I just ask that you turn around and head back out of California the same way you came in. And do it as quickly as you can."

Lexi took the papers, set them down on the passenger seat, and wrung her trembling hands together. "You just want me to leave?"

"That's right. Go back home if you can or find somewhere else to settle down. Even if it were legal for you to stay, there's no place left. That's why they put the ban in place. There's no place to rent. All the hotels and motels have been converted into apartments. Not enough jobs to go around. It's that bad. And crime rates—well, I don't need to tell you about that."

"Thanks, Officer."

He nodded and touched the brim of his helmet. "Good luck, ma'am. Take care of yourself." He sauntered back to his motorcycle and drove off.

Lexi watched him go, then took a deep breath to steady her frayed nerves before putting away her papers and starting the car. Once traffic cleared, she pulled a giant U-turn right there across the highway. If it was illegal, too bad. A cop just told her to turn around and get the hell out.

And that's exactly what she intended to do.

CHAPTER 46

Lexi took the exit for the first rest stop she saw. Better take advantage of the strong cell reception along the highway while she could. She'd lose it soon enough when she turned off to make her way back out of California. She shook her head. Amazing that cop didn't arrest her on the spot. Best not push her luck by hanging around any longer than absolutely necessary.

Popular place. Lots of people—kids or dogs in tow—hitting the restrooms, having a drink or a snack before getting back on the road. Where the hell were they all traveling to or from? Didn't matter. She had her own business to tend to and wanted to be left alone to do it. She never had been the type who struck up conversations with strangers anyway. She chose a parking spot way at the end, away from most of the other cars and foot traffic.

She took out her cell. *Halleluiah!* Max bars. For the first time since they left I-80, back in another lifetime. At least she got that much right. Taking the main highway did get her the cell reception she wanted. Of course, if she'd stuck to the side roads, she probably wouldn't have gotten pulled over.

But maybe that was a blessing in disguise. After all, he didn't arrest her, didn't even give her a ticket. And he probably saved her from getting into more trouble, or wasting a lot of time and gas, by telling her what living conditions were like. He probably wasn't lying, either. Not based on what she'd experienced so far.

Lexi checked her phone, suddenly hungry for news. It felt like she'd been on another planet, out of touch with everything, for months. Hard to believe it'd only been a week and a day. She gasped. The Nebraska fire was *still* going. No spare water to fight it and no estimate when it would be contained. The drought had turned everything to tinder, and peak summer temperatures only made things worse. Unchecked, the fire was simply devouring everything in its path. The only hope for it stopping was if the swath of land west of it that had burned last summer was wide enough to act as a fire break.

Trembling, she dropped the phone in her lap and clapped her hands to her face. Too much, too much. She was terrified to even touch her email. Probably nothing but more bad news lurking in there, waiting to deal a final blow to her will to survive. She stood on a knife's edge right now, with no good options.

She'd lost everything. And she belonged nowhere.

She couldn't stay in California. Nowhere to go, and even if there were, the next cop might not be so forgiving. But she couldn't go home, either. Not anywhere near it. Incinerated. Nothing left on the map through there. Just a horrible blankness. And the fire was chewing into neighboring states now.

Lexi clenched her teeth, grabbed fistfuls of hair and tugged. She wanted to scream, to tear her hair out. To beat something with her fists until she smashed all the bones in her hands. How could all this have happened to her? How could she ever recover from so much loss? Every time she turned around, more tragedy, more disaster. When would it end?

A tap on her window. Lexi jerked around in her seat.

An elderly couple stood just outside her door, looks of concern on their weathered faces. The woman's mouth moved as she pointed a bony finger toward her.

Lexi started the car and backed out, tires squealing, then cut the wheel and barreled out of the parking lot and back onto the highway. She checked her mirrors. No cops that she could see.

She wiped unshed tears from her eyes and focused on the road. Clenching the steering wheel like a lifeline, she stole a quick glance at the speedometer and edged off the gas a little. Better not blast past a cop and risk another stop.

By the time the adrenaline eased off a few miles later, Lexi felt sheepish. That elderly couple probably only wanted to help—and she likely scared the shit out of them. But they startled her, and she just...reacted. She'd never in her life been on such a hair trigger. Some sort of survival instinct must have kicked in. Maybe she did still have something left to fight with.

Lexi drew a deep breath. All right, keep moving. It's the only thing left to do, at least for now. Retrace her steps back out of California, the way they came in. Best thing after that would be to head north to I-80 at the first opportunity after crossing back into Nevada. There'd be more options along I-80, including good cell reception.

If she followed the interstate long enough, something would present itself. It was as good a plan as any for now. Sooner or later she'd find someplace to land—and put an end to this disastrous journey.

CHAPTER 47

Lexi kept driving through the rest of the morning and into the afternoon, putting the miles behind her as quickly as she could. Even so, time seemed to stand still like she was in some other plane of existence—though the dash clock said otherwise. Her encounter with the cop changed everything. Before that, she had time to wander, to find what she needed no matter how long it took. Or at least she thought she did. But now she had to move her ass, get over that border as fast as she could.

She shuddered at the sight of the sign up ahead: the turn-off for the road where Jake was killed. Horrible images forced themselves back into her mind's eye for what felt like the millionth time, replaying the whole thing as clearly as if it were happening in real time. She wiped away a tear and forced herself to focus on the road, to push the visions away before they broke her completely.

Jake never stood a chance. And those murderers would roam free because she couldn't go back and report them. How ironic. If she lingered in California a minute longer than necessary, *she* risked being the one thrown in jail. Lexi sighed. No point in taking that risk. No point in wasting time and energy even thinking about it. Nothing could bring Jake back to her now.

Later that day, she rounded the curve and saw Ray's beat-down little enclave up ahead in the early afternoon heat haze. The place looked abandoned, but she knew better. He'd be lurking somewhere in there like the desert rat he was. She smiled as a thought came to her. She could talk to Ray. He'd know what to do, and he'd been so helpful before. Surely, he'd have some advice on the best and fastest way to get through Nevada and back to civilization. Her smile faded. But he'd wonder why she was traveling without Jake. He'd ask. How could she answer without coming completely undone?

Lexi bit her lip. That's just the way it would have to be. If she couldn't even talk about it, how could she hope to go on living with everything that had happened? Jake and Ava were gone. And she damned well better deal with it, one way or the other.

She parked in front of Ray's old gas station and got out of the car. He opened the door and poked his head out. The threatening glare melted from his face the moment he recognized her. He gave her a broad, yellow-toothed smile.

"What're you doing back here?" He glanced around. "Where's Jake?"

Lexi hesitated, trying to hold herself together, to explain what happened in a calm, matter-of-fact way. "He—" She leaned back against the car, put her face in her hands. It was no use fighting it. The tears began to flow.

"What's the matter? What happened?" Ray came over, put an arm around her shoulder, and led her to the wooden bench. He sat down next to her and looked her in the eye. "Tell me, now."

Lexi sniffed, then took a deep breath to try to control her sobs. "We were trying to find a place to stay the next town over, and these men…these men tried to rob us. They…shot him."

"Oh my God," Ray whispered.

"They…killed him. I took off in the car, fast as I could. I thought they'd kill me, too. They chased me for a while, then I got away."

"I'm so sorry. Is there anything I can do, anything I can get you?"

"I have to get out of California. Quick as I can. Cop stopped me, told me I could be arrested just for being here. I need to know the fastest way to I-80 once I get back over the border." She hung her head and wiped her eyes. No point in mentioning what happened to Ava in that godforsaken desert. Just get to the freeway and somewhere else, anywhere else.

"Sure, sure. I can help you with that, and whatever else you need." He stood. "Let me have your gas cans and your water bottles. I'll top them all up. I have some food you can have, too. Basic stuff, but I don't want to see you leave here short of anything."

Lexi wiped away a tear. "That's so nice of you."

He tipped his head. "Least I can do. You have a long road ahead of you in many ways. I wish I could do more."

"You've done a lot already."

"You know, I can't offer you anything fancy, but you're welcome to stay a while if you want. Rest up as much as you need before you go on. Cops rarely come out this way, and we can hide your rig out back just to be safe. You're not likely to get arrested here."

The offer was tempting. Lexi glanced at her watch and shook her head. "Thanks, but I think I better get moving. There's still enough light to make it over the border and then some. I want to make the most of the day…and put California behind me."

"I understand." He clapped his hands together. "Then let me top up your gas and water, get you some food and directions, and you can be on your way."

Lexi opened the SUV's rear compartment. Ray sorted through the gas cans and water bottles, taking those needing topping with him out back. While she waited by her car, she glanced around the place and again marveled at how someone could have the nerve and the strength to live alone way out in the middle of nowhere like this, depending on no one. Did Ray ever wake up in the night, frightened in the darkness? Did he ever long for someone to talk to? Or did he just not think about it? How did he cope with the isolation, year in and year out?

A short time later, Ray brought out the gas cans, then the water and what looked like some jerky, and loaded it all into the back of her SUV. He pulled a rumpled piece of paper out of his back pocket and pointed at the penciled scrawl.

"Here. I drew a map for you. That there's the first direct route to I-80 once you cross into Nevada. A pretty long drive on a rough road, but it'll get you there sooner than looping around to the next major northbound road." He handed her the piece of paper.

"Thanks, Ray."

He placed his hands on her shoulders and gazed into her eyes. "Travel safely, Lexi. I'll be thinking of you. Wish I could do more to help. I'm so sorry about Jake."

She reached out and hugged him. "Thank you. I truly appreciate all you've done. But I'd better go now, before I start crying all over again."

Ray smiled and waved as she drove off. She watched him and his little outpost grow smaller in her rear view, and tried not to imagine what might happen next.

At least she'd be out of California soon.

CHAPTER 48

Lexi clenched her jaw as she spotted the bullet-ridden wooden sign up ahead: *Nevada.*

Welcome to hell.

She loathed this place and always would. This place with its deceptively empty terrain. Looked like nothing out there. Nothing but death, that is. The desert would forever remind her of what happened to Ava, how they might as well have been on Mars when she got sick. No one to help, no way to save her. And how they had to bury her like a dog somewhere out in that endless sand. She chewed her lip. Probably couldn't even find her little grave now if she tried.

One good thing about Nevada, though: it wasn't California, where she risked being thrown into jail. And where she lost Jake. Gotta look on the bright side, right?

Lexi squinted through the sun's glare at the landscape surrounding her. No one around. No cops to stop her. Odd, the isolation felt almost freeing all of a sudden. No one to hassle her. Nothing left to lose. She'd never felt that way before. Never thought she *could* feel that way.

A dust plume kicked up behind her as she barreled along on her way to the turnoff Ray'd suggested. The sooner she could get through this damned desert and onto I-80, the better. But then what? In a matter of days, she'd lost her entire family, her home, her job. What the hell was left? What kind of life could she have now after so much loss? She hadn't had a chance to envision anything beyond getting back on I-80. Everything past that was an empty canvas. From the looks of things, now she'd have hours of solitary driving time ahead of her to think about it.

Speeding down the gravel road made her feel like she was doing *something,* anyway. Might be completely futile, but at least she was on the move.

Everything had changed in ways she was only beginning to grasp. For starters, she never would have envisioned driving any great distance by herself, let alone through an endless desert with nothing more than the stuff she had in the car. No one to talk to. No one to be responsible for. No one else to depend on. If anything went wrong, she'd have to figure it out on her own. She hoped she was up to the task. Because even after all that had happened, she could still envision countless ways things could get still worse.

Food and water shouldn't be a problem, though, at least for now. Thanks to Ray and her earlier stay at Don's, she had enough to last a week or so—if she was careful with the water. Should be plenty. Unless she got stuck somewhere. She imagined what it would be like, slumped in the hot sand at the side of the road, delirious. No food, no water. No shade. Hungry vultures circling ever closer. She shook her head to clear the image from her mind. Better not to think that way.

But that spare.

Ray warned them the fix might not hold because of where the puncture was. Better than having no spare at all, but maybe not by much. Lexi shook her head. Just another way things could go horribly wrong. The problem with the spare wouldn't matter a bit if she couldn't change a tire on her own. And she probably couldn't. She'd never done it before, and the SUV's wheels were huge. Likely way too heavy for her to wrangle. The hell with it, she'd drive on the rim if she got a flat. Better than dying in the blazing sun over a stupid fucking tire.

She glanced at the GPS. Only a couple more miles before she'd hit the north-south road Ray told her to take. It would give her a pretty straight shot to I-80, but he warned her it was also one of the least-traveled roads in a state famous for thinly traveled roads. She'd get there faster, but she'd be very much on her own.

Lexi took the turn and headed north. The road was much narrower than the one she'd been on, and it consisted of some of the most poorly maintained asphalt she'd ever laid eyes on. Afraid to risk damaging her tires or suspension, she slowed down a little so she could dodge the potholes and avoid skidding in the loose sand that crept across the surface. Definitely a slower road than she'd hoped, but still better than retracing their outbound route, with that fake accident site. Those creeps might still be lurking there, waiting to catch someone in their trap.

There was just plain nothing along this road. Not even sagebrush. Maybe this was a nuke-testing site back in the day. Sure looked like it. Flat as hell, nothing but blinding white sand. Not a stick, not a hill. Not nothing.

She grabbed her cell and snuck a quick look. No signal whatsoever. She turned it off and tossed it onto the passenger's seat. Hardly a surprise. The thing had been useless for most of the trip once they'd left the interstate. She hated being without a working cell, feeling so vulnerable. But on the other hand, who the hell would she call if she *did* run into trouble out here, anyway? There was nothing for miles and miles around.

Lexi dodged another pothole and nudged up her speed. So what if there was some sand on the road? So what if she skidded a little? Not like there was a ditch to slide into or any traffic to crash into. She swerved around another pothole, fishtailing a little. She laughed out loud. Not a chuckle, but a good, long belly laugh. Felt like the first laugh she'd had in years. And it felt pretty damned good.

No one to write her a ticket. No one to tell her to slow down. It was eerie, like having the world—such as it was—to herself.

She entertained herself that way for some miles, pushing the speed as much as she could without taking it too far. She got pretty good at it, rolling along at a good clip, swerving from side to side, kicking up sand in her wake—and not hitting a single pothole. It was a better way to occupy her mind than thinking about Ava or Jake. Or the future. At least for now.

Lexi glanced at the console to check her speed, maybe push it a little more, make even better time. The temperature gauge caught her eye. Not in the red, but higher than the SUV normally ran. She'd been blasting the air conditioning, creating a cool cocoon for herself against the raging heat outside. She shut off the AC and pulled over. Better let it cool some. Overheating and blowing the engine out here was not an option. Not if she wanted to live long enough to see I-80 again.

She cut the engine and got out to stretch a little while she waited. No wonder nothing grew out here. The sun's heat felt as intense as a nuclear blast, and the bright sand reflected it all back up, multiplying the effect right through her sunglasses. She shielded her eyes and forced herself to walk around just long enough to restore the circulation in her legs.

Sweating, she sank down onto the sand in the tiny pool of shade cast by the car. From where she sat, it looked like the only shade left in the entire world, as if nothing else existed but this white-hot desert around her. And even the shade was hot as a frying pan.

Lexi closed her eyes and tried to imagine she was sitting beside a gurgling stream in the shade of a stand of pine trees. Green, healthy, living pine trees that actually smelled like pine trees, not those dead snags the color of flame near the California-Nevada border. Anything to distract herself from the sun's assault while she waited for the SUV's engine to cool down.

It wasn't working. Her imagination was nowhere near strong enough to overpower the brutal reality around her.

Clenching her jaw, she glared at her watch and willed the time to pass so she could get back into the car's air-conditioned comfort and out of this goddamned sun.

And back on her way.

CHAPTER 49

Kevin Oakley switched on the overhead lights, bathing his office in a sickly fluorescent glow that matched his mood just perfectly. He plodded in, dreading the day before it even started. Just as he did each and every day lately. Only today, he had even more reason than usual to detest what his responsibilities would force him to do.

He dropped into his chair and slammed his Starbucks down a little harder than he intended. The lid popped off, unleashing a shot of hot coffee across his desktop. Expensive mistake, with the price of a cup of coffee these days. He stared at the steaming brown puddle and decided to deal with it later. At least it didn't splatter onto his computer or anything important.

Right now, he had just enough time to prepare for his daily status meeting. He always kept his prep time short. It was a little trick he used to force himself to look at the endless parade of gloomy statistics that he had to digest. It was the only thing that worked for him anymore.

Kevin let out a deep sigh, then pulled up the latest water supply report on his computer and scrolled through the charts. The news was even more depressing than usual. No surprise, given how all the key indicators had been trending in recent weeks. Every single aspect of the situation was hurtling toward absolute and inevitable disaster. Construction on the new desalinization plants was still running way behind. They wouldn't be online for months at best. Summer was in full force—with record-breaking temps, no less. Demand for water was the highest he'd ever seen it. And supply was at an all-time low.

His shoulder muscles tightened, sending a burning sensation

up into his neck and the back of his skull, as he scanned the state-by-state charts. More cuts had to be made. Without them, national water reserves would go from critically low to nonexistent. And he knew perfectly well that for some people, any further cuts would be a death sentence. But many, many more would die if he allowed the reserves to run out completely.

He covered his face with his hands, wishing he could unsee the doomsday data in front of him. He never dreamed his job would force him to choose who lived and who died. But he never dreamed a drought this long, this intense, could ever happen. If only he'd chosen some other career. Anything but this.

But it *was* his job, whether he liked it or not. And he had to do it the best way he knew how. He'd been putting off ordering new cuts, hoping for a break, any little change in the situation that would make more cuts unnecessary or allow him to delay them further. But the drought showed no sign of breaking anytime soon, and the desalinization plants were too far behind schedule to help soon enough. With no new water sources, he had no other choice.

Kevin clicked the icon to start the Skype call and watched the screen as his staff joined, one glum face after another popping up in its own tiny square. He cleared his throat and began.

"Good morning. Have you all had a chance to look at today's report?" He waited for the murmured "yesses" to subside. "Good. Well, as you can see, the stats are worse than ever. This leaves no choice. We'll have to make some more changes."

Almost as one, the faces in the boxes across his screen donned concerned looks and shook their heads. Several of his staff started talking at once.

"Kevin, water allocations are already set to the absolute minimum per capita, and that's according to the American Medical Association. We can't ask for people to do with less than the current allotments. We'll start losing—"

"The allotments are *already* too small for people with chronic health issues. Studies have already shown higher-than-normal mortality rates from certain conditions. You might as well—"

"The economy's tanking. The allotments are affecting businesses. Unemployment's at an all-time high. The stock market's dropped to its lowest level in years. Another hit and we'll have a crash on our hands."

Kevin waved his hands for them to stop. "Enough! None of you is telling me anything I don't already know. Look, you all saw the report. And it's not a blip. The stats have been trending that way for weeks." He paused, took a deep breath, and wished he didn't have to go on. "Facts are facts. Even with the strict rationing we already have in place, if usage continues at the current rate, we will deplete all our reserves within a few more *weeks*."

The faces on his screen froze, mouths open. Silent.

"That's right. Weeks. That's all we have if we don't make some immediate changes. Maybe when the new desalinization plants come online, we can loosen the restrictions. But last I heard, they're months away—and no one has any brilliant ideas for how to speed them up. Every one of you knows what'll happen if we let the reserves run down completely."

Kevin paused to let his words sink in, then continued. "You're right. We can't cut allocations across the board without widespread mortality. But it's clear we must cut usage somehow, or we'll simply run out of water."

"Well, what the hell do you propose?"

"I propose to cut water distribution to Alaska, New Mexico and Nevada. At least until we have some positive developments in the overall water supply. Those are the states with the least dense populations that don't also produce much in the way of food."

"Are you insane? That's a death sentence!"

"If you have any better ideas, believe me, I'm all ears. You all just agreed we can't cut per-capita water allotments any further. But if we don't cut somewhere, we run out. For everyone. Simple as that."

Kevin terminated the Skype call and tried not to think of what he left unsaid.

Even this cut was likely only putting off the inevitable. How much longer could he stave off complete disaster? Would the desalinization plants come online in time, or was this all for nothing?

He closed his eyes and put his head in his hands. There had to be something more he could do, but what? No matter how hard he tried, nothing came to him.

Nothing whatsoever.

CHAPTER 50

Lexi glanced at her watch again. Somehow, the better part of an hour had passed while she sat scrunched in the tiny patch of shade beside the SUV, baking in the heat and imagining all sorts of menacing doomsday scenarios. Enough already. Had to be enough time for the engine to cool down, at least some. She pushed herself to her feet and trudged to the front of the car.

Not quite sure what to look for, she popped the hood and gazed down at the engine. The plastic coolant reservoir looked to be at or near the right level. But could it look okay even if the radiator really was low or something else about the cooling system was somehow screwed up? Out here all alone, she'd better be extra careful about everything. No sense in trusting a plastic part that might be lying to her.

But she didn't know shit about the car's engine, and opening the radiator—or messing around with anything inside there—scared her. What if it was still hot? You had to take the cap off just so, or steam could shoot up in your face and burn the hell out of you. That's what she'd heard, anyway. Better get something to open it with. She went to the back and dug around in the cargo area for something to protect her hand. A diaper. Not like Ava would be needing it. *Ava.* She pressed her lips together. Focus on the here and now—and staying alive. Nothing else matters. Not anymore.

Lexi stared at the radiator cap for a moment, unsure if it was safe to take it off yet. She frowned at the sun's angle. The afternoon was getting away from her. Better get this over with and move on. She folded up the diaper, pressed it onto the cap, and gave it a twist.

Nothing bad happened. She peered down into the radiator but couldn't quite see the fluid level. Damned if it wasn't dark in there, even with all this sun beating down. She fetched a small flashlight and peered inside. The level looked okay.

Puzzled, she switched off the flashlight and put the radiator cap back on. Then why did the gauge climb like that? Either it was just so damned hot it was unavoidable, or there was some problem other than low coolant in the radiator. Great. A mystery. If it had been low, at least she would have known the reason. But then, she would have had a leak to deal with. And that would have presented yet another problem. She had no spare coolant with her, and no way to fix a leak.

No matter the cause, she couldn't let it overheat. That would wreck the engine. Game over. She gazed at the emptiness surrounding her. No one would pass by in time to help her, not out here. She'd die alone in the desert. She wondered how long it would take, how agonizing it would be. She shook her head. Better not think like that.

She got back into the car and started it, then forced herself to glance at the gauges. She blew out a long, relieved breath. They all looked okay, at least for now. She turned the air conditioning to the lowest setting, rationing out the coolness to minimize the load on the engine.

Lexi got back on her way, one eye on the temperature gauge and one eye on the broken-up asphalt that lay before her. She turned on the radio and searched for a station while she nimbly skipped past the potholes. Terrible reception out here, even though there was nothing around. You'd think radio waves could travel forever in a landscape like this.

Finally, she picked up a station. Reception was weak, but it was audible. Barely. It felt like she'd found a lifeline out here, surrounded by nothing. Sounded like a news station from Reno. She strained to pick out the words.

California has now indefinitely extended its moratorium on travelers crossing its borders. While some drivers are simply turning around and heading eastbound, others have chosen to pull off the interstate and set up camp nearby. At first, there were only scattered campers. But now, as more and more have been denied entry at California's border, these camps have consolidated into several major encampments. So far, given the circumstances, local law enforcement has allowed the encampments to stay. The governor and his advisors are discussing how best to address the mounting humanitarian problems.

The station crackled, faded, and fell silent. Lexi messed with the radio, desperate to hear the rest of the report. Nothing but silence. She smacked the console and let out a frustrated scream. It was gone, at least for now. She felt more alone than ever.

She glanced at the temperature gauge, couldn't decide if it had crept up a millimeter or if it was just her imagination running wild. Maybe the problem earlier had been a blip, and everything was fine. Or maybe it wasn't. Maybe it was the first hint of something about to go terribly wrong with the car. So many things could happen. None of them good. Maybe she shouldn't be out here all alone.

She thought about turning around, heading back to Ray's place. He might be able to fix whatever was wrong with the car…but then she'd be back in California. And that's if she could even get in. If they were getting that hardcore about not letting people in, they might start watching more of the entry points. Risky to turn around, drive all that way, and not be able to get to Ray's after all. A dangerous waste of gas and supplies. No, she had to keep going no matter what, and just baby the car along if it heated up again.

The encampments could be a good thing—as long as she found one that was relatively peaceful and crime-free. Someplace to stop, rest up, figure out what to do next. There'd be people there, with plans, information. Maybe even someone with some car-repair skills. And surely there'd be radio and cell reception that close to the interstate. She felt so cut off without reception, like the entire world could catch on fire and she'd have no clue. Maybe it already had.

The sun was dipping closer to the horizon. Much as she wanted to make more miles, she didn't want to drive at night. It had already been a long day, and she was bone-tired. Way too easy to make a mistake under those conditions. But…it'd be much cooler driving at night, probably easier on the car. *No.* If she had to pull over and check something under the hood, no way did she want to do it in the dark. It would be so much harder to see what she was doing. And she didn't know what sort of creatures might come out under the cover of darkness, wanting to hunt for their food in the relative cool.

Better pull over and prepare for the night while she still had some light left. Maybe even get some sleep, if she was lucky.

CHAPTER 51

Frank Delano shoved his computer monitor aside and clapped his hands over his eyes. Enough already. The emails were out of control. So were the voicemails. And the snail mail. Every single day brought a fresh deluge of pleas, demands. Even threats. Whatever possessed him to want to be governor of Nevada? Whatever it was, running was the worst decision he'd ever made. If only he'd lost the race.

Maybe he should resign, go do something—anything—else. Move to another state, get out of this goddamned desert. Dig ditches, even. Who cares? Anything had to be better than this. He didn't even feel like a governor, spending all day every day fielding complaints from citizens. Complaints he couldn't do a damned thing about anyway. For crissake, he didn't control the weather. Or the federal government, for that matter.

Everyone wanted more water. No one had enough. But he couldn't influence water policy, no matter how hard he tried. And he couldn't magically make more water appear out of thin air. Not in Nevada, of all places.

His phone rang. He peered at the caller ID and groaned. That goddamned water czar, Oakley. He never called to deliver good news. He reached out his hand to answer the call, hesitated. No. Not answering it wouldn't change anything. He picked up.

"Hello, Kevin."

"Hello, Frank. How are things out there?"

"We're doing as well as can be expected, for the most part. Say, I was going to call you, see if we can get a break on our allocation. Even a temporary one would help. We don't have a lot of livestock out here, but the ranchers we do have are experiencing serious losses. And Vegas is a ghost town." He sighed. "To be honest, Kevin, we're hurting. We're hurting bad."

After a long pause, Oakley spoke. "I'm sorry to hear that. I really am."

"Then what can you do to help us out?"

"I wish I could, but I can't."

"Don't you have the authority to shift allocations if you see fit? Look, I'm not asking for anything huge or permanent. Just give us a break out here, just for a little while."

"Can't do it, Frank. Water reserves are at an all-time low—dangerously so. We've considered every possible alternative, and there's no other way out of this. We have to make some immediate changes."

"What...what sort of changes?"

"We have no choice but to terminate water distribution to several states. I'm sorry to have to tell you this, but Nevada is one of those states."

A sickening flutter passed through Frank Delano's chest. He couldn't possibly have heard correctly. "What?"

"It's like this, Frank. We have no new water sources to tap right now. Construction on the new desalinization plants is way behind schedule, and no other country has surplus water they're willing to sell to us—not at any price—"

"But why single out specific states? Can't you make it up by shaving the per capita allocations?"

"Can't do that, wish we could. Per capitas are already so low that any further cut would trigger a significant increase in the nationwide death rate. But if we don't cut somewhere—and quickly—we will deplete our national reserves in a matter of *weeks*. You can imagine the consequences. On the other hand, Nevada has one of the least dense populations in the country, and little to no agricultural activity to speak of."

Frank ran a trembling hand over his bald head as he tried to process what this asshole was telling him. The population *had* dwindled, especially since Vegas emptied out a couple of years ago. The idea of coming to a hot, dry desert in the midst of a drought didn't attract many tourists, the town's economy imploded, and residents had fled in droves.

"Look, you can't do this. There are still people here. They need water. We're barely getting along as it is."

"Perhaps they can try moving to other states. I'm sorry, Frank, but there's no other choice. Water distribution to Nevada will end first thing next week."

"California already shut its borders! Where's everyone supposed to go?"

Oakley's silence gave him all the answer he needed.

"You're letting people die. That's what you're doing."

"It's this or we all die, Governor. Don't think for a minute I take this decision lightly."

"You do realize there are people from other states here now, right? Lots of them. There're encampments all along I-80. People passing through, trying to get to California and getting turned back at the border. What about that?"

"Non-residents are free to go back where they came from."

"Jesus, you're a cold son of a bitch, aren't you?"

"I'm sorry. Truly I am. If I could do this any other way, I would. I promise, I'll lift the ban as soon as the new desalinization plants come online."

"And when will that be? You already said they're way behind schedule. It'll be too late by then."

Frank slammed down the phone and stared into space.

Too late. My God, it'll be too late.

CHAPTER 52

Bones picked clean and sun-bleached as white as the sand around it, a full skeleton of some large animal lay at the side of the road like a warning sign. *Too late for that. I entered this hell long ago.* Lexi shivered as she drove past the thing. She couldn't help but watch it in her rear-view mirror as it shimmered in the heat, then disappeared as she left it behind, almost as if it had never been there.

The carcass proved there must be animals living out there, but where? This road ran through a ghastly, desolate area, flatter than anything she'd ever seen, and completely devoid of ground cover, much less shade. The other roads she'd taken though Nevada looked lush in comparison. Maybe the poor damned thing had gotten lost, wandered around for days before dying some horrible death under the unrelenting sun. She glanced at the GPS. I-80 was only about forty miles farther on. Hard to imagine.

The temperature gauge ticked up a notch. *Not again.* She'd checked and rechecked the coolant level in the radiator since the trouble started yesterday. And every time, it seemed okay. Even so, something wasn't right—and whatever it was, it was getting worse. The time between stops to convince the gauge to retreat was getting shorter and shorter.

All this stop-and-go, fussing with the car, and worrying were sucking away time and sapping her energy, when all she wanted was to get to I-80 as fast as she could. Almost like the desert didn't want her to leave, didn't want her to ever get back to civilization and safety. Maybe it was just her imagination getting the better of her, but she felt some kind of malevolent presence tracking her, wanting her to fail.

And if she wasn't careful, it might just win.

Lexi pulled over once more and hesitated, her finger linger-ing on the ignition button. What if it didn't start up again this time? Start walking, and hope she didn't wind up like that skel-eton? The gauge ticked a little higher. But if she let the engine burn up, she could count on being marooned out here. No choice but to hope for the best. Off it goes.

She gulped some tepid water, then got out to stretch a little. The engine would take around twenty minutes or so to cool down again, maybe a little more this time if it kept to its pattern. Might as well get some circulation back in her legs while she killed some time.

Shielding her eyes from the sunglass-piercing glare, she trudged around the car, eyeing the tires as she went. The dash gauge showed normal pressures so far. Better stay that way. With those big-ass tires, she'd have to suddenly develop some serious upper-body strength to manage a tire change on her own. Besides, between the god-awful heat and the brutal road surface, the spare's iffy patch job would likely fail and strand her anyway.

She made herself circle the car a couple more times to work the stiffness from her legs. Her blood felt like it was boiling inside her head, pounding in her ears, against her skull. What she wouldn't give to be lying on cool, white sheets in a frosty, air-conditioned motel room right now. Just lying there, her mind empty, numb to the pain. Away from this awful, disori-enting place, with its crushing heat and blinding bright sand, flat and unchanging in all directions.

Lexi got back in the car, wiped the sweat from her face, and downed some more lukewarm water to stave off dehydration. She tried to conjure up the sound of clinking ice cubes in her mind to make it taste a little cooler. It didn't work. But at least she *had* water.

Biting her lip, she pressed the ignition button and hoped for the best. The engine roared to life and the temperature gauge backed down to near-normal. Better get moving. No telling how long her luck would hold. Glancing at the GPS, she pulled back onto the road. Forty miles. Not that much farther. She skirted a few more potholes, then took advantage of a relatively smooth stretch of road to make quick work of the last miles.

Lexi squinted, blinked, then blinked again. Up ahead in the distance, shimmering in the heat. Something on the horizon. She pressed even harder on the accelerator, eager to see. Tents. Lots of tents. And a little farther beyond that, I-80.

Screw the temperature gauge. Almost there. Breathless, Lexi gunned it.

CHAPTER 53

Trent Dillon stepped up onto the makeshift wooden platform and squared his shoulders. Never in his life did he imagine—let alone wish—anything like this would happen to him, of all people. He'd always been the loner, the guy who was busy doing his own thing. Never ran for class president. Never wanted to. Hell, he'd even dropped out of college after only one year. Too many people, too much groupthink. Been on his own for the nearly eight years since. And happily so.

But somehow in the past few weeks—so gradually he didn't even realize it was happening—he'd become the de facto leader of a desert tent city just south of I-80. A little enclave born of desperation. There'd been no formal election, no proclamation. But the motley mix of people who'd landed here looked to him to lead them as if it were the most natural thing in the world. He couldn't put his finger on the tipping point, when it happened. But it had.

The whole thing was one big cosmic accident. People from all over the country—himself included—were fleeing the ravages of the drought, trying to get into California to make a new life. Like a new gold rush, only this time cheaper water was the prize everyone was after. California had the most working desalinization plants of all the states, and the most coastline to put them on.

But that optimistic gold rush for water turned into a Grapes of Wrath-style death march when, without any advance warning, California slammed its border shut, stranding refugees out there in the desert.

Many couldn't return to their homes if they wanted to, like

those people from western Nebraska, where they had that massive fire. Parched and dying, his native Wyoming held nothing for him anymore, either. What hadn't burned in previous fires was ripe as kindling now for the next big blaze. And there was nowhere left to stay anywhere along the I-80 corridor. Hotels and motels had long since filled to capacity. So began the tent city.

Trent took a deep breath and looked out over the crowd of forty or so people waiting to hear him speak. Some older, some younger. All different levels of physical abilities and skills. Some coping with the situation pretty well, some shell-shocked and unmoored, barely able to face their new reality.

In some ways, he felt he was the right person to lead them. He was good at planning, organizing, solving problems of all kinds. Always had been. He could always work his way out of a tight spot. But so many lives depended on him now. He didn't like to be responsible for others. He only ever wanted to be responsible for himself alone. But it was too late for that. All eyes turned to him as he spread out his arms and nodded.

"Some of you may have heard the news already. Water supplies are at an all-time low, so the Water Czar's decided to cut deliveries to some states—and that includes Nevada—starting next week."

The crowd erupted into angry shouts and murmurs. Mimi, a young single mom from Oklahoma who seemed to take the border closure as a personal rejection, burst into tears, leapt up from where she sat, and ran for her tent, clutching her crying baby to her chest.

"And there's no more water on the shelves of any store within twenty miles of here. Stores farther out'll run out of stock fast, if they haven't already," Trent continued.

Stan, who fled Montana after having to shut down his ranch for lack of water, yelled from the back of the crowd, his face beet-red with fury. "What're we going to do? We can't just stay here and die!"

Everyone turned, their mouths moving in unison, "What do we do, Trent?"

"We still have some water here in camp. That'll last us for a while if we're careful. For now, I want some volunteers to drive out every night and tap water from unguarded spigots in the residential neighborhoods on the other side of I-80. Do it while we can, before the local reservoirs run dry."

A chorus of voices shouted, "Then what?"

The inevitable question. Trent wished he had a ready answer, something he could feel confident in. Something that would satisfy the crowd—and actually work, too. "I don't know yet. But that should help bolster our supply, at least for the near term. Local reservoirs'll still have some water in them for a while even after they cut off new deliveries. We have to take advantage of that as best we can for now."

Veronica, fresh from Kansas after being laid off from her accounting job at the dairy, stepped forward, waving her fists in the air. "I heard all the states surrounding Nevada are planning to shut their borders, too. They're going to leave us here to die! It's not fair!"

"Where'd you hear that? I haven't heard that." Trent's mind raced. He hoped it was another false rumor. Too many problems to solve already. If they closed them in like that—

"What's that?" Stan pointed to his left.

An SUV approached from the south—fast—dust kicking up in its wake. Murmuring, all heads turned in its direction. It skidded to a stop at the edge of the camp and a young woman got out. She stood for a moment, leaning on the open driver's door.

"Get out of here, we're full up!" shouted Veronica.

Trent waved a hand to shush the crowd and shouted to the intruder. "Ramp to I-80's about five miles up that way. California's closed. You'll want to take it eastbound."

"Please...I can't. I can't go any farther." The woman's voice faltered.

Trent rested his hands on his hips, tried to look authoritative. "We can't take on any more people here. Our supplies are already low and they're cutting off water deliveries to Nevada. *And* they may be sealing up the border soon. You'd best get out while you still can."

The woman wobbled, gripped the car door to try to stay

upright. "Oh my God, no. I can't go anymore."

Trent stepped down from his stand and approached her. "I'm really sorry, but—"

Sobbing, she fell to her knees, her face buried in her hands. "I've lost everything. I can't go home. It burned in the fire. My baby died, my husband was murdered. I can't keep going. I can't."

She collapsed right there in the sand at Trent's feet.

CHAPTER 54

Wet…water…rain? What is that?

Lexi startled awake and batted something off her face. A young woman bent over her and pressed a cool, wet cloth onto her forehead.

"Where am I?"

The woman adjusted the cloth, smoothed Lexi's hair, and whispered softly. "Lie still. Relax."

Lexi tried to sit up, fell back, and squeezed her eyes shut. Her head throbbed as if her skull were two sizes too small. "Who are you? What happened?"

"I'm Katie. You showed up here out of the clear blue and collapsed right out there by your car."

Lexi opened her eyes and glanced around. She lay on a low cot in what looked like a family-sized canvas tent. *Here? What is this place?"

Katie smiled, sat back on her heels, and pushed a stray lock of her long, strawberry-blond hair from her face. "It's hard to say what we have here. No one's even tried to name it. It just sort of happened. No rhyme or reason, just a bunch of people from lots of different places looking for a better life. Got blocked at the California border and wound up here." She sighed, her smile fading away. "Unfortunately, things didn't work out like any of us had hoped."

"How many people live here?

"Oh, a few dozen now, I think. I've only been here a few weeks. Others have been here longer."

Lexi pushed herself up on her elbows and peered out the open tent door. From what she could see, the rest of the place was festooned with tents of various types and sizes. Even so, it seemed tidy, with an air of organization about it. She could just see I-80 off in the distance, its image flickering in the waves of heat rising from the parched desert sand.

"So, what's *your* name, and how did you wind up here? What happened to your baby and your husband?"

"How do you—"

"Right before you collapsed, you said something about losing your baby and your husband."

"Oh."

Lexi stared into space as those few minutes came back to her with gut-wrenching clarity. She'd felt as if her heart would explode, she'd come so far and been through so much, only to be turned away at the first sign of civilization she'd seen in what seemed like forever. This Katie person was probably just trying to get her in good enough shape to send her on her way.

But every minute she managed to remain here was time spent somewhere safe, a brief respite from what she'd already been through—and whatever might lay ahead. Might as well tell her whole story, see if they'd change their minds and let her stay, at least for a while.

She lay back down, took in a deep breath, let it out slowly, then began. "My name is Lexi. Lexi Morgan. My husband Jake and I had to evacuate because of that big fire in western Nebraska. We had so little time to get out." She clenched her fists, the feeling of helplessness returning as clearly as if she'd been transported back in time.

"There was almost no warning. Just like that, the fire was nearly at the edge of town. We threw everything we could into the car and took our baby, Ava. Didn't even have a plan where to go, just...go. No time to think. Not then." Lexi wiped a tear from her eye. That night seemed a lifetime ago. She supposed it was.

Katie nodded, her brow furrowed. "I heard about that fire. You must've been terrified."

"We sure were. We just took off, got on the freeway and headed west as soon as we could get through all the traffic. Finally found somewhere to rest up and plan. Someplace in

Utah. Decided to try California, but heard they were blocking the borders. We thought we could sneak around, get through on a backroad, so we turned off I-80 at West Wendover, went through the desert. Ava got sick and...died out there."

"Oh my God, what happened?"

Lexi shook her head. "I don't know. Guess I'll never know now. Wish I did. She'd been fussy off and on, but we figured she was just upset from being on the road like that, you know, the heat and all. All of a sudden, she couldn't breathe. We were out in the middle of nowhere. Absolutely nothing around, and no time to get anywhere to find help." She touched her throat. "Jake tried to help her, but it didn't work. She just...we had to bury her out there." She sobbed.

Katie reached out and laid her hand on Lexi's shoulder. "I'm so sorry. I can't imagine how horrible that must have been for you." She sniffed and wiped a tear from her own eye.

"We had no choice. Had to keep going, try to get into California. We did get in at a pretty isolated stretch of border. God, I wish we hadn't. I wish we'd turned around, done just about anything else. But we kept going, trying to find a place to stay for the night. That's when some thugs tried to rob us." She swallowed, her throat tight, dry. "They shot Jake dead, right there in the street."

Katie's blue eyes grew wide. "Didn't anyone help you?"

"There was no one around. I just took off, fast as I could. Barely got away. Didn't dare go back there."

"I can't believe all you've been through. But how'd you end up here?"

"Well, I was trying to find somewhere safe to stay, to think things through. Then I got stopped by a cop. He said I could be arrested just for being in California. But he let me off, told me to get out fast as I could. So I did. Figured I'd head up to I-80, find someplace to stay, get some more supplies. Get my car fixed and figure out what to do next."

Katie gently rubbed Lexi's shoulder. "I am so sorry. You've been through so much."

Lexi looked away. "But I can't stay here, can I?"

"How's she doing?"

Lexi glanced up. It was the young man who seemed to be in charge, a rail-thin twenty-something with choppy black hair and a sunburned face. He stepped inside and offered his hand. She set aside her wet cloth, sat up, and took his hand.

"Hi, name's Trent."

"Trent's our leader. Sort of by unofficial vote." Katie smiled. "He's gotten us organized and working together. Before, we were all just scattered around here, everyone trying to do their own thing. Really inefficient. No organized way to supply ourselves, pool resources, those sorts of things."

Trent gave a half-smile and waved her off. "Thanks, Katie. Just doing what needs to be done." He looked into Lexi's eyes. "You feeling better now? Kinda scary how you just went down like you did."

Katie stood, arms folded, smile gone. "She's been through hell, Trent. Worse'n any of us, I'd say. I think we should let her stay."

"Katie, we're running out of water—"

"If we're running out, we're running out, and we have to find more anyway. Meantime, I'll share mine with her."

Trent hesitated, gave a single nod, then turned back to Lexi. "Welcome to the camp, then. Everyone here contributes their skills one way or another. We'll find something for you to do to help out, but for right now, just rest and feel better, okay?"

"Okay. Thank you for letting me stay."

Katie handed her the wet cloth for her forehead. "Here. Put this back on and try to sleep. I'll be back in a while to check on you."

"Thank you."

Lexi lay back down on her cot, adjusting the compress over her eyes to hide her tears. What skills could she contribute? If she couldn't provide something useful in return for them letting her stay and share their food and water, they might kick her out after all.

And if she couldn't stay here—at least for a little while—she had no idea what else she could do, where she could go. Especially with her car acting up like it was.

Lexi rolled onto her side, utterly drained. She couldn't

believe she just told Katie—a total stranger—the entire horrible story. But in a way, she felt a little better now. Odd how that worked. Didn't change a damned thing that had happened, but the burden somehow felt a little lighter.

She curled up in a fetal position, tucked her hands under her cheek, and closed her eyes. She was safe, for now. But tired, so tired. A thick, heavy blanket of exhaustion descended on her, taking her down into a deep, dreamless sleep.

CHAPTER 55

Katie lay in her sleeping bag with her eyes closed, savoring the relative cool at daybreak's edge. Funny how life here in the encampment felt even more rigidly scheduled than the life she'd left behind: working two jobs to put herself through school, constantly rushing, fighting her way through traffic to be on time for everything. That damned sun was, as they say, a harsh mistress. That and the water supply. All activity in the camp revolved around conserving water and picking the cooler—or at least the less blast-furnace-like—times of day for more strenuous activities.

She rolled over, picked up her water bottle, and gave it a little shake. Pretty low after making sure Lexi got enough yesterday. She'd have to ask Trent for a small advance on her share of the main supply. And hope he didn't give her a ration of shit about it. She sat up, took a sip, and capped the bottle back up.

It was her choice to share her water, though. No one put a gun to her head. She felt bad for that Lexi. No one should have to go through that much shit. And certainly not in such a short amount of time. Amazing the poor thing was even remotely able to function after all she'd been through. She gave the bottle another little shake, set it back down, and hoped the camp's water supply would last until Trent figured out what to do.

She opened her tent fly and watched the sun push its way up through a band of the sweetest pink. So beautiful, yet so deadly. Soon it bathed the entire camp in a gorgeous warm glow. She wished she could sit there and paint the scene, but she'd sold off her art stuff and everything else, thinking she could start over in California. Travel light and restock when she found her new home. Great idea, big mistake. Now she had nothing to go back to, and no way to move forward.

Katie put on shorts and a T-shirt, grabbed her water bottle, and stepped outside to greet the day while it was still a relatively pleasant temperature. Tents of all sizes, shapes, and colors dotted the sand around her. The makeshift general assembly area lay to one side of the camp, along with a small stage-like platform for Trent to speak from. Canvas awnings provided shelter from the sun during group meetings. One larger tent off to the side of the assembly area held the communal supplies in one place. All the vehicles were parked in a tidy row on the opposite side of camp.

Pretty well organized, considering they'd all arrived as strangers to each other over the preceding weeks. Trent was amazing. She'd noticed a big difference in camp operations since he gradually assumed leadership. Before, everything was helter skelter. No supplies—like food, water, or tools—were pooled or even inventoried. Lots of bickering over small things, no one trusted anyone. Pretty intense, and not in a good way. Almost certainly a lot of wasted resources, too.

He'd changed all that, and he somehow did it without being forceful or overbearing in any way. Everyone was still an individual, for sure, but he had the group working together, sharing what they had in far more efficient ways. She doubted the food and water supplies would have lasted as long as they had if he hadn't stepped up to the job.

Katie glanced toward his tent and wondered what he was really like. He kept to himself a lot, was hard to know. Not in a snooty kind of way, not like that. More like he took his role really seriously and didn't want anyone to think he played favorites. Probably in case he had to make any hard decisions along the way. She frowned and hoped it didn't come to that. But it very well might. He also didn't make it a practice to sugarcoat things. Their water situation was getting dire. How they would resolve it, she had no idea. But if anyone could come up with the answer, it was Trent.

She went over to Lexi's tent, bent down, and listened. Probably still asleep. She'd slept a good part of the day after she arrived yesterday. Likely the first decent rest she'd had in her entire horrible journey. Better not to wake her. She'd check on her again in a little while, make sure she drank some more water and got something to eat.

Katie stood back up and saw Trent getting out his tent and heading in her direction. And not for the first time, she felt the beginnings of a crush—maybe something more—developing. She admired what he'd been able to accomplish already. He was smart. And more than a little cute. She hid a shy smile.

"How's she doing?" He tipped his head toward Lexi's tent.

"Okay, I think, given everything that's happened to her. She slept almost straight through yesterday, and I didn't want to wake her now. The rest'll do her good."

"Glad to hear it." He looked her in the eye. "How's your water?"

"She still had some of her own to drink. I shared some of mine when she ran out of hers. It's...a bit low." She glanced down at the bottle dangling from her hand. "I wouldn't mind a little advance on my share."

Trent folded his arms, looked off into the distance. "That's exactly what I was trying to avoid, why I wanted to send her on her way. But you were right yesterday. If we're running out overall, we're running out. And we need to try something new to solve the problem. Help me spread the word through the camp. I want to hold an all-hands meeting a couple of days out, to give everyone a little time to think, prepare to bring their ideas. That way we can make a decision and move on it while there's still time."

"Sure thing. Lexi, too?"

"Lexi, too. We need all the ideas we can get, and we need everyone to do their part in whatever plan we come up with. Get her back on her feet and ready to help. Take a little more water from the stash if you have to."

"Thanks, Trent." Katie watched him go. If there was a way out of this mess, he'd find it. But what if there *was* no way out? She shivered. Better not think like that. Just trust in Trent.

CHAPTER 56

Time for Trent's mandatory planning meeting. Lexi wondered what to expect as she followed the others to the row of canvas canopies that made up the assembly area. She chose a spot up front near the makeshift stage and seated herself on a shaded tarp, a little away from the rest. She'd kept mostly to herself since arriving, assuming some of the camp members likely viewed her as an unneeded drain on already scarce food and water supplies. She still felt very much the outsider, so she took care not to intrude on others' space and conversations. As she settled in and waited, she thought back over her first few days in this place.

Katie had been incredibly kind to her, giving her food and water out of her own allocation and letting her get all the rest she needed. And it worked. Physically, she felt pretty good now, almost restored. Physically. But not emotionally. She wondered if she would ever heal from losing Ava and Jake. Probably too much to hope for.

Trent had scheduled the emergency all-hands meeting this morning to decide what to do about water. The camp was down to the very last of its supply, and those sent out on reconnaissance last night had come back empty-handed for the first time. No more water to be found in any stores within reasonable striking distance of the camp. No luck finding accessible taps, either. Nothing. Not a bit of water to be had within several hours' drive. Something had to be done. Something very inventive, indeed.

Water delivery to Nevada had only just stopped, but the effects were swift and dramatic. Virtually overnight, all local water reserves dried up. Housing developments looked like ghost towns. Some speculated the residents had taken all the water they could and fled north for Canada, only to face an uncertain border crossing. Not like there was much choice. Desperate to protect their own water supplies, neighboring states only allowed travelers from Nevada to take major interstates straight through and out.

Trent got up on his rickety wooden stand and signaled for everyone to settle down. He seemed an odd combination. On the one hand, leadership appeared to come naturally to him. Yet he didn't seem at ease in the role. Lexi wondered how he came to be chosen. Maybe it was one of those things where he didn't step aside quickly enough, and *bang*, it became his job because it needed to be done and no one else would or could do it.

She shook her head and thought about her own situation. Sometimes life was that way, wasn't it?

"As I think you've all heard by now, last night's water run was a bust. Now we're days away from running out entirely here in camp."

The crowd gasped and murmured. Lexi felt a chill down her back despite the oppressive heat. Where *was* the nearest water? Likely not far as the crow flies—they were very near the border. But California was off limits. No way could they sneak inside and get water there. The entry west of Reno would be heavily guarded, no excuses or sad stories accepted.

"Ideas?" Trent glanced from side to side.

A woman in back spoke up. "Relocate farther east along I-80? Maybe more sources left there."

A man shouted her down in a voice laden with barely concealed panic. "How do you know there aren't others like us east of here? Then what? They've probably already dried up their sources, too!"

Another woman called out, "Those bastards in Washington hung us out to dry. It's a death sentence and they know it. Keep the water for the states with more voters. That's what they're doing!"

A man in the back yelled, "They won't give us our fair share of water, so we *take* it!"

Trent pointed at the man. "Jack, what are you suggesting?"

Jack, a middle-aged man with a slight paunch and a blond crew-cut, got to his feet and pumped a fist in the air as he spoke. "We take it. They still have to ship the water out from California. And they have to use I-80. So, we hijack a truck full of water. The way we conserve, it'd last us a real long time."

Trent stood silent, weighing the suggestion. "They use two drivers in those trucks. Heavily armed. What about that?"

"We set up a trap, some kind of blockage they have to stop for, then we ambush them. A lot of us have firearms and ammunition. If there was ever a good use for it, it's this."

The crowd grew silent. Trent pressed Jack further. "Let's say we managed to get the truck, then what? It's not like they won't notice a missing water truck."

"Well, I don't know, Trent. Drive it out here and guard it. Maybe build some kind of reservoir to store the water and destroy the truck. We can worry about that later. Right now, I don't see any other viable source of water we can get at. And if we don't get water soon, nothing else'll matter anyway."

Trent rubbed his chin, shifted his weight from foot to foot as he considered the plan. Lexi glanced around her. All eyes were on Trent, waiting for his response. She tried to think of some other way, something less violent, less risky. But all other doors seemed to be closed. Even if they could freely go to neighboring states, it wasn't as if water supplies were abundant anywhere else—except maybe in California. And even that was a big maybe.

Trent cleared his throat. "Any other ideas?"

Silence.

He stared down toward his feet and shook his head. "I can't think of anything else, either. I agree. I don't think we have a choice. But this is so risky. So many unknowns."

Trent made eye contact with everyone in turn before continuing. "We must all understand what we're saying here—and what it could mean. We're talking about ambushing two heavily armed, well-trained guards. That means some of us could get injured—perhaps badly—and we only have rudimentary medical skills and supplies available here in camp. We may even lose some people. Are we prepared to accept these risks? Because if we're not, the time to speak up is now."

The crowd shifted, people glanced at each other and had hasty, muted conversations amongst themselves, while Trent stood, arms folded across his chest, waiting for them to decide their future.

Lexi's mouth went dry. She'd already seen what bullets could do, from just a handgun. God knew what kinds of weapons some of the others in camp had. Those water-truck drivers probably had the kind of guns that could cut you in half in a single burst, like in the movies.

Trent unfolded his arms and put his hands on his slim hips. "Well? It's up to you. If you decide to go through with this, I'll do my best to organize and lead the ambush. I won't guarantee we'll succeed, though. I can't."

Jack cupped his hands around his mouth and shouted to the crowd. "If we succeed, we have a chance to live. If we don't, or if we don't even try, we die anyway. Simple as that."

Trent pointed. "Show of hands."

Hands went up right away through much of the crowd. Other hands rose soon after to join them. Lexi took a deep breath and raised her hand shoulder height, then high above her head. Jack was right. Doing nothing meant sure death.

Trent nodded. "Then we do it. Let's start planning right away. There's no time to waste."

CHAPTER 57

Trent wiped the sweat from his forehead and allowed himself a small sip of water as he assessed the camp's progress on their plan. Everyone had worked feverishly in the past days to prepare for tomorrow's hijack. He hoped with all his heart it went off without a hitch, but something nagged at him. What had he missed? He had to have missed something. They didn't have the time or resources to plan for every possible contingency, and he had to somehow make peace with that. But he knew he never would.

No matter how well they executed on the plan, there were likely to be injuries, even deaths. And he'd have that on his conscience the rest of his life. He shook his head. Can't think about that right now. Because if he thought about it too long, he'd be tempted to call the whole damned thing off. And that would sentence them all to slow and painful deaths, without a doubt. No, they had no choice but to go through with it and do the best they could.

He paced the length of the trench dug out by one of the teams. They'd only been able to do the work in the pre-dawn and early evening hours, else risk sunstroke. Hard work, and well done. The trench would let them offload water from the truck into their stash of containers, then bury the supply for safekeeping. He figured they'd have to dispose of the truck sooner rather than later. Couldn't have it sitting there in camp, like some beacon. Cops would see it as incriminating evidence. Others desperate for water would see it as a prize to be captured, no matter the cost to either side.

Everyone had also dug a small hole beside their tent to bury a personal supply of water. Too bad they couldn't just keep the truck as their own camp-wide reservoir. It would be so much less work than all this digging with hand shovels. But they likely couldn't make the truck disappear right away. And that's why he'd had everyone move their vehicles nearer their tents, kind of like circling the wagons in pioneer days. Provide a little more protection in the event of an attack. And a faster getaway if they had to flee than having the vehicles all parked on one side of camp as they had been.

Repercussions. They hadn't done much planning for that. The actual hijack, they had pretty well worked out. Lexi'd been elected to create the distraction that would force the truck to stop. Everyone knew their part once that happened. But they hadn't had the time—or the stomach, to be honest—to come up with a plan in the event someone came after the truck. Might not even be possible, anyway. Too many potential scenarios to consider.

Who would come? Police? Government? Other would-be hijackers? How would they be equipped, how heavily armed? How fast would they come? Would they simply arrest them all and take them away? To where? Maybe somewhere with water and better supplies than they had here, but without their freedom. And if other desperate people came after the truck before law enforcement got there, how would that go down?

Trent clapped his hands to the sides of his head and willed his brain to stop spinning in those terrifying circles. That part was impossible to predict, impossible to control. Better focus on what they *could* control for tomorrow. And just be ready for anything after that.

CHAPTER 58

The day had come. Lexi waited alone in the decoy car near the on-ramp, terrified at all that could go wrong as the plan played out beneath the murderous desert sun. Clamping her trembling hands on the steering wheel, she took a deep breath, held it, and let it out as slowly as she could. But her heart refused to slow its panicked rhythm.

The others waited in several larger vehicles parked nearby. She wondered if everyone else was as on edge as she was, despite all the preparations. True to his word, Trent had organized the ambush as rigorously as possible under the circumstances. Everyone involved had been extensively briefed. They'd even done some limited mock runs, though nothing could fully prepare them for the real thing. She wondered—not for the first time—if she would be able to play her role effectively, or if she'd let everyone down and cost people their lives.

Ready or not, they had no choice but to act now. The camp was down to only a few gallons of water in total. As Jack had so plainly put it, as risky as the plan was, not executing it was a sure death sentence.

In the short time they'd had to prepare, they'd worked hard to boost the plan's odds of success. Hours upon hours had been spent in the past week planning every aspect of the hijacking, thinking through all the potential scenarios and filling in as many details as possible. Even so, many unknowns remained. One of the biggest was when the next water truck would pass by. Two from the camp had driven out west, right near the California border, so they could spot the next truck and call it in to Trent on a cell phone. Then everyone would have time to move into position.

Each of the last two mornings, the go-team had set up near the on-ramp, ready to execute on their plan if the spotters called in that a truck was coming. But both days, they'd waited for hours, poised for action, only to have Trent call it off for the day so they didn't lose their edge when a truck finally did come along.

The first day, Lexi'd nearly hyperventilated, she'd been so nervous. But now, sitting on stand-by for the third day running, she was plenty nervous, but not so overwhelmed as before. She hoped it was a sign she'd do better—not worse—than if they'd carried it out the first day. She hoped the same held true for everyone else on the go-team. They all had to be on their best game, or many of them might not make it out alive.

But even if everything went according to plan, some would likely die. Trent had drummed that into them to prepare them for the worst.

Trent got out of his car and came up to her window. "Truck's coming. We probably have just under half an hour before it gets here. Move out in about twenty. I'll let everyone else know." He nodded, tried to smile. "Good luck." Then he strode off to where the others were parked.

Lexi tried the deep breathing again, but it didn't work at all now. Her heart felt like it was right up in her throat, trying to choke her. She had the starring role in this desperate plan, and she had to be convincing. She rehearsed it in her mind once more, hoping she could just do it without thinking when the time came. If she blew it, the entire plan would fail. And she'd undoubtedly be shot dead on the spot.

Can't think like that...can't think like that. Focus!

Twenty interminable minutes later, she started the engine and headed for the on-ramp. The others fell in behind her, but they would stay at the top of the on-ramp while she positioned herself right on the highway and waited for the water truck.

Lexi drove onto the freeway and parked her car at an angle, blocking two lanes. It felt so weird to just park on a freeway, though nothing felt normal out here anyway. I-80 was basically a dead-end westbound, and—aside from water trucks and maybe occasional other government-related vehicles—no one in their right mind came eastbound out of California, so it was pretty much deserted day and night on this stretch.

She lit a couple of flares and arranged them on the asphalt, then popped the hood and stood beside the car, doing her best to look like a helpless woman, desperate for help. Even if they didn't offer her any other assistance, the water-truck drivers would have to push her car aside so they could get by. And that's when everything would happen.

Lexi glanced at the top of the on-ramp out of the corner of her eye. Several cars waited there, those inside ready to come pouring out, weapons drawn, to ambush the water-truck drivers when they stopped to help her. She turned away from them, not wanting to envision what was going to happen next—and not wanting to risk drawing the drivers' attention to them before the time came. It was all on her now to set everything in motion.

She paced around the decoy car a couple of times, getting into her damsel-in-distress character. God knew she'd had plenty of practice since the fire. But this time, so many lives depended on her. She tried not to think about that. To think about that would be to freeze up. And to freeze up would mean death. For everyone in the camp, whether by bullets or by dehydration.

Lexi shielded her eyes with her hand and peered west, into the glare of the mid-day sun. There it was. Had to be. She watched as the water truck came into view, its image rippling in the heat waves, then started waving, flagging it down for help.

CHAPTER 59

"What's that over there, Jess?" Len leaned forward in the passenger seat and pointed.

Jess slowed the water truck a little as he peered through the glare. Metal glinted in the harsh sunlight up ahead. A car with its hood up, stuck and taking up two lanes. And some girl standing right there on the road with it. Some people didn't have any sense at all.

"Looks like a breakdown. But what the hell would she be doing out on this stretch of road, anyway?"

"Nothing good, I'd say. Better call it in." Len reached for the microphone on the dash.

"No, hold on. Let's see what's going on first."

"Standard procedure—"

"I know standard procedure, Len. It's just a girl, not a sniper, for crissake."

"She shouldn't be out there. There's never any traffic on this stretch. I don't like it."

"It's not like this section is blocked off. She could have gotten lost, then had some trouble. Doesn't take much to overheat out this way, you know." Jess geared down as he drew closer.

"What the hell are you doing? We're not supposed to stop, not for anything. Standing orders. If you're that worried about her, let me call it in. Get someone else out here to deal with it. We don't have time to deviate from schedule for something like this."

Jess sighed. Len was a rookie, with rookie nerves and an unhealthy attachment to the procedure manual. Too green to know when to ignore the literal language in the book and use common sense.

"Len, I'm well aware of standing orders. But she's blocking

the way. Are you suggesting I just ram into her car and hope she gets out of the way in time?"

"Can't you get around her?"

"Not with this rig."

"Then our orders are to push it aside, right? We're not supposed to let anything get in the way. We have the authority. The responsibility. They drummed that into us in the Academy."

There had to be a better way to handle this, a reasonable way. Jess reached for the microphone, then hesitated. What did he expect if he called it in? They probably *would* tell him to ram his way through, to hell with any collateral damage. After all, that's why they had the heavy-duty reinforced grilles on these babies. The water came first. Anyone who got in the way of delivery was…expendable. Ignoring Len's blithering, he studied the scene carefully as they drew closer.

Young woman standing there by the car. Looking upset, as any young woman broken down on the freeway in the middle of nowhere *would*. Flares on the asphalt. Car parked catawampus, blocking up not one, but two, lanes. Concrete center divider, unforgiving. Metal guard rail and not a lot of shoulder on the side. He calculated his odds of passing by her without hitting something.

Nil.

"I'm gonna stop. Help her get out of the way, anyway."

"Are you crazy? They'll suspend both of us quicker than you can say 'no pay'!"

Jess glanced at Len. "If neither of us says anything, who's to know?" He gestured toward the disabled car. "We can push the car aside pretty fast, make sure she's okay and can get hold of a tow, and move on—all without creating enough delay for anyone to suspect we stopped. And if anyone does ask, we can just say we needed an extra-long rest area stop because of something we ate." He chuckled.

Len leaned forward in his seat, his brow furrowed. "Well, I suppose you're right. She's just a little thing, doesn't look like much of a threat. Probably won't take that long for us to be back on our way. Okay, let's go for it. But if anything goes wrong, it wasn't *my* idea to stop."

CHAPTER 60

The truck drew closer. Lexi adjusted her stance. If it couldn't stop in time, she'd have to jump out of its way and let it collide with her car. The truck flashed its headlights and halted a few car lengths away. Relieved, she put on a huge smile, pointed at her car, and shrugged her shoulders.

Nothing happened. She strained to make out what the drivers were doing in there. The glare on the windshield made it impossible to read their expressions. Were they coming out, or would they just sit in there and radio for help? She tried to keep the helpless smile plastered on her face. They hadn't thought of that in all their planning. What if the drivers *wouldn't* get out, or weren't allowed to? That could be, especially since traffic on this stretch was so rare. She tried waving and wiping her forehead to show how overheated and distraught she was to break down right on the freeway.

Sweat trickled down her torso beneath her T-shirt. Finally, the truck doors opened and two men stepped out, loaded with gear and dressed in guard uniforms. One stayed next to the truck; the other slowly approached. He looked stiff, like he was wearing a bulletproof vest under his shirt. His belt bristled with frightening things: handgun, Taser, plastic cuffs. Lexi found it hard to keep up her façade in the face of all that menacing equipment.

"Can you help me, please?" She giggled and smiled harder. "I don't know what happened, it just quit on me right here. Just like that."

"Ma'am, we're under orders to proceed without delay, so we'll need to push your vehicle off the road. I'm sorry, but we can't stop to do more."

"Oh." Lexi turned and absently ran her hand along the car's fender, trying not to give away what she knew was about to happen.

The guard turned and signaled to his partner. Before the driver could get back up in the cab, the others took their cue and came running from the top of the on-ramp, carrying a motley assortment of firearms.

Lexi clapped her hands to her ears as bullets flew all around her. Nothing prepared her for the intensity of the sound. It felt like the ground—the very air around her—was being shattered by the blasts.

The guards took position and returned fire with their professional-grade weapons. The powerful blasts made the go-team's guns sound like toys. Lexi heard some of her fellow camp members cry out as they were hit. She scrambled for cover on the other side of the car, but not fast enough. Something whizzed by, followed by a searing pain in her upper right arm. She clamped her hand on it, trying to stop the pain, the blood. No time to think about it now. She ducked lower and watched everything unfold from where she crouched, trapped.

One of the guards lay sprawled by the water truck's front end, half his face blown off. The other had taken refuge in the cab, shut the door. The windshield glass appeared to be bulletproof. Her side's bullets weren't penetrating—but the remaining guard couldn't shoot out, either.

A standoff. They hadn't planned for that. They'd figured on hitting both guards when they came out to assist her. The shooting slowed, then stopped, but her ears still rang.

Lexi remained crouched behind the car with her hand clamped around her injured arm, unsure of what to do, as the minutes played out. The remaining guard stayed in the truck's cab, a vague silhouette through the tinted windshield. The camp members stood their ground. Then a group of them ran past her—some carrying long guns, some carrying handguns—and rushed the truck.

Someone ran up to the truck's passenger side, jammed the end of his shotgun onto the lock, and fired. Others mobbed that side and forced open the damaged door. Several fell, hit by the other guard's fire from inside.

At last, the remaining guard flung open the driver's side door and jumped out. Blood soaked his left sleeve. The mob sprinted around the truck and fired wildly. The guard turned and fired once more before a bullet caught him in the throat and knocked him down, out of Lexi's line of sight.

Silence again. Then cheers.

Lexi tried to stand so she could get a look at what was going on, but instead wobbled and fell on her ass beside the car. She spread her fingers and peeked at her wound. Still bleeding, but it seemed to be slowing down. Maybe. Or maybe not. Spatters and a small puddle of blood lay on the asphalt beside her. She'd never bled so much in her life.

She giggled. Of course not. She'd never been shot before. Not something she'd ever have thought to put on her bucket list. Dizzy, she sagged against the side of the car as darkness rolled over her like a soft, gentle blanket, erasing all pain.

CHAPTER 61

"With all due respect, sir, you can't be serious."
"The hell I'm not."

Kevin Oakley stared at the satellite image on his computer, wishing he were looking at some kind of optical illusion. But there it was, clear as day. The stolen water truck, sitting right there beside a bunch of tents, a little south of I-80 in the Nevada desert. His hands clenched into tight fists. If he didn't have the evidence right on the screen in front of him, he'd never have believed anything like this could happen.

There'd been no advance warning that the truck was in any kind of trouble. No one radioed in. Nothing. He'd only realized something had gone wrong when the truck didn't make its next scheduled checkpoint. Someone had to have broken protocol for this to happen. The trucks were not supposed to make unscheduled stops—not for anything. And the drivers were authorized to use deadly force to stay on schedule and keep that water safe. Middle of fucking nowhere, with highly trained, armed guards driving, and somehow a bunch of transients took the truck—and killed the guards.

"But there's no way to know which individuals were actually involved. Can't be all of them."

Kevin switched away from the satellite picture and glared at the row of faces displayed in the Skype window. As soon as he'd found out about the truck heist, he'd called a special emergency meeting. Everyone was in a foul mood at having their day interrupted—especially by something like this. Understandable. But his staff didn't seem to want to take the necessary action. And that was not acceptable.

They all looked stunned, like they thought he'd lost his mind. They'd lost *their* minds, if they thought water theft of this magnitude shouldn't trigger the severest of consequences. People got locked up all the time for stealing a few gallons of water from their neighbor's unwatched spigot. But this. An entire, fully loaded water truck—and the cold-blooded murder of the two guards. Crime like this could not be tolerated. It deserved the maximum response.

"One or two people didn't plan and carry that out by themselves. No way. The whole encampment had to be complicit. So we go in. I'm going to activate a National Guard unit to take care of it and I want each of you to help provide logistical support as needed. The press hasn't gotten hold of this yet, and I'd prefer it stay that way, if at all possible. But if not, I want you to coordinate with me and present a united front in any communications with the press."

"Wait a minute. Even if everyone in that camp *was* complicit, where would they take all those people anyway? Can't process and hold them in Nevada, not with the water supply cut off."

"No need to worry about that."

"What do you mean?" All the faces across his screen wore the same puzzled look.

"No prisoners. It's a capital crime. No point wasting a single drop of water on them."

"Kevin, no one's disputing that this is a very serious crime. But they deserve fair trials. Some of them may not have been involved, may be completely innocent. There has to be a proper investigation. You can't—"

Kevin slapped his palm down on his desk. "Are you all forgetting? We're dealing with the longest and most widespread drought in recorded history. Every single day now, people are dying from lack of sufficient water. And there is no end in sight. This is a national emergency, God damn it! Play-nice rules don't apply anymore. I want that camp destroyed, everyone in it *eliminated.*" He ignored his staff's collective gasps and went on. "If we respond in any other way, these people could try it again or they could tell others how to do it, and incidents like this will spread across the country in no time. We'd lose all control of water distribution. And even more people will die."

The faces all protested at once, eyes wide, mouths frantic.

"Enough! Anyone who feels they can't do their job can tender their resignation, effective immediately. And one more thing. From now on, every water truck gets a two-vehicle armed escort. One in front, one behind. No exceptions. This cannot be allowed to happen again, no matter the cost."

Kevin slammed the mouse so hard it shattered. The faces all disappeared from his screen, once again revealing the satellite image of the camp and the stolen truck. He turned away, fighting the urge to throw the monitor across the room. Anything to get that image out of his sight, out of his mind.

If only he'd handled things differently. Instead of selecting individual states to cut off, he should have reduced the per capita allocations again. The models showed a lot more people would have died had he done that, but at least *nature* would have chosen who lived and who died. Weakest first. Nature's way. Instead, he tried to minimize the overall death toll by picking the winners and losers himself. *Of course* the losers wouldn't just happily accept their fate. They'd fight to survive as best they could. He should have thought of that.

The truck heist was his own damned fault, the direct consequence of his decision. And now he was about to compound his guilt by destroying the encampment and everyone in it. But he was backed into a corner. If he let this go, there'd be heists all over—or at least attempts. Water distribution would be severely disrupted, and he'd have even more deaths on his hands.

Kevin put his face in his hands and sobbed. He'd chosen the lesser of the evils.

But he'd still chosen evil.

CHAPTER 62

"You did great, Lexi. Rest now. You lost some blood, but you'll be okay."

Lexi smiled and gave a slight nod as her eyelids drifted shut.

Trent checked her bandage once more, then glanced at her face, so ashen it scared him. He'd run up to help her as soon as he realized she'd been hit. Blood spattered the asphalt where she fell, making it hard to tell how much she'd lost. Might have been as much as a couple of pints, maybe a little less.

He sat back on his heels, ran a hand through his hair, and let out a long, slow breath. The drills had really paid off, far better than he expected. With only minor exceptions, everyone knew their part, knew what to do and when to do it. As the hijack unfolded, he'd dashed from one end of the scene to the other, keeping an eye on things and lending a hand everywhere he could. He hadn't had to waste time reminding people of what they were supposed to be doing.

With the truck captured, all efforts shifted to the mop-up phase. First priority had been to get the wounded back to camp for triage and whatever first aid could be rendered with their limited supplies. Anyone needing more than some heavy bandaging was likely going to be out of luck. No IVs, no blood transfusions—and the strongest thing they had for pain was ibuprofen. The vehicles had already been cleared from the highway. Even now, the tanker was parked in camp, with a tag team filling all available water containers and placing them in the main trench and the holes by each tent that had been dug in the days leading up to the hijack. Another group was starting to backfill the trench where containers had already been placed.

And they'd brought in the dead.

Trent stepped outside Lexi's tent and crossed over to the assembly area, where the bodies had been laid out on tarps beneath the canvas canopies. He stood, hands on hips, gazing down at them. Five—so far. A couple of the wounded didn't look like they'd last the night. Not that he'd had any medical training beyond a first aid class at the local community center a couple of years back, but with the heat and lack of medical supplies, they'd likely lose a few more before it was over.

With the high-powered weapons those guards had, they were lucky to have escaped with as few casualties as they did. He'd known—they'd all known—this was a risky thing to even try to pull off. But they'd had no choice. Do nothing, and they'd all die, slowly and painfully, from dehydration.

But still. He'd hoped they could maybe get away with it and not lose anyone. Wishful thinking, for sure. They all knew there would be some losses, though they hadn't planned on how to handle the dead. It was one thing they all agreed to figure out when the need arose, instead of spending precious drill and prep time on it. Looking back, Trent still believed it was the right thing to do. Surely more would have died if they hadn't been as well prepared.

Trent knelt on the ground and bowed his head. The practical thing to do would be to wait for the cool of the evening or early morning and bury the bodies a little outside of camp. But these were heroes. Every one of them had died trying to bring life-saving water to the camp. They should hold some kind of ceremony for them as soon as the rest of the mop-up activities were done. To honor them as they deserved.

And maybe to relieve him of a small part of the guilt and responsibility for these deaths that he'd carry for the rest of his life. They may have willingly accepted the risk, but they'd still died under his leadership.

Wiping a tear from his eye, Trent stood and gazed out on the rest of the camp in the late afternoon light. Amazing, what they'd accomplished together. Now they had the water they needed to survive, and lots of it.

Even if they did pay for it in blood.

CHAPTER 63

Ben Stratton did as he was told. He got into the truck, quickly slid to the end of the wooden bench, and wedged his rifle between his knees. More uniformed men toting rifles filed into the troop transport truck, filling the benches on both sides before the back gate slammed shut, leaving them with just the bare overhead light bulb in the vehicle's windowless back section. A claustrophobe's worst nightmare.

The engine rumbled to life and the truck got underway. Ben stared down at the battered metal floor, avoiding eye contact and the possibility of conversation with the others. This wasn't how it was supposed to be. He'd joined the National Guard to help people. And, so far, in his time with the Guard, he'd been deployed all over the country to help bring order to chaos after natural disasters of all kinds. He was proud of that. He loved the look on people's faces when they realized someone had come to help, to make their worst hour just a little less horrible. That's why he joined. And he was damned good at what he did.

But along the way, he'd learned that wasn't the only reason other people joined. He glanced around out of the corner of his eye. Some of them joined just so they could get a rifle in their hands, so they could strut around in their uniforms, feeling invincible and superior. They found the recovery work a little tedious, a little boring. Those were the guys who thirsted for some action, maybe some blood—but didn't want to deploy overseas in some all-out war where they couldn't go home at night to relative safety and the comfort of their own beds.

Those guys'd be happy today.

The order came from Oakley, that water czar. Confirmed

by the President. All in a matter of hours late yesterday, so they could deploy in time to reach their target no later than mid-day today. A matter of national emergency, they said. A full water truck had been hijacked and the guards driving it had been killed. All by some bunch of people who'd been camped out in the Nevada desert.

Ben stared down at his rifle, the cold dark metal glinting in the dim light like the wink of some malevolent being. He'd never before used it for anything more than target practice. But today, orders were to shoot to kill. And he wasn't at all sure he was ready for that.

How desperate must those people have been? Stuck in Nevada, baking in the endless desert heat. Nowhere to go and running out of water fast. Fleeing to a neighboring state wasn't even an option for them. What were they supposed to do, just lie down in the sand and graciously accept their slow and painful deaths by dehydration?

He knew the crime was serious, but he couldn't find it in himself to blame them. After all, water distribution to the entire state of Nevada had been cut off, leaving them to die. Had he been in their position, he might have done the same thing.

And now they'd all been sentenced to death for the crime of trying to stay alive. Whoever was there. Men, women, children. Old and young, sick and able. Didn't matter. Shoot to kill, take no one alive. Destroy everyone and everything in that encampment and take back the water truck. Didn't matter who'd been the ringleader, who'd stayed behind. Everyone. No exceptions. Ben bit his lip.

The truck's back gate opened with a metallic clang.

"Go-time. Get in position. You know what to do."

The men ahead of him leapt from their seats and poured out of the truck. Ben brought up the rear, jumped down onto the shimmering fawn-colored sand, and scoped out the scene while he waited for the next signal.

About a dozen Guard transport trucks were parked in a line, noses toward the encampment so the men could assemble behind them before moving in. Ben peered between two of the trucks. A motley assortment of tents of all shapes, sizes and colors dotted the landscape about a hundred yards away. Various passenger cars, SUVs, and light pickups were parked amongst the tents, and he could just make out the water truck farther into the camp. The sun hung high overhead, beating down on the entire scene. The camp was quiet, no one moving around. They were probably all sheltering themselves from the peak heat of the day.

"We go in three...two...one!"

The Guardsmen formed a tight line and trotted toward the camp, rifles raised and ready. Ben took the rightmost end position, sweat already trickling beneath his bullet-proof vest. As they drew near the edge of the camp, an older man emerged from one of the tents with a puzzled look on his face.

He shouted "Hey" and raised his hands, then danced a bloody jig as he was cut to shreds by bullets. His body slammed to the ground, twisted and motionless on the bloodstained sand.

Heads poked out of tent doorways, only to be blasted away by rifle fire like doomed targets in a shooting gallery. Screams and rifle shots merged into a symphony of terror. A few people came out of their tents firing away with weapons ranging from shotguns to tiny revolvers. All were cut down where they stood before they could do any damage.

Ben advanced with the rest of the line, his rifle unsteady in his sweating hands. His legs moved on their own, like they weren't even a part of him. Like he was an unwilling passenger being taken on a ride he hadn't chosen.

The others had broken formation and were now running from tent to tent, making sure whoever was inside was dead before moving on to the next one. Knees wobbling, Ben went up to the tent nearest him and looked inside.

A young woman with a thick white bandage wrapped around her upper arm sat on the tent floor with her knees pressed up against her chest, arms encircling her shins. She looked up at him, face pale and lips pressed together, silent, unmoving. As if she were steeling herself for the bullet to come.

Ben lowered his rifle and reached out his hand. "Come on. Hurry."

She took his hand, confusion on her face. "Why?"

"Just go. *Now*. Don't look back." Ben pulled her to her feet and out of the tent. "Take some of the others from this side, get in a car. Get the hell out of here."

She turned and ran to the next tent over. A young woman with long strawberry-blond hair emerged and the two ran to another tent. An older couple got out, holding each other close and looking confused. Ben made sure they all made it into nearby cars, then fired shots into the empty tents, hoping the others were too busy with their own carnage to notice what he'd done.

He watched as the cars sped off into the distance in a speedy single file, dust kicking up behind them. At least some of them would survive. But without water, probably not for long.

Maybe it would have been more merciful if he'd just shot them like he was supposed to.

CHAPTER 64

Lexi took one last look at the soldier who'd let her go, setting his image in her mind for later, when there would be time to think back on what happened, on what he'd done for her. Then she ran straight for Katie's tent, reached inside with her good arm and pulled Katie out and onto her feet in one fluid movement.

"C'mon!"

"What about Trent?" yelled Katie. She glanced from side to side, frozen in place by the horror surrounding her.

"Can't wait for him. Might be dead already."

Lexi ran to the next tent over, yelled at the older couple inside to get out while they could. They emerged from their tent, holding each other tight and blinking in confusion. She gave them a gentle push.

"You guys, Katie, get in your cars. Follow me—now!"

Ignoring the throbbing in her arm where the bullet nicked her during the hijacking, Lexi raced to her car as the others got into their own cars to follow her. Thank God for Trent's planning. Before the hijack, he made everyone move their cars near their tents. And once they got the tanker into camp, he'd had them store as much water as possible in all the vehicles, in addition to burying as many water containers as possible. He figured the government would find out what happened and might come after the truck before they could find a way to dispose of it, or at least hide it better. He just didn't realize how fast they'd come.

And he hadn't counted on an all-out slaughter.

The afternoon had started out like any other. Scorching

hot, a good time to rest in their tents, saving up the energy to hold a memorial and bury their dead when the heat leveled off later in the day. Maybe if they had someone standing guard, it wouldn't have gone down this way.

But they'd killed those two guards in the ambush...no way would they let them get away with that. Even so, Trent had figured worst case, some type of law enforcement would come out, investigate, and make some arrests at some point—not carry out an annihilation.

Lexi flung herself into the driver's seat and hit the Start button. Good thing one of the guys had figured out the problem with her radiator and fixed it soon after she arrived. She took off southbound down the road that brought her to the camp, sand kicking up behind her. She took a quick glance in her rear view, saw that Katie and the others were following in their cars.

They had a head start. A slim one, but a head start nonetheless. Didn't dare waste it. If they could just get out of sight—or far enough to not be worth chasing—before the armed men realized they'd escaped. Who were those men, anyway? Soldiers, or maybe some special cop force? They weren't state troopers, or anything she'd ever seen before. Whatever they were, they didn't plan to take anyone alive. That much was clear.

Why did that one let them escape? She shook her head and glanced again in the rear-view mirror. No one following their little convoy. At least not yet. Too busy murdering the rest of the camp. She sped up, then veered around a pothole, the SUV's rear end fishtailing on the sand-blown road. She spun the wheel, regained control, pushed her speed up again. Last thing she needed was a wrecked tire.

Her mind spun as she fled. Best to just put as much distance as possible between them and the camp and hope no one came after them. Sure couldn't stick around and make a stand. Not against that firepower. She wondered where Trent was, if he—or anyone else—would get out alive.

At least she had several days' worth of food and water, right there in the car. The others should, too, if they'd followed Trent's instructions. They could hold out for a few days together, wait for it to be safe to return to camp, while she figured out what to do next.

Lexi steered around another pothole and sped up, hoping the others would take her cue and haul ass.

CHAPTER 65

Lexi eyed her rear view. The others were falling behind. She glanced at the GPS map. She'd rather stop farther away from the camp, but maybe this was good enough. She didn't want the others to get separated from her. They clearly didn't have the confidence driving this stretch of desert that she did, and probably wouldn't know what to do come sunset. They should all stick together and figure out what to do next. She pulled over, got out, and signaled them to stop as they drew nearer.

Katie was the first to arrive and step out of her car. Face pale, eyes wide, she had her arms wrapped around her torso as if she were cold. "What the hell was that? What just happened?"

Lexi went over and gave her a hug as the older couple pulled up. "I don't know. I didn't see or hear anyone start trouble. Cops shouldn't open fire like that, not without some reason." She shook her head. "Seemed like soldiers of some kind. I just don't know. Let's get the others. Not sure I've met them before."

"That's Bill and Martha. Nice people. Tend to keep to themselves." Katie glanced back in the direction of the camp with a longing look. "I hope Trent's okay."

"We're likely the only ones to get out of there in time."

"Oh, no." Katie began to cry.

"Come on, there's no time for that right now. Let's check on Bill and Martha. They looked pretty shaken."

Lexi gave Katie's shoulder a squeeze as they walked up to the couple's car. Bill sat in the driver's seat, hands clenched tight on the wheel. Both he and Martha looked like they'd just witnessed a nuclear explosion. Lexi knocked on the window and leaned in when Bill lowered it for her.

"Hey, you guys okay?"

Martha just stared, her pale blue eyes a little glassy. Bill mumbled, "What do we do now?"

Katie turned to her, "Yeah, Lexi. What now?" She pushed the hair off her face with a trembling hand.

An almost palpable feeling of weight settled on Lexi's shoulders as she took in the looks on all their faces. They needed someone to make sense of what just happened, to help them take their next steps, whatever those might be. Lexi hesitated. She didn't expect this, didn't want it. Hard enough being cast adrift on her own, responsible for herself. But to take responsibility for others?

Suddenly she understood what it must have been like for Trent. He hadn't sought out that role, either. She could tell. There was a tension inside him. He knew he had to take the lead, for the sake of the others. He didn't want to, but it had to be done, and it had to be done right. Lexi squared her shoulders.

"Let's all go sit down by my SUV. It's casting a better shadow than either of your sedans."

She opened the driver's side door and helped Bill out, then nodded to Katie to go help Martha. She led them all to the pool of shade beside her car, then sat down in the sand and waited for the others to settle in. Martha leaned up against Bill, and they clung to each other as if they were afraid to let go. Katie drew her knees to her chest and wrapped her arms around them.

"Trent was worried about someone coming after the truck, whether law enforcement or someone else trying to take it for themselves. And he planned well."

Katie winced at the mention of Trent and rubbed her eyes.

Lexi continued, ideas forming in her head as she went. "You all stored food and water in your vehicles, like he told you to, right?" Everyone nodded. "Good. So we've all got days of food and water right here with us. Let's just spend the night here tonight. Get some rest and regroup in the morning. Sleep in our cars."

"In our cars?" Martha looked horrified.

"That's the safest thing to do. We'll take turns on watch while the others sleep."

"What do we do if someone comes after us?" Katie's brow furrowed.

"Whoever's on watch wakes the others. Then we all haul ass southbound on this road. It intersects something a little more major south of here. It's a getaway plan...if it comes to that. But I suspect if they saw us escape camp and wanted to come after us, they'd have done it by now."

"You think so?" Martha spoke in a choked whisper.

"I can't be completely sure, but I think so."

Martha buried her head in Bill's neck and sobbed.

"Let's have a little food and rest up as best we can. I'll go check out the camp in a day or so, see what's left, what we can salvage. Maybe figure out what happened."

Katie leaned forward and gasped. "You want to go back there? Are you crazy? They *shot* everyone!"

"Don't *want* to. Have to. We can't just camp out here forever. Need to know what's left, what we can use. If nothing else, they might not have figured out we buried a good supply of that water. Don't want to leave it behind to waste."

Katie leaned back against the SUV. "You're braver than I am."

The irony of that remark made Lexi smile. She never thought someone else would think her the slightest bit brave. She certainly never thought of herself that way before.

Of course, it was all fine to *say* she was going back to the camp. She hadn't gotten there yet, let alone had she seen the horrors that likely awaited her there.

She stood up to go get her water bottle, then leaned against the SUV for a moment, fighting off a wave of dizziness. Her upper arm throbbed beneath the bandage. She'd forgotten all about it in the rush to escape. She took a deep breath, straightened up, and strode to the other side of the car to get her water... and some ibuprofen. She had to be strong for the others, had to keep them as calm and functional as possible until they got into a more stable situation.

CHAPTER 66

Lexi waited a couple of days before returning to the camp. Better chance the soldiers—or whatever the hell they were—would have taken what they came for and gone, thinking they'd left no witnesses behind. And to make sure she was ready to handle going back to face whatever there was to face.

Katie came up to her as she was getting in her SUV to go. "Are you sure it's a good idea to go back there?"

"Good idea? No. Not really. I'm not looking forward to seeing what happened to everyone. But it needs to be done. I don't know if I'll be able to figure out what happened, who did it, but I need to know what's left of the water and any other supplies. That'll help us decide what to do next, how far we can travel on what we have."

"All right. Well, good luck." Katie reached out, and they clasped hands.

"Thanks."

Lexi got in her car, gave a quick wave to Bill and Martha, who were sitting in the sand together next to their car, and started off on the twenty-odd-mile trip back to the camp. She'd chosen to do it alone, with no one to interrupt her thoughts, no one to have to worry about babysitting through the experience. Not that anyone volunteered to go with her anyway.

She pulled up in the early morning light and got out of the car, her breath catching in her throat at the sight of so much death and destruction. Their little enclave, gone. All gone. Wiped clean off the map. Whoever was responsible for this had been determined to obliterate the camp and everything in it.

Not a single tent remained.

Just black rings, ashes blowing in the fickle dawn breeze.

Lexi moved closer, bent down to touch a charred shred of canvas. She knelt for a better look, running her fingers through the warm sand, streaked with black. Fragments. Like bone. She stood, walked deeper into what used to be the camp. The camp that—albeit reluctantly at first—took her in and saved her life.

Even the little makeshift podium Trent used to speak to the group. Incinerated. Lexi shielded her eyes from the sun with one hand and turned, looking, looking...for anything.

She strode over to where they had buried the bulk of the water offloaded from the truck, knelt in the ash-strewn sand, and began digging with her hands, the wound on her arm throbbing in protest. *Please be there...please be there.* Her fingers touched something solid, a container. Frantic, she scooped more sand out of the way. *Thank you, Trent.* The water supply was still there. She stood, nearly dizzy with relief.

But they'd left almost nothing else behind. Just scorched desert sand and ashes. The vehicles were charred skeletons, nothing more. They'd taken the water truck...and they'd taken their revenge.

No mercy. Except for that one soldier, the one who'd pulled her out of her tent and set her free. Who he was and why he'd done it, she'd never know, but she'd always be grateful to him. He must have gotten away with it without anyone noticing, or she and the others would surely be dead now, too.

Lexi trembled with rage and sorrow both. They'd shot the others down like dogs, then torched it all—burning the bodies along with everything else like so much garbage—as if that erased what happened.

Never.

She'd always remember, no matter what.

But she would not let it break her.

Lexi stood amid the ashes of the camp, amid all the ashes of her former life, gathering strength. A new strength, unlike anything she'd ever felt in her life. She took a deep breath, felt the blood coursing through her veins, through her arteries. Something shifted inside her, and she knew what it was.

The old Lexi was gone forever, erased from this earth like the encampment in front of her.

She reached down, touched the sheath clipped to her waistband. The knife Jake bought to protect them, back in that other lifetime. She took it from its sheath, extended the blade, then raised the knife high in the air and let out a primal scream.

CHAPTER 67

Lexi sat down in the sand, crossed her legs, and settled in. She took a deep breath and savored the air, still cool this time of day with the sun barely peeking over the horizon. A new day. A new start.

The others took their seats in the sand and silently waited for her to speak. Lexi watched their faces, the faces of the only other survivors, as far as they knew. Katie and the older couple, Martha and Bill. Four people out of that entire camp who made it out—and only because that one soldier had mercy on them for whatever reason.

They still had no idea who carried out the raid, and likely never would. Sure wasn't local cops, not with those heavy-duty weapons and gear. Had to be some sort of hush-hush government operation to get back that water truck. And to punish by total extermination. They killed—without exception for children, the old, and the frail—every single other person in the camp. They'd shot them where they stood. They'd shot them as they lay inside their tents. They'd shot them as they tried to flee. Precious few even had time to try to defend themselves.

And they'd so thoroughly destroyed the camp that there was nothing left, except the water Trent had them stockpile and bury right after the hijacking—and the food and water he'd told them to stash in their vehicles. Damned good thing he did. Because of his careful planning, they would survive. Lexi assumed he'd been killed in the raid, and could only hope his death had been as quick and painless as possible.

In the week since the raid, the four of them had rested up in their temporary base just off the road twenty or so miles south of the camp. No point in returning to the camp until they were ready to take their share of the water stash and move on. None of them could stomach the idea of setting back up on the site where so many of their friends had been murdered in cold blood.

So, they'd bided their time, mostly in silence, each mourning what had happened in their own way. Lexi'd kept an ear to the car radio for news. Nothing about the raid, nothing at all. Of course, if the government was involved, it wouldn't want to advertise what it had done—and it undoubtedly thought no witnesses had been left behind.

Lexi cleared her throat. All eyes turned to her, expectant. "I think it's time we leave here and split up. But first, we need to head back to the camp and load up all the water we can from the stash. It'd be a shame to waste it after all we sacrificed to get it."

"Why?" asked Martha, her brow furrowed. "What can't we stay together?"

"Well, we can't stay here in Nevada, cut off from water supplies. That water stash won't last forever. And I think it would be dangerous to stay together. What if they're still looking for anyone who might have been associated with the camp or the hijacking?"

Bill nodded, wrapped his arms around Martha, and gave her a gentle squeeze. "Makes sense, Lexi."

Katie rubbed her arms. "I'm afraid. I still think we're safer together, in what numbers we still have."

Lexi gazed out at the desert, its bright sand gleaming and already heating up with the rising sun. She felt like she'd lived in the desert her whole life. In a way, she had. *This* life, anyway. Her old life was dead and gone. Never to return.

She smiled at Katie. "You'd be surprised what you can do when it means surviving—or not." She got to her feet and dusted the sand from the seat of her pants. "Let's get going."

Lexi got into her SUV, waited for the others to get into their vehicles, then started it up. Splitting up was the right thing to do for all the reasons she'd said. But still. She worried about the others, whether they'd make it out okay. She knew *she'd* be fine, whatever happened.

She pulled onto the road and headed back to the camp. She

hoped the others were readying themselves to see the camp for the first time after the raid. She'd told them what to expect, prepared them for it as best she could. But she knew it would still be hard for them. She dreaded seeing it again herself. But it had to be done.

Everyone looked grim this morning, like she'd sentenced them to death instead of a new beginning. Maybe she had. But she hoped not. She hoped they'd all find some new strength inside them and survive. Maybe even thrive, eventually.

It had been a lot of work, but they finally finished digging out and distributing the water containers amongst their vehicles. Hopefully no one got pulled over carrying that much water, but better to have it and hide it than to leave it behind. It had certainly been wise to get started early in the day, else they'd all have had a heat stroke by now.

Lexi wiped sweat from her forehead and leaned against her SUV, taking a much-needed break along with the others. "So, where's everyone thinking of going?"

Martha and Bill glanced at each other. Bill spoke up, his arm firmly around his wife's shoulders. "Back where we came from. Nebraska. Don't know what's left back there, but we'd rather be home than wandering around like this."

Katie just shrugged. "I have no idea. I left everything behind, burned all my bridges thinking I could start a new life in California." She sighed and stared down at the sand. "See how well *that* turned out."

Lexi reached out, touched her shoulder. "You'll be fine. You'll figure something out."

"Yeah?"

"Sure you will."

Katie gave a slight smile. "Well, I hope you're right. Where are *you* going, Lexi?"

"Oh, I don't know. I don't have anything specific in mind yet. There was a time I wanted to get back to Nebraska more than anything. Not anymore. And the Golden West didn't work out so well for me. I think I'll go up north somewhere. See what's up that way."

Katie shook her head, an incredulous look on her face. "I don't know how you do it, driving around the middle of nowhere by yourself with no specific plan. You're awfully brave."

"I just do what I need to do. That's all. That's all anyone can do, right? Well, I guess this is it. Good luck to you all. I'll wait to make sure you all get going okay."

The others muttered awkward thanks and goodbyes to her, then everyone traded hugs, dabbing at their eyes, before parting. Bill and Martha got into their car, and Bill gave a big thumbs-up before taking off toward I-80. Katie walked around for a few minutes, her eyes trained away from what was left of the camp's core, before getting into her car and driving off in the same direction as Bill and Martha.

Lexi watched as they all drove off into the distance, more than a little relieved to be back on her own, responsible only for herself. She got into her car and glanced at the bandage on her arm. Sweat had loosened the tape, and the whole thing was twisted sideways. She peeled it off and checked her wound. Didn't look that bad anymore. She chucked the bandage out the window, then pulled onto the road, pointed north. She cast one last look at what remained of the camp on her way to I-80.

If she took I-80 east for a few miles, she could pick up a decent north-south road and try her luck in eastern Oregon. Maybe Washington if that didn't work out. One way or the other, she'd figure something out. Get off the road and settle in somewhere. Make a new life.

SIX MONTHS LATER

CHAPTER 68

Lexi relaxed in the tired old recliner and allowed her gaze to drift up to the shadow-strewn ceiling. The recliner looked its age and then some, but its appearance didn't matter to her. What mattered was being able to lean back into its soft cushions and put her feet up after working hard all day. That was heaven, right there.

The work was strenuous, and she faced another long day of it tomorrow out at the job site, clearing dead trees and brush. Endless dead trees, it seemed. The drought continued to kill, but at least it brought paying work to those who could handle it. Forget about fancy software jobs, all cushy behind antiseptic desks. Fire prevention was the new hot career these days. It was tough—made even tougher by the relentless heat—but it paid well, allowing her to afford a place to live in this converted motel in central Oregon.

She idly flexed her arm, admiring the taut, well-defined muscles she'd built—and the scar she bore on her deltoid from being shot in the raid. The raid. Seemed like something that had happened to someone else. And it had, really. She'd showed up at that camp broken, beaten, stripped of everything and everyone she loved. But in spite of everything, she left that camp transformed. She didn't just survive. She felt...reborn. The person she used to be didn't exist anymore—and that no longer seemed like a great loss to her. She ran a finger along the ropy pink scar. *No. No loss at all.* Some days she could hardly believe what a weak, dependent little thing she used to be. Pathetic, really.

She checked her watch and sighed. Better get to bed. She

pushed herself up and out of the comfy recliner, then headed for the bathroom to clean up for the night.

Lexi flicked on the bathroom light, slapped some toothpaste on her brush, then stopped. *What's that?* She set down the toothbrush and cocked her head at the unfamiliar noise. Couldn't be the person next door taking a late-night shower. Not the right sound. She was on the top floor, no one above her, yet the sound seemed to be coming from above. But what the hell was it? Better not be a leaking pipe in the wall or ceiling.

She padded into the center of her little motel-room-turned-apartment and listened. Still there, maybe a bit more distinct. She went over to the front window and peered out between the blinds. Something shimmered, sparkled in the outside lights. *No way.* She yanked open the front door.

Rain!

Heart pounding, Lexi stepped out onto the concrete walkway, raised her arms and let the rain come down on her, soaking her sweaty T-shirt and shorts. She lifted her face, mouth open, and drank it in. Her tears mingled with the raindrops.

She couldn't even remember the last time she'd been in the rain—any rain, no matter how light. She twirled and danced, letting the rain pelt her, soak her. She wanted to drink it all in through her skin, it felt so good.

Doors up and down the landing flew open as the other residents emerged from their rooms. Some fell to their knees, weeping. Others hopped and whooped. Residents from the bottom floor flooded out into the parking lot, running and shouting.

One of them yelled, "It's over! It's finally over! They're saying the drought's finally broken!"

Lexi ran back inside and turned on the news. She stood in front of the television, dripping rainwater onto the threadbare carpet.

For our top story this hour, we turn to our meteorologist, Skip McAdoo.

The camera cut to the U.S. weather map, with the usually stoic Skip McAdoo standing beside it, hair disheveled, sleeves rolled up. He waved his arm at the map as he spoke in a breathless rush.

Rain storms have broken out all across the western states as of this hour. Anticipated rainfall amounts range from one to two inches to as much as eight inches. The ground has been so dry for so long, widespread flooding and landslides are expected. The storms are on track to spread across the entire country within the next few days.

The drought is finally over. Our predictive models show this is just the first in a round of storms expected over the next week or so, and then the weather patterns appear to return to normal, pre-drought patterns.

He shook his head, stared down at the floor, then cupped his face in his hands and sobbed. *It's finally over.*

The camera cut back to the anchorman, who sat grinning like a kid at the circus as he continued:

And this just in. Water Czar Kevin Oakley issued an official statement a short time ago. Water restrictions and rationing will be lifted on a rolling basis as the reservoirs begin to refill. Oakley was seen openly weeping as he left the podium, right before he collapsed and was rushed to the local emergency room. He was pronounced dead on arrival. Doctor Miles McClendon, the treating physician, suspects Oakley died of a massive cerebral hemorrhage. An autopsy is scheduled for tomorrow. Oakley will be replaced by his deputy czar, Sheldon McDonald, until a new Water Czar is appointed by the President...

Lexi switched off the television and went back outside to drench herself in the rain. She imagined herself a seedling, breaking through the ground, thirsting for growth, renewal.

The drought—and all the miseries that came with it—was over at last. Now she could begin again. *Really* begin again. Set aside all that had happened, all she'd lost, and grow into her new self, without restriction. Stronger. Better.

A survivor. Afraid of nothing..

About the Author

Lisa began writing dark fiction just after the turn of the century. Her very first short story appeared in Greg F. Gifune's small press 'zine *The Edge* in 2002. After working in Information Technology for 25 years, Lisa dropped out of everything—including writing—to attend the University of Minnesota Law School. She graduated magna cum laude in 2009, and now practices law and writes in the Seattle area. On the writing front, she's made up for lost time since law school and is now the author of the thriller novels THE GENESIS CODE, THE JANUS LEGACY, BLOCKBUSTER, BROKEN CHAIN, DOWN THE BRINK, and INCIDENTAL FINDINGS, as well as the novellas ASH AND BONE, SKINSHIFT, and MOON OVER RUIN.

Curious about other Crossroad Press books?
Stop by our site:
http://www.crossroadpress.com
We offer quality writing
in digital, audio, and print formats.